The Saga of Kate and Molly

The Rise of Kate

VICKI PEARSON

The Rise of Kate
by Vicki Pearson
St Paul, Minnesota

ISBN 979-8-9852449-0-8

Library of Congress Control Number: 2021923966

Black Parrot Publishing
www.blackparrotpublishing.com

Fiction Disclaimer

TABLE OF CONTENTS

List of Names
(Pronunciation Help)

The Ersland Family
Kate's Father – Karle (k-AA-r-l)

Kate's Mother – Birgitta (bihr-GEE-tah)

Kate's Sister 1 – Ylva (EEL-va)

Kate's Sister 2 – Brenna (bren-e)

Kate Sister 3 – Katherine, they called her Kaija (KHA-ya)

Séamus Flanagan – (SHAY + MUHS)

Maurice – (maw-rees)

Graceann O'Connell – (gracean-n) (oh-kon-l)

Ex-slave encampment – Tendaji (Tehn-dah-jee) Swahili, East Africa, Makes things happen

Mambo Nicole – (mäm-(ˌ)bō) mother of magic, priestess (ni-KOHL) victory of the people

Ikemba Kamara – (ikem-ba) strength of a nation, power of the people (kuh-MAR-uh)

Cataline – (kah-tah-LINE)

Valentina – (vaa-lehN-TIY-naa)

Lakshmireet – m Lucky Soul – prefers Laxmi (l-ah-k-sh-m-ee) Lakshmi f goddess

Thank you!

First, I want to thank my husband, Tim Pearson. Without his love and support, this book may never have happened. Every step of this journey, he has been by my side, encouraging me. On days that I had doubts, he was quick with reassurances. On days that I felt like I could conquer the world, he agreed with me. Throughout this process, he has been my sounding board, my creative inspiration, and my courage when mine faltered. I cannot thank him enough for all that he is. I feel very lucky to be walking side-by-side with him in this lifetime.

Next, I want to thank my children. Their belief in my ability to make this book happen was unwavering. They allowed me to talk incessantly about my characters, my doubts, and the possibilities of my success. They stepped in with suggestions when my creativity stalled and they cared about my characters as much as I did. I love them to the moon and back and I am fortunate to have them in my life.

I also want to thank my beta readers. This trusted group of people were the first to lay eyes on my written words. It was daunting and frightening to release this creative project out into the world. My beta readers took on the task with love and kindness. They gave me honest feedback and encouraged me to continue. With their help, Kate and Molly became stronger characters and I became a stronger writer. I cannot thank them enough for their important role in bringing this book to market.

Finally, I want to thank everyone else who has encouraged me over the years to write. Once I found my voice and my inspiration, these same people cheered me on. They generously gifted me with their inspirational words and have helped me more than they will ever know.

Special Acknowledgements
Leesa Ellis, 3 ferns books
www.3fernsbooks.com

I want to thank Leesa for her guidance. With her help, I made educated decisions on all aspects of the self-publishing process. Plus, she kept me on track with deadlines and Zoom calls. Because of her extensive knowledge, she took the worry out of publishing my first book.

Marcelo Simonetti
www.marcelosimonetti.com
Instagram: @simonetti.marcelo_art

I would like to thank Marcelo for all of his help. Working with him was a genuine pleasure. He patiently hung in there with me during the creative process and helped me to bring my characters to life. I am thrilled beyond measure.

STORY 1
KATE ERSLAND

Going Home
The American Colonies

Standing on a small knoll, Kate surveyed the scene before her. This cannot be right. She must have forgotten the way.

Please, please let me be in the wrong place.

Her heartbeat was deafening in her ears. Her body knew what her mind was refusing to accept. A tear slipped down Kate's cheek as she gazed at the burnt-out cabin before her. It was clear to Kate that no-one had cared for the cabin in a long time.

Maybe they moved.

Kate walked down the small hill, making her way toward the cabin she had been born in. Her eyes frantically roved over the area, looking for any sign that her family was alive, that they had moved on after the raid. She took in the trees and bushes that were growing wildly around the cabin. The Ersland family had kept the wilderness at bay while they'd lived here. Now the wilderness had taken back much of the area. Kate's stomach clenched. She fought against the bile hitting the back of her throat.

Now is not the time to be sick.

She pushed the horror of that day out of her thoughts. She was young. Maybe her recollection of the day was wrong. She'd convinced herself that her family had survived. They were alive somewhere.

Kate remembered the small garden that her mother tended. For their mother's birthday, Kate and her sisters had made a sign that hung on the garden gate. Her mother loved it and would never have left it behind. If it wasn't there, her family was alive. If it was still there, the unthinkable had happened.

Kate made her way around the cabin to where the garden was. She paused when she saw them. Kate's breath came in shallow gasps and her vision faded until finally everything went black and she dropped to the ground in a heap.

It was dusk when Kate finally came to. She felt disoriented as she sat up. Where was she? Where was her family? Kate's gaze landed on the graves. "No! No!" Kate's sorrow poured out of her in cries of desolation and pain. She sat on her knees, arms wrapped around her stomach, rocking back and forth. The graves she saw beyond the cabin couldn't hold her family. They just couldn't be the graves of her family. She had to find out.

With heavy steps, Kate made her way to the markers. She needed to know. The dread in her stomach was heavy and gnawed at her insides.

There were four. The names on the wooden crosses were worn but they held the names of her parents and two sisters. Kate collapsed, thankful that she was once again blacking out and the intense anguish was pushed to the outer edges of her consciousness.

Kate spent the rest of the day and that night sitting with her family, singing the soothing lullabies she remembered from childhood. Her mind drifted to the happier times in the cabin. Her father, Karle Ersland, had been a large man with an even larger laugh. She and her sisters would hear him walking back from the fields, singing as loudly as he could. The girls would run down the path to meet him and he would gather them up in his arms, squeezing them in a tight hug. Kate cried as she remembered how he smelled of horses, dirt, and sweat. His thick, blond beard would scratch them as he kissed them. Their Norwegian roots were clear in her mother and sisters. Her mother, Birgitta, and her sisters, Ylva and Brenna, were all beauties. Kate, the youngest of the Ersland clan, shared that beauty with their white-blonde hair and their brilliant blue eyes. Birgitta loved Kate and her sisters. She taught them folk magic from the old country and the songs of their ancestors. Her father didn't like that her mother was bringing the old country to this new country but he loved his wife and allowed her to keep that connection to their homeland. Kate sat by the graves, trying to remember every detail of their happy lives before that fateful day when it was all shattered by the Indian raiders.

Kate removed the blanket she had tied on her back like a makeshift pack. She unrolled the blanket and set aside her few belongings. Kate kneeled on the blanket and and stayed there late into the night. Her grief and anger came in fits and waves. She cursed the Indians who had killed her family and stole her away. Kate screamed her hatred of the gods who'd brought the Erslands to this place. She grieved the loss of her family. She cried aloud as loneliness settled deep within her.

As the moon rose high above, the cool evening became a cold night. Kate was not ready to leave her family so she gathered wood and started a fire. Kate placed her blanket beside the fire. Across the flames, she could see the graves of the Erslands. Beyond the graves, the full moon shone down. Kate took a knife from the belt around her waist. She held her arms outstretched, and in the native language that they had taught her during her years with them, she sang the song of mourning and of loss. She held the knife in her right hand and began making small cuts in her left forearm. Each cut moved the pain from her heart to her arm. Kate moved the knife to her left hand and continued to cut her right arm. Kate leaned toward the fire and watched the blood drip from her arms. The pain in her arms would go away sooner than the pain she felt in her soul but, for now, it was a relief to not feel such deep sorrow.

As the sun rose the next morning, Kate knew it was time to leave her family and her memories behind. Somehow, she had to begin again and make a life amongst the white settlers that she remembered from her time here. She tried to remember where the settlement was and turned in all four directions, attempting to get her bearings. The landscape was unfamiliar but she vaguely recalled riding in the wagon with her family to pick up supplies. She was uncertain but decided east was most likely the right direction. Pausing, Kate hoped she was remembering accurately. She walked to the cabin and placed her hand on one wall, her head bowed. Could she still make out the smell of burnt wood? Was it only her memory that brought back the sickening stench of the Ersland home burning to the ground?

The horrible memories of that fateful day hit her. She sank to the ground as the images overwhelmed her. Kate recalled the sounds of the Indians riding around the cabin and her mother yelling for her and her sisters to get into the root cellar. She remembered hearing the door breaking, her mother screaming in pain and how her older sisters clambered out of the cellar to help her. Their efforts were in vain. The Indians slayed Ylva and Brenna. Their dead bodies fell next to Birgitta. Kate retched as she remembered her father's booming voice, silenced in death. She shook as she relived watching one of the Indians climb down to the cellar and spot her.

Young Kate had stood and stared at him, her blue eyes wide with fear. He stared at her for a moment, his face void of emotion. He motioned for her to come to him. She had been so frightened but she couldn't resist walking to him. He crouched in front of her and touched the eagle feather Kate had tied into her braid. He stood and held his hand out to Kate. She put her small hand in his. Kate recalled how pale her hand had looked against his dark skin. The Indian looked down at her for a few moments, almost as if he was unsure. As he studied her, the man seemed to contemplate something. He looked toward his fellow warriors and back down at Kate. He pulled her along with him up the stairs onto the main floor of the cabin.

Thinking back, Kate barely recalled being put on a horse and the man jumping on behind her. She remembered hearing a lot of shouting in a language she didn't understand. Her captor had the last word and kicked his horse. With that, they left behind her home, her family, and her happiness. They rode hard and arrived at the Indian village late that night. She remembered waking up in her captor's tent. His wife fed her, cleaned her, and let her sleep through the night. From then on, he was no longer her captor. They made her a part of the family and she learned to have a happy life with them. Until the night her brother helped her escape.

Kate stopped and berated herself. These thoughts of the past wouldn't help her start her new life. She had to get up and find the settlement. It had recently rained. The wet ground gave way under her feet. Kate lifted her head and took in a deep breath. She loved the smell of fresh rain. A wagon carrying a young family came toward her.

Good! Maybe they will give me a ride to the settlement.

As she tried to stop them, the people on the wagon looked frightened. The man urged the horses on faster. Mud splashed underneath the wheels of the cart and landed on Kate's dress. She looked down at the droplets of mud. Kate hadn't considered how she looked. She was tall, her blonde hair was in loose braids, and her beaded buckskin dress was obviously native. She needed to be careful and get to the safety of the settlement before someone stopped her with questions about her appearance.

After walking for two hours, Kate made it to the settlement. It didn't look that different from when she'd left. It was bigger and busier but still familiar. The large wooden gates that were once shut and guarded were now open and people were free to come and go at will. She recalled her mother's favorite mercantile and headed there. Maybe her mother's friend still owned it. Kate walked to the store, trying to keep her head down and not draw attention to herself.

As she entered the shop, she felt relieved. It looked very much the same as it did when she was last here many years ago with her family. Like everything else, it was larger and there were more people. Her gaze stopped on Bertha, her mother's friend and the owner of the store. Kate started toward Bertha when she heard a scream.

Kate turned to see a woman pointing at her and screaming. All eyes turned toward Kate. Bertha took in a quick breath and rushed over. The woman was still screaming and holding her children close to her. Bertha turned and told the woman to be quiet. With tears in her eyes, Bertha grabbed Kate's arms. "Katherine? Kate, is that really you?"

All Kate could do was nod. She couldn't speak. Her throat was thick with a mixture of suffering and relief.

The woman grabbed her in a tight hug and sobbed. "I knew it was you. You look just like your mother."

The store full of people stood staring with their mouths open. Kate wanted to run when a man shouted, "Why is there a savage with white hair in your store, Bertha?"

Bertha called to her husband.

He came out of the backroom and didn't say a word, but his eyes grew wide when he saw Kate.

"Owen! Quit yer gawking and get these people out of here!" Bertha ordered.

Owen herded their patrons toward the front door, promising they would be open again the next morning. Bertha had her arms wrapped her arms around Kate's shoulders, urging her to a set of stairs that led to the rooms above the store that served as their home. Kate slumped over on a small sofa while Bertha made her food. She could lie down on this sofa and sleep for days. As Kate ate, Bertha and Owen got a bath ready. They left her soaking while Bertha went downstairs to gather some suitable clothing. Kate could hear their voices drifting into the small kitchen.

"Bertha, you know she can't be here. Folks will turn against us if we allow her to stay." Owen was desperate for his wife to see reason in this matter. The girl could not stay with them.

"That is nonsense. No one would expect us to turn Karle and Birgitta's daughter out into the cold."

"Yes, yes they can and they will. She's been living with those Indians all these years. They will see her as one of them. If we let her stay, this is going to be bad, Bertha. Very, very bad."

"I do not believe that. Look what she's survived. She is a miracle. We are not sending that precious child away."

Kate smiled. At least some things hadn't changed in her absence. Bertha was still a feisty, stubborn woman who couldn't be intimidated or pressured by those around her.

Bertha helped Kate clean herself. The small bathing bucket was only large enough to sit in. Kate's knees were even with her chin and the water just hit at her waist.

Bertha laughed, "You surely did grow tall, Katherine. Your papa would proud as can be of you. Now, step on out of there and so I can wash your hair."

Kate stepped out of the bathing bucket, knelt down and leaned over it.

"Do you remember the color of my mother's hair, Bertha? I think it is the same as mine, but I'm not sure."

Holding back tears Bertha undid the braids in Kate's hair and gently washed her long, blond hair. "Yes, it is the same. Your mother's hair shone like the sun even on the darkest night. Your hair is just as beautiful, Kate."

Kate sighed. "Good. I am happy to carry something of my mother with me."

Bertha helped Kate dry off, stopping at the fresh cuts on her forearms. Bertha shook her head and patted the wounds dry.

"Now what happened here, child?"

Kate didn't answer. How could she explain what she had done to herself and why? Bertha helped Kate dress. She felt restricted in her new attire but she knew if she was going to fit in, her clothing was the first step in doing so. She sat in a chair as Bertha put her hair in one long braid down her back. As she did this, she whispered reassurances to Kate. Everything was fine. Kate was home. She could stay with them. She was safe now.

Kate quietly cried, her heart breaking as she slowly started to accept her family's deaths. During the years she'd lived with the Indians, Kate had always hoped that her family was still alive. That they had somehow survived the raid. As the years passed, she imagined her sisters growing up. What did they look like now? As Kate grew taller, she wondered if her sisters were the same height. She often envisioned her family sitting around the fire after dinner, wondering what she looked like.

Now, her mind felt like her enemy. It held in the forefront the sights, sounds, and smells of the day the Indians slaughtered her family. She'd loved her new family. Kate had wonderful memories of laughing with them and living in happiness with them. The guilt of that almost sent Kate over the edge to oblivion again.

"Kate, you need to sleep. You've had a shock to your mind and body today. Sleep will help," Bertha urged. Kate gladly curled up on the sofa and quickly drifted to sleep.

Kate awoke to Bertha making supper for the three of them and then they sat around the table to eat. She remembered the Ersland's time around their table. Sharing meals. Laughing and talking about the day's events. Her father lighting his pipe after supper and telling Kate and her sisters stories of the old country. The weight of Owen's gaze resting heavily on her face jerked Kate out of her reverie. She felt uncomfortable under his scrutiny and looked at him. "I… I guess you are wondering where I've been."

He nodded, saying nothing. Bertha rested her hand on his arm and said to Kate, "Only if you are ready to tell us, dear."

Owen wasn't as patient as Bertha. "Of course you can tell us where you've been when you're ready but you lived with the savages. Any fool can see that. They put their mark on you." Owen sighed heavily. "Bertha, this girl is not fit for polite society any longer. No one will accept her in their homes, their businesses, or their churches with those marks on her face."

Bertha shook her head and smiled at Kate. "It will all be fine, dear."

Owen snorted, giving Bertha his best *there is no way this is going to be fine* look he could muster.

Kate looked down, covering her chin with her hand. She hadn't seen herself in a long time. Sometimes in a calm stream, when the light was just right, she could see her reflection. Most of the time, Kate didn't think about the marks on her face. They'd given her the first tattoos out of fear. It was their way of protecting themselves, and her, from the evil spirits the tribe thought she brought with her. The newer ones they'd given out of love. Kate was not ashamed of the life she had with the Indians but she wasn't ready to talk about any of it just yet. Even when she did finally tell Bertha and Owen about the past few years, she would leave out the love she had for her second family. Kate was sure they wouldn't understand.

"Do you know who buried my family?" Kate tried to move the conversation away from things she wasn't ready to talk about.

Bertha set her fork down on the table and folded her hands in front of her. "We did. Owen and I found your family dead and the cabin burned. When we didn't see your family for two weeks, we became concerned. We rode out to the cabin and found them." Tears rolled down Bertha's cheeks.

Owen put his big hand over Bertha's, comforting her as she continued. "Owen and I organized the town to dig graves and have a memorial for your family. We couldn't find you, of course. We feared that the raiding party had taken you with them." Bertha looked at Kate's face and reached out, gently stroking Kate's chin and the lines tattooed there. "I am sorry for whatever those savages did to you, Katherine." Bertha choked down a sob and forcefully stood up. "Now, if you will excuse me, I am feeling tired. I think I will go to bed now."

Kate watched Bertha make her way to their bedroom. She couldn't imagine how horrible it had been for Bertha and Owen to find the Ersland family slaughtered and, for these years, not knowing what had happened to their youngest member. Would it make it easier or harder for Bertha to know that the Indians had treated her with love and kindness? Would it make Kate seem like a terrible daughter if she thought of Red Eagle Feather and Small Snow Fox as her parents as well? Could either of them understand how desperately she missed her brother Kan?

She kept that knowledge to herself. No one needed to know. After experiencing the reactions in the shop that morning, she didn't think it would be wise to share too much of her time with the Indian tribe. It would be her secret. Kate's eyelids felt heavy. Tonight, she needed rest. Tomorrow, she would begin building her new life.

Bertha woke Kate up from her deep slumber with a bright, "Good morning, dear! Are you ready for a wonderful day?"

Kate smiled at Bertha. The poor woman was trying so hard. She had determined that Kate would be fine. She believed Kate would begin a new life and no one would hold her time with the Indians against her.

As Kate folded the blankets that they'd given her the night before, Bertha rushed over. "Look at this fabric!" She shoved the folded blue fabric toward Kate. "Just as I thought. The blue is the same color as your eyes. The pink flowers will show everyone just how sweet you are. Look at this beautiful lace. It will be pretty at the collar and wrists. It is perfect. We will make a dress for you today."

Kate wasn't sure. The blue did match her eyes, but the small pink flowers dotted over the field of blue seemed too young. Too innocent. Would people really look past her face and her faltering English because of pink flowers?

Kate hugged Bertha. "I love it. Thank you."

Bertha sewed all day. Owen tried to talk her into coming down to the mercantile to help customers but she refused. He and Kate made lunch but she wouldn't eat. Bertha's disheveled hair and red eyes from both the strain of sewing and bouts of crying showed the stress she was under. Kate could hear Bertha mumbling a promise to Kate's mother.

By the late evening, she'd completed the dress. Bertha helped Kate put the dress on and put Kate's hair in a tidy bun at the back of her head. She stepped back, studied Kate's look, frowned and shook her head. After letting Kate's hair fall freely down her back, she swept up some of her hair into a knot. Bertha stood in front of Kate, pulling her blonde hair forward and partially covering her face. This time when Bertha stood back, she seemed satisfied.

Bertha led Kate downstairs to find Owen. Owen looked up as they approached. Kate looked uncomfortable. Bertha looked as if she had created something magical that would hide Kate's obvious time spent with the Indians.

Bertha waited, her eyes sharp. "Well? What do you think? Isn't it perfect?" She turned to Kate, fussing with the long sleeves and high neck.

Owen gazed at Kate with pity. Bertha had made this dress, intending to cover as much of Kate as she could. The sleeves were very long and hung past her wrists. The collar was severe. It was tall and buttoned closed just below her lower jaw. The small amount of lace peeking out of the collar and wrists did little to ease the fact that the blue dress looked like a suit of armor meant to keep the world at bay. Even Kate's hair covered much of her face.

Owen put his arm around Bertha and hugged her. Regardless of whether his well-meaning wife hadn't meant to, she was clearly trying to protect Kate by hiding as much of the girl as she could. She may have said that Kate being there was fine but the thought of Kate's probable fate upset her. She was as worried as he was about this young woman.

Looking down on Bertha's beaming face, he smiled. *Yes, they were going to pretend all is well.*

"You look beautiful Katherine." Owen said through a tight smile.

Traveling Down the Mississippi
Minnesota to New Orleans

To ease the burden she'd put on Bertha and Owen, Kate attempted to find work. Each morning, she would don her blue dress and arrange her hair so it covered much of her face. Kate talked to every person she could to find work, despite them treating her as an outcast and a heathen. Most people would simply ignore her. Some would rush away from her while others were blatantly rude, telling her she should go back to those murdering Indians because she no longer had a home amongst civilized people. Kate realized her wish to return to the life she once knew was going to be harder than she expected. The years she spent as an Indian captive made her somewhat of an interesting oddity. Her hesitant use of the English language and her face tattoos made it impossible for people to forget that, for a time, she had been one of those Indians.

In Bertha and Owen's home, Kate found a small mirror hanging on the wall. She stood in front of it, inspecting her face. Kate decided she looked a lot like her mother. Her striking hair and eyes were her most attractive features. Kate wasn't as pale as she remembered her mother and sisters being. Kate had lived a lot of her life outside in the sun. Her darker skin just made her blonde hair and blue eyes stand out more. Her tattoos were the problem.

To Kate, they were art. They were spirit. They were symbols of protection. She trailed her finger down the line that started on her lower lip and ended with a diamond shape on her chest. Kate traced the lines going down her chin from either side of the long line. These two lines had smaller lines leading out. Each short line had three dots on the top and underneath. She also had several dots above each eyebrow.

In the years that Kate spent with the tribe, the length of the midline and the dots were added. The dots marked the number of years she spent with the tribe. As Kate studied her tattoos, she reminded herself why she had them. The tribe believed the tattoos to be spiritual marks that protected themselves and Kate as well. She couldn't bring herself to hate the people or the marks they placed on her.

Kate was never sure what the original reason was behind the tribal elder's orders. She was the only person in the village with tattoos on her face. Then again, Kate was unfamiliar territory to them. She was the only white person in their village. Kate considered her open palm. The elder had initially forced the tattoos on her but in the following years, Kate insisted that on her tribal anniversary that they add to her facial tattoos. The small tattoo on the palm of her hand just below her pointer finger had also been her choice. She and her brother had given each other a matching tattoo. Kate's mark was on her right hand, her brother's on his left hand, a reminder of their bond. When they touched their marks once again, the time and space between them would be erased. It was a reminder of the love her Indian family had for her and she for them.

A month after her return, things still hadn't gotten better for Kate. She couldn't find work. The people wouldn't accept her. Bertha struggled to find ways for Kate to blend in but nothing worked. Even the traveling minister wouldn't welcome Kate into his flock. He flatly told Bertha that he didn't minister to heathens. Every night, Kate listened to Bertha crying. Kate knew something had to change. She just wasn't sure what to do or where to go.

One evening, the three of them sat silently eating supper. The people in the area had to shop at Bertha and Owen's mercantile. It was the only one but many didn't like the idea of them housing Kate. There were whispers that Bertha and Owen should leave the settlement.

Owen, clearing his throat, broke the silence. Kate jumped, startled by the sound. "My cousin owns a shipping company in New Orleans. The stories making their way up the river sounds like the perfect place for... someone like Kate to make a life. We should send her. The sooner... the better."

Owen nodded his head while speaking. It looked to Kate like he was trying to convince himself that what he was saying was the truth, that Kate needed to go and her destination should be New Orleans.

"Owen! I am shocked that you would suggest such a thing. You would send this sweet child away like she is an inconvenient dog?"

"She cannot stay here, Bertha! These people won't accept her. You would let one stray girl ruin everything we have? Everything we've built with our hard work? I'm sorry, Kate, I truly am, but I won't allow Bertha and myself to suffer because of your presence in our home."

Bertha stood up quickly, the chair scraping harshly across the floor. "You listen to me, Owen Anderson! I won't turn out Birgitta's only surviving child! Her home is here with us. We are her family now. That is final!" Bertha stalked to their bedroom and slammed the door behind her.

Owen sighed, shaking his head. He and Kate sat in uncomfortable silence as they finished their supper.

That night, Kate tossed and turned in her makeshift bed on the living room floor. She overheard Owen and Bertha quietly arguing well into the early morning. Kate considered Owen's offer. The new and wild town sounded more promising than this God-fearing settlement in the north. These people had not only refused to accept her but they weren't kind to Bertha and Owen about sheltering Kate. Bertha insisted the people just needed more time to adjust. Kate wasn't so sure. She didn't expect these people to accept her, even if they had thousands of years to do so.

Kate was tired of being treated so poorly. Since she couldn't find work elsewhere, Kate worked in Bertha and Owen's store. People whispered about her just loud enough for her to hear. Daily, she heard them talking about her.

"There's the blonde heathen that turned her back on her own people. She doesn't care one bit about the death of her family. She should have killed herself before letting those Indians do that to her."

There were days that Kate's heart would ache with doubt. Were they right? Should she have fought the Indians when they took her? Maybe she would be better off if she was buried next to her parents and her sisters.

One cold rainy day, Kate was sweeping the store. The gray day amplified Kate's misery. Her mind was swimming with dark thoughts. She contemplated going back to the cabin and taking her own life. At least then she would be with her family. Would the people of this place think her death was more honorable than her life? Would they come to bury and mourn her as they had her family? Kate was deep in thought when a mother and her two children came into the store. They lived on a farm far from town and hadn't seen Kate yet. Kate looked up from her task of sweeping the floor when the shop bell rang as the door opened. The woman froze when she saw Kate.

She started screaming. "Bertha? Owen? Where are you? Are you here?" Her face was red and her eyes bulged out of fear as she screamed at Kate. "You stay away from us! Bertha! Bertha!" Bertha ran from the stockroom to see what was wrong. Seeing Bertha, she stopped yelling. Angrily, she stabbed a finger toward Kate. "Who is this?"

"This is Katherine Ersland, Karle and Birgitta's youngest daughter. You must remember her! She found her way home. Isn't it wonderful?"

"Wonderful? Wonderful?" the woman sputtered, shaking her head in denial. "No! It is not wonderful that you have a savage whore working here. I heard the rumors but I didn't want to believe them! What has gotten into your head, Bertha Anderson? You know what the Indians do to their captives."

Bertha tried to calm the woman. "Lettie, this is Katherine Ersland. You must remember the Erslands? They went to our church. They shopped here often. Kate is a miracle! If you heard rumors surrounding Kate, then you know she survived her time with the Indians and returned to us. Lettie, please. We couldn't be happier that Kate has come back to us."

Lettie pushed her children behind her full skirts, vehemently shaking her head. "No! She isn't safe. She was one of them. What if she kills you and Owen in your sleep?"

Bertha looked exasperated with Lettie's hysterics. "That is nonsense, Lettie Baker, and you well know it."

Lettie's face hardened. She glared at Kate. "We won't be back in here as long as you have that filthy thing here. I will talk to our church pastor and members of our lady's prayer group. Soon enough, no one will buy their goods here. How is that for wonderful?" With that threat left hanging, Lettie turned and dragged her children after her. Bertha watched from the window as Lettie angrily walked down the street with her poor children attempting to keep up with their mother.

That night's supper was quiet. Owen wouldn't look at either of the women sharing the table with him. He sat stiffly in his chair, stabbing his food and shoving it into his mouth. Bertha would occasionally glance sideways in his direction but she wouldn't give in. Kate felt horrible that Owen and Bertha were suffering from her presence in their lives. She sighed quietly, knowing what she had to do. Kate put her fork down and gripped her hands tightly together.

Before she lost her nerve, Kate blurted out, "I think I would like to try a life in New Orleans. Working for a shipping company in a new town would be exciting. An adventure. What if my tattoos are not a problem there? Wouldn't that be wonderful, Bertha? Owen, you are certain that your cousin would give me work?"

Both Owen and Bertha turned toward her. Bertha was shaking her head no but Owen looked relieved. "I'll write a letter. He's a good man. I know he would take good care of you, Kate."

"When can I leave?" Kate reached out to Bertha and touched her arm. "I have loved being here with you and Owen but I am ready to start a new life." Kate tried to sound and look more confident than she felt, however the tears streaming down her face told the truth of her fear and pain at the thought of leaving Bertha and Owen. It took all of her resolve to stay in the chair and not run to the chamber pot and lose her dinner.

The following morning, the three of them sat around the small table and discussed Kate's departure. Bertha couldn't stop her tears. The guilt was eating away at her. Birgitta had been her friend. How could they do this to the youngest Ersland child, especially after she lived through a horror and then made her way back to them? Bertha was certain they were betraying the Erslands. "If that dear woman is looking down from Heaven, I'm sure that Birgitta is very disappointed in me. I can feel it, Owen! I can feel Birgitta's displeasure with our actions. We should give it more time. Maybe send Kate later in the summer?" Bertha pleaded.

Owen ignored Bertha's tears. After all, this shop was their entire life. Without it, they would starve and be homeless. He would not allow one wayward waif to interfere with that. "Bertha, my cousin is doing very well there. It's a newly established town and, while yes, it's a little rowdy, it is more accepting of all types there." "Rowdy? Rowdy? What does that mean, Owen? You want to send this poor girl who survived so much to a rowdy town because she has a few marks on her face?" "Yes. Those marks on her face set her apart from every other person in this territory. My cousin is a kind man and he will care for Kate. She will be just fine. In fact, she will probably do a lot better there than she's done here. Her new life has not been a great success, Bertha, and you damn well know it!"

Owen instantly felt bad. He never used foul language with Bertha. Despite her stubbornness, he loved her dearly. Owen gathered Bertha to him in a tight hug. "She can't stay here, Bertha. She just can't. She will ruin us." Bertha leaned into her tall husband and sobbed. Bertha knew he was right. Kate couldn't stay with them.

Two days later, Bertha and Owen were feeling both relief and sorrow at sending Kate away in the company of a trusted friend. Claude had been a French fur trapper in the area for years. He was a good friend to Owen and he had been around long enough that he still remembered Kate's father. The man shook Owen's hand and hugged Bertha. "I promise I will treat Kate as if she were my own daughter. I will get her safely to New Orleans."

Owen handed Kate a bag. "Here are some provisions. Claude is an excellent trapper, he will catch fresh meat along the route but I'm sure you will want to eat something other than raccoon and beaver on your trip." Kate laughed. "Thank you. I can also forage for herbs and berries, I'm sure." Owen hugged her. "Take care, Kate. I am praying that life treats you kinder where you are going." Kate's eyes filled with tears and she hugged him tight.

"Your blue dress is wrapped up in that bag, Kate. Keep it safe and clean until you reach your destination. You want to make a good impression on your future employer." Bertha could barely speak. The emotion was thick in her throat. Kate took the bag. "Thank you for all of your kindness. I know that my parent's are looking down on you and thanking you for being so good to their youngest child."

"Bless you for saying so, child." Bertha straightened the plain brown skirt and simple ivory top Kate was wearing. "You take good care of yourself, Katherine Ersland. Do you hear me?" Kate nodded in response, unable to speak. "You must promise to write as soon as you're settled in New Orleans. Do you promise?" Bertha pressed Kate for an answer.

Kate nodded again. She knew this was the best decision for all of them. It didn't make it any easier or any less painful though. These people were the last connection to her childhood and the happy times she had with her family. "I promise. Thank you for everything you two did for me. I love you both and I will miss you." Kate's voice was thick with emotion.

She gave them each one more hug and turned to follow the old trapper to the river where his canoe was waiting. As she was about to round the corner and leave them for good, Kate turned one last time to see her mother's friend sobbing into her husband's shoulder. Owen lifted his hand in one last wave. Kate waved back. With that, she turned and didn't look back again. She was ready for whatever came next.

STORY 2
THE MEETING OF KATE & MOLLY

Frightened Rabbit
New Orleans

Kate stepped out of the canoe onto the bank of the Mississippi River. She turned to the French trapper whom she had spent weeks traveling with. His weathered face showed he was concerned for her. Kate smiled. He spoke little English but she still said, "I will be just fine." She hoped she sounded and looked more confident than she felt. He tossed Kate the one bag she had. Kate thanked him and turned to make her way into town.

In the bag Kate carried were all the belongings she had in the world including the letter from Owen introducing her to his cousin. She glanced down at the bag and her clothing. Everything was dirty and ragged. It had been a long trek down the river from the far north. Her father's friend had seen her safely here and she appreciated his kindness. Still, the smell wafting from her — wet fur, mud, and smoke from the fires she huddled next to each night trying to stay warm — was horrible. She stopped and attempted to brush off the dirt and muck on her clothing. She also tried to smooth her hair. This was the last stop on the river. She had to make a home here. If the stories were true, she should be able to settle in and make a new life.

Kate made her way into New Orleans. This new, bustling city already had a reputation for accepting wild French citizens. Kate needed to find her place here and hoped for honest work. As she watched the divergent throng of people walk down the street, Kate prayed that her tattooed face would be an interesting benefit and not a hindrance in her ability to earn money. Owen was certain that his cousin would take her in and give her a job. Kate hoped he was correct. If not... Kate refused to think about that. First things first.

Kate only had a few coins in her sack so she needed to start work soon. She hoped Owen's cousin had a generous nature and wouldn't only give her a job but lodging as well. Kate's exhaustion felt like a wet blanket weighing her down. She needed to find a quiet place to sleep for an hour or two before she sought her future employer. She looked for a secluded area where she could rest and change into her blue dress. Kate wandered down an alley that was far away from the view of the crowded main street. She found a tight corner behind a shop and sank to the ground. She wedged in, wrapping her arms around her bag and hugging it to herself as she tried to keep warm. The minute she stopped moving, mental and physical fatigue took over, and she drifted off to sleep.

Kate awoke, startled, with a man standing over her. In a thick French accent, he asked, "What do we have here?"

Kate gasped and struggled to stand up and run. The filthy man, dressed in furs, grabbed both sides of her hair and slammed her against the wall.

"Where do you think you're going, *petit lapin?*" He looked closely at her mouth. "I have a perfect use for that tattooed face of yours." With both hands still in her hair, he roughly kissed her, jamming his tongue into her mouth. Her back against the wall, he pressed harder against her. He released one side of her hair and dragged a hand down her body.

She cried out in pain when he squeezed her breast and desperately struggled to get loose but he had a firm grip on her hair and she couldn't break free. His disgusting stench was overpowering. Kate was sobbing, trying to push him back so she would not throw up from his putrid odor and foul taste.

He growled at her. "If you bite me, wench, I will slit your throat." He once again pushed his tongue deep into her mouth. Grinding against her and roughly groping her body. Kate fought the man but he was larger and stronger than she was. Fear clenched her belly. Did she travel all this way for this terror? Kate tried to scream, but the large man grabbed her upper arms and slammed her against the wall again.

"Be quiet, little rabbit. Maybe I let you live once I'm done." His wicked smile told her he had no such plans.

"Excuse me."

Kate stopped struggling. Did she hear someone?

"I said, excuse me, good sir. The lady doesn't seem to be a willing participant in your fun. Did you forget to pay her?"

"Go away!"

"As I said, the lady looks to be doing her best to escape you and your brutish behavior. I'm quite sure she would like you to release her." Kate didn't recognize the person's accent.

"Leave now or I will kill you!" the dirty man yelled without releasing his grip on her.

Kate's rescuer responded in a more serious tone. "Let her go at once or you will lose any future ability to have relations with women — willing or otherwise."

The man let out at an angry bellow and threw Kate away from him. She flew to the side and hit the ground hard. For a moment, her world went dark and all she could see were shooting stars as her head bounced off of the side of the wooden building.

The man turned and came face to face with a woman staring calmly back at him. He took her in slowly. Her long, red hair was thick with braids and curls. She kept the mass at bay with a black headscarf that covered part of her forehead, ran under the curls, and tied at her neck. She had one brilliant green eye and a patch covered her other eye. A large scar ran from her forehead, through her eyebrow, and down to her cheekbone. Her ankle-length coat, fitted pants, and knee-high boots looked more suited for life on a ship. Her white shirt was tucked into the waist of her pants and silver belts were slung low on her hips. She looked relaxed and had a slight self-assured smile on her face. A sword could clearly be seen under her coat. Perhaps that was the reason she didn't appear frightened of the large trapper. It gave him pause for a moment. Most men avoided conflict with him. Why was this woman facing him without fear? He shook off the doubt. There was no way a woman could ever beat him in a fight.

The man laughed. "You? A *chienne* like you thinks she's going to best me? What's your name? When I tell this story tonight at the tavern, I want a name to go with the one-eyed, Irish pig that lost her life over a *lapin effrayé.*"

The woman raised her eyebrows in feigned surprise. "I am Molly Malone." She cocked her head to the side in contemplation. "You haven't heard of me?" His short, harsh laugh told her he hadn't.

"Pity. If you had heard of this, Irish pig, you might have lived through the day."

The Frenchman drew a large hunting knife from the sheath on his hip. He leaned forward and in a hushed, coarse tone threatened Molly. "First, I am going to kill you and fuck your dead body. Then, I will finish by slitting the throat of that white-haired bitch. When I am done, I will leave you both here so the rats and the starving can feast on your flesh."

Molly looked irritated. "I agree. You do have the size and probably the experience to beat me in a fight. Yet, I'm confident that I will kill you. My mates are always telling me I have more bollocks than brains." Molly's brows met as she pondered that statement for a moment. She looked the filthy man in the eye. "Perhaps that is true. I, however, feel that we're all headed to the devil's dance floor. I just want to live in such a way that makes my attendance there worthwhile."

Molly quickly flung back her coat and drew her sword. The man's eyes widened in shock. "Where did you get a sword like that?" The trapper took in the sword's curved blade, ornate hilt, and intricate golden etchings.

Molly kept her eye squarely on him. She lifted the sword so he could see the weapon better. "It was a gift from my first captain. I saved his life and in doing so lost my eye." Molly motioned to her missing left eye. "He wasn't able to give back my eye, so he gave me this sword. It's called a scimitar. He took it from a Moroccan merchant captain. I'm not sure what a Moroccan is but this beautiful sword is something to behold. Do you not agree? It thirsts for blood and hasn't let me down in a fight yet."

The man reconsidered his earlier confidence and backed away from her.

Molly's smirk grew. "So, you are smarter than you look. Go and I will spare your life. Go! Run away, *lapin effrayé,*" Molly said throwing his insult back at him.

The Frenchman stopped, his face darkening with rage. "Me? A *lapin effrayé*? Fortune is smiling down on this trapper. For tonight I will not only have the story of your death to tell, I will also have a sword to sell."

The man rushed Molly, the large blade glinting in the sun. As he came closer, Molly spun away and slashed downward against the man's shoulder and back. The trapper roared in pain. He still held his knife but Molly could see he was struggling. He turned and again he ran toward her. With a quick step forward, Molly gripped her sword and rammed it through his belly. Molly watched his blood spill out as she slid her sword out of his body. He dropped his knife and sank to his knees, his hands on the fresh wound. The shock on his face was plain to see as he stared up at Molly. He saw nothing on her face. No anger. No pleasure. No remorse. Nothing. She stood over him, waiting for the moment when he realized his fate was fixed. He was leaving this life behind and was going to Hell. After she was certain that he was close to death and couldn't ever do harm to another woman, she wiped her sword on the man's clothing. After returning her sword to its sheath, she turned to walk away.

"Please! Please! Do not leave me. I need your help."

Molly stopped, turned around and looked at the woman she had just saved. Kate's blonde hair and clothing were dirty and disheveled. Her entire demeanor was that of a broken woman in a desperate situation. Molly had her own problems and didn't want another burden. Her soft spot for hard-luck cases had already given her another mouth to feed and cost her coin she couldn't spare. Molly started to turn away when Kate's tattoos caught her eye. She strode back and knelt before Kate to she could get a closer look. "Why do you have these?"

Kate reactively covered her mouth and chin with her hand. "When I was a girl, I was captured by Indians. They tattooed my face."

"Why?"

"It was their belief that the marks would ward off evil. It was a way to protect their people... and me."

Molly stood straight up, remembering the words of Mambo Nicole, who had told her to watch for a blond woman with tattoos on her face. She had said this woman would be her friend, her greatest ally, and would signal a great change in Molly's life. Molly could barely contain herself. "What's your name?"

"Katherine Ersland, but most people call me Kate."

Molly nodded. "All right then, Kate. You may come with me."

Molly helped Kate up off the ground. Kate could barely stand. She was bent over, leaning against the wall, shaking. She started crying, then violently threw up. Molly felt for this woman. She understood the feelings of being helpless and hurt but allowing her to continue like this wouldn't help either of them. They were in a dangerous city. Molly needed to get her back to the room at the boarding house. She did not want to fight off anyone else while trying to keep this woman safe. They really didn't need anyone finding them standing over a dead French trapper.

"Kate, we have to go. That Frenchman was correct. You look like a frightened rabbit, an easy target for just about every person on these streets."

Kate didn't move, her arms wrapped around her midsection. Her sobs were getting louder. Molly grabbed her arm and turned her around. "Enough! We must get off these streets." Molly pulled out a cloth and wiped Kate's face. Kate took in a deep breath to calm herself. She wasn't sure she could survive another attack. She really wasn't sure her rescuer would want to save her once again. They had to get to safety. She nodded to Molly. Molly picked up the bag and motioned for Kate to follow her. Kate stumbled seemingly unable to hold her own weight. Molly put her arm around Kate's waist and helped her walk. They headed toward the boarding house as Molly debated how she was going to explain this latest addition to Séamus.

Shelter

New Orleans, Boarding House

Séamus knelt in front of a five-year-old ex-slave boy. The boy sat slumped in the chair and didn't want to eat or drink. *Where the hell is Molly?* She was the one who had bought this boy. She was the only one he would respond to.

He pushed the food closer to the boy. "You must eat, Maurice!" The boy didn't look up or move. Séamus sighed. The boy might look like he was starving, but Séamus was sure he wouldn't waste away before Molly got back.

Both Séamus and Maurice jumped as the door swung open, hitting the wall with a bang. Molly was half-dragging a tall, blonde woman through the door. She dropped the woman onto the bed and went back to kick the door closed. Séamus turned to Molly, his hands on his hips. He opened his mouth to yell at Molly but she put up her hand to stop him.

"I can explain!"

Séamus waited to hear her explanation. Molly was struggling to find the words to explain how she had managed to add to their ranks.

"Out with it, Molly!" Everyone in the small room jumped. Maurice ran to the corner and curled up in a ball. Séamus motioned to Maurice, exasperated. "You go about the town with your bloody heart wide open and bring back every poor soul who is in a hard situation. Life is hard, Molly! If you don't believe me, take out that wee looking glass of yours and look where your eye should be!" The madder Séamus was, the more Irish he sounded. "Molly!"

"I found her getting attacked on the street. I couldn't leave her behind."

"Yes! Yes, you could have, and you should have. Molly! We cannot keep taking in strays."

"I know! I do! But Séamus, look at her face."

Séamus stalked over to Kate and grabbed her chin, jerking her face upward so he could get a closer look. He ignored the shock on Kate's face. The anger in his face softened when he saw her tattoos. He looked at Molly, his mouth agape. Molly nodded. Séamus dropped his hand. He rubbed his forehead for a moment while Molly waited for him to talk to her. Instead, he grabbed his coat and left the room.

Kate didn't understand. *Why did both Molly and Séamus change their attitude towards me when they see my tattoos?* It didn't matter. She needed them right now. Time for questions would come later.

Molly went over to Maurice in the corner. With his bowed head resting on his knees, he was curled up, making himself as small as possible. Molly crouched down and put her finger under the boy's chin and gently lifted it until his eyes met hers. Molly smiled.

"I understand, little man. This must be so frightening for you. You probably don't understand anything I'm saying to you." Molly sighed. How could anyone do this to an adult, let alone a child? She picked his small body up and cradled him in her arms, sitting in the chair with him in her lap. She moved the plate of food in front of him. "You need to eat, Maurice. I didn't rescue you from that slave market to watch you starve and die." She took a piece of beef and put it in his hand. He didn't move and just held it. Molly moved his hand toward his mouth. "Eat. You must eat."

Maurice looked at Molly, his large brown eyes wet with unshed tears. His long eyelashes and shaved head made him seem so fragile. She wanted to cry with him.

"I know but you must eat." Again, Molly moved his hand toward his mouth. This time, he took a bite. His stomach gurgled loudly. Molly smiled and rubbed his head and back while Maurice finished every morsel on the plate.

Her next task was to get Kate cleaned up. Kate smelled like a dead animal. Molly went downstairs and spoke with the innkeeper's wife. After much arguing and a lot of haggling, the woman agreed to set up a bath in the kitchen before the tavern started getting busy for the night. Kate needed some clothing. Everything she was wearing was filthy and had a pungent smell that made Molly want to retch. The innkeeper's wife suggested a seamstress shop that sold previously owned clothing out of her back room. As long as Molly didn't ask where she got her clothes from, she would cut a good deal.

Molly set out, keeping watch for Séamus. She also kept a careful eye out for one of the less friendly types that skulked around this place. Molly wasn't looking for any more trouble today. Following the innkeeper's directions, she found the shop easily enough. She knocked on the small door and waited. A short French woman opened the door. The woman had dark hair piled high on her head in a bun, helping her seem sightly taller than she actually was. She had a beautiful accent and a soft voice. "*Oui?*"

"I was told that this is the place to come if I want clothing pieces that are already sewn."

"And who told you about me?"

Molly assessed the woman. She was small and seemed frail. Her voice was soft but her crossed arms and hard, dark eyes gave her away. Molly noticed the scissors held in her right hand. She was sure the woman's frail demeanor was an act. Molly smiled. It was better to get what she needed with charm and gold than to test this woman's skill at using sharp scissors as a weapon.

"I need women's clothing. I need it right away and I have gold to compensate for the speed of our transaction."

"Who sent you?"

Molly cocked her head to the left and sighed, impatient with the question.

"The innkeeper's wife at the River View Lodging House said that you may help me."

The woman hesitated and studied Molly carefully. "You are Irish?"

"Yes, I'm Irish."

"Why are you dressed like a man?"

"I'm a sailor on a ship. Skirts and petticoats are not practical so I'm dressed like a man."

"What happened to your eye?"

"I lost it in a fight," Molly said flatly. "The clothing? I'm in a rush. *S'il vous plaît.*"

The woman eyed Molly warily. Finally, she motioned for Molly to follow her inside and led her toward the back of the building. They walked down a dimly lit hallway and came to a locked door at the end of the hall. The woman glanced in Molly's direction, then took a key out of her pocket and unlocked the door. The room was filled with clothing of all kinds. Molly looked around, surprised by the number of pieces in the room. She tried not to think about where all of it came from.

Molly explained to the woman that Kate was very tall and not at all petite. They found skirts that were sewn, but not hemmed. Molly pulled several out of the pile. Nothing too bright. She did not want Kate to stand out any more than she already did. Molly finally settled on a deep gold skirt with blue, tan, and burgundy stripes running vertically down the fabric. None of the women's blouses looked like they would fit Kate. They found a man's shirt that had a feminine flare. The color was close to the tan stripes in the skirt. The seamstress pulled out a deep blue, shortsleeved overcoat and offered it to Molly. Molly took it and noticed the brown belt attached. Perfect. The blue would tone down the entire look. Molly put the pieces side by side.

"Do you have stockings?"

The French woman nodded and brought Molly an off-white pair that seemed long enough for Kate. Molly placed them with the rest of clothing. She tried to recall Kate's shoes. It didn't matter. They would have to do. Molly doubted she could find anything to fit Kate here. Molly assessed her choices. Nothing would fit Kate as they should, but they had to do. The French seamstress gave Molly a price for the clothing she chose. It was higher than expected but worth not having to explain her needs to a nosy and possibly gossiping seamstress. Her small band didn't need additional attention on them. Molly was about to pay when she had a thought. "I need boys' clothing. About five years of age but tall for his age."

The woman shot Molly a quick look but said nothing. She pointed Molly to a section of children's clothing. Molly dug through the clothing until she found two shirts, a pair of pants, and a coat she guesstimated would fit Maurice. Molly paid the woman and walked to the front of the shop.

As Molly reached the front door, something caught her eye. It was a black hat displayed in the shop window. The bill of the hat dipped low on the left side and the right side was bent upward. Molly absently touched the patch covering her missing left eye.

"How much for the hat?"

"It is a fine item. New, not already worn like the other items you purchased." The French woman said in a tone that told Molly she wasn't willing to budge on the cost.

"I asked, how much. Not its condition," Molly countered.

The woman gave Molly a price. Molly raised a brow and cocked her head. The woman shrugged and lowered the price some. Molly paid and left the shop with all of her purchases. Time to get her small crew ready for whatever was coming next.

Molly walked into their rooms and found Kate asleep on the bed. Maurice was sitting at her feet, watching the door. He had the table knife gripped in his hands. He seemed relieved when Molly walked through the door. Molly walked over and took the knife from him.

"I'm not sure what you thought you could do with this dull blade, but I am impressed that you intended to defend yourself and Kate with it. At some point, Séamus and I will need to get you a proper knife. Just not too soon." Maurice gazed up at Molly, not seeming to understand anything she was saying. Molly smiled down at him and rubbed his head in a quick gesture of affection.

Molly shook Kate. Kate slowly opened her eyes. "What do you want? I'm tired and I need to sleep."

"You can sleep once you've had a bath. I cannot tolerate your stench any longer."

Kate frowned. *Do I smell that bad?*

"Yes, you do," Molly said, seemingly reading her mind. "Now, let us go downstairs and get you two cleaned up."

They went down to the kitchen where the innkeeper's wife was filling a small tub with heated water. Kate went first. It felt wonderful! The bathing tub sat next to the roaring fire in the kitchen fireplace. Kate could have soaked all night but Molly was getting impatient so she quickly washed from head to toe. The soap was much nicer than she expected it to be. It smelled slightly of jasmine.

Molly had obviously paid extra for this soap.

Maybe I really did smell that bad, Kate thought. Her face flushed with embarrassment. She came to this city in need of help. Little did she know she would be in so much need that someone had to purchase soap for her.

Once she was clean, she stepped out of the tub and stood naked in front of the fire so she could dry. She enjoyed the feeling of heat on her body and listening to the crackling of flames and the occasional pop from the logs. For a moment, it transported Kate back to the days of sitting around the fire with her Indian family as her father told stories of hunting and bravery in battle. A deep pain pierced Kate's heart. She missed them.

The sound of a child growling and crashing around the kitchen broke Kate's revere. She turned to watch Molly wrestle Maurice out of his clothes and then try to get him into the bath. It was a battle of wills. Maurice was determined not to go in that water but Molly was using her larger size to make sure he did. Kate laughed. Molly looked up and swore. She had stripped down to her breeches and a shirt, both now soaked from her struggle with Maurice. She finally got him settled into the tub and he wailed while Molly bathed him. Until that point, Kate hadn't heard him make a sound. Kate giggled as she dressed in the clothing Molly laid out for her. Molly was swearing and Maurice was crying like he was being murdered. As Kate braided her hair, it surprised her that no one had come into the kitchen to investigate the commotion.

After their bath adventures, the three of them ate dinner in the tavern. They sat in a dark corner so little attention was paid to them. A one-eyed, redheaded female in men's clothing, a slave boy, and a blonde woman with a tattooed face and ill-fitting clothes would be cause for curiosity, even in a city like New Orleans. Molly's gaze stayed trained on the doorway for most of dinner. Séamus had been gone for hours. She was sure that he wouldn't abandon her. The new addition had angered him, though. Enough to leave her and strike out on his own? Molly felt a twinge of doubt and worry.

To take her mind off of Séamus, Molly turned her attention to her latest problem. "Kate, what brought you to New Orleans?"

Kate looked surprised. Oh, her reason for being in this city. She forgot about Owen's cousin. Strange. She glanced at Molly. This seemed right. Once she had met up with Molly, all else faded.

Molly cocked her head and raised her eyebrow in a silent question.

"I came here to find work with a friend's cousin. This friend sent a letter of introduction that I was to give to his cousin. I was on my way to find him when... when... you found me."

"I see. Would you like me to help you find him?" Molly asked, trying to hide how anxious she felt about Kate venturing off on her own.

"No. At least not today. Maybe on the morrow?"

Molly nodded. She wouldn't stop Kate from leaving if she wanted to find her friend's cousin and ask for work. Fate had brought them together once. If their paths separated, it would more than likely do it again.

They finished dinner in silence and went back to their room. Molly pulled a well-worn pamphlet from her bag. It was a collection of poetry written in her native language. Molly smiled and held the pages to her face and breathed it in. Her mother used to read it to her and her siblings by the fire on cold evenings in Ireland. Her mother had secretly given the pamphlet and a small gilded mirror to her on the day she left Ireland. Of everything she had, these two things were Molly's greatest treasures.

She read to Kate and Maurice, allowing the Gaelic to roll over her tongue. She hadn't spoken her language in a long time. It felt like home. Molly finally stopped when she noticed Maurice struggling to keep his eyes open. Molly closed it and helped Maurice to his pallet on the floor. She tucked the thin blanket around him. "*Codladh go maith fear beag. Sleep well, little man.*"

Kate seemed to fall asleep as soon as her body was prone on the bed. Molly paced around their room. Where was Séamus? Molly felt sick. Did she finally push his good will to the breaking point with the addition of Kate? She stopped and gazed at her sleeping wards. If she had to choose, she would send Kate on her way. Molly was sure Séamus would never ask Molly to find another place for Maurice. Neither one could assure his safety if he wasn't with them.

It was late when Séamus came back to the room. He walked straight to Molly, who was dozing in the chair, her head cradled on the table in the crook of her elbow. He grabbed Molly by the shoulders and set her up. Molly gasped when she woke to find his face close to hers. "I found us a ship!"

Molly stood up. "What? How? You found a ship? How? Where?"

Séamus laughed. He took Molly by the shoulders and eased her down in the chair. He sat on the end of the bed and took a deep breath. Séamus and Molly sat face to face as he explained his wild and fortunate night.

Séamus could barely contain his excitement as he told Molly how he had gone to a tavern to drink his anger away. In that tavern, he found a ship's captain throwing around coins, purchasing food, drink, and female attention. Séamus watched him throughout the night as the captain drank heavily and became increasingly incoherent and incapacitated. Pondering how he could take advantage of this man and acquire his ship, he felt the call of nature and went to the alley behind the tavern to relieve himself. As he was heading back into the tavern, he overheard a group of men talking excitedly.

"He is in there spending our pay! We should go in and drag him out of there!"

"No! Let him come out and then we kill him!"

"It would be better to kill him after we make way. We can take the ship out and drop him overboard in the middle of the ocean."

"If we kill the captain, who's going to be captain?"

"Me. I'll be captain."

"You? Ha! No one would accept you as captain!"

"Why not? I'm more qualified than you!"

Séamus heard what sounded like them pushing and shoving each other. Another man hissed, "Stop this! We need the captain gone. After, we can decide who will be captain."

"We cannot take him back to the ship. He has men loyal to him. They won't take kindly to the captain's death. We have to make them think someone else killed him. Maybe robbed him and killed him."

"Yes! That's it! The captain got drunk and was robbed and killed. That's why he didn't make it back to the ship!"

Séamus heard the drunken captain loudly announcing his departure and inviting all the ladies to accompany him. The captain stumbled down the dark street alone. Apparently, no one had taken him up on his offer of spending the night with him on his ship to enjoy fine wine and his purportedly generously-sized body parts. The sailors trailed behind their captain. Séamus rushed down an alley and stepped out in front of the men. They stopped, instinctively pulling their knives and pistols.

Séamus put up his hands to show he didn't mean harm and smiled. "Good evening, gentlemen. I couldn't help but overhear your discussion and I believe I have the perfect answer to your captain dilemma."

STORY 3
THE ACQUISITION OF A SHIP

The Dousa
New Orleans

Three days later, as if being pulled by the twin forces of fate and fortune, Séamus, Molly, Maurice, and Kate stood on the dock waiting for the longboat to take them to the ship moored in the bay.

"Well, Séamus, boarding the ship is either going to fulfill my destiny or it's going to carry us to our deaths." Molly said softly.

"How could it not be fate that I was in that tavern when I was? We are meant to be boarding this ship. Let's go, your destiny is waiting."

Séamus went to place their belongings in the boat but Molly hesitated. She wasn't just risking her own life with this insane plan. There were the others to think about. Séamus was an experienced sailor and was, because of her rash decisions, now a pirate. The other two were innocent.

Molly took a step back. Kate and Maurice were walking into danger they didn't understand. Molly turned and walked away from the ship. Séamus rushed to stop her. Kate and Maurice followed closely behind.

"Molly, what's wrong?" Kate asked.

Molly's gaze roamed over the ship. It was large. Larger than she expected. It looked like a galleon with the lavishly gilded sculptures decorating the bow and stern but it sat lower in the water than a traditional galleon. The lines of her hull streamlined to help with speed. Despite the size of the ship, it seemed capable of outrunning a pirate ship, or in her case, overtaking a ship laden with bounty. The large cannon ports were designed to warn off anyone with an eye on taking the ship. If need be, those heavy cannons would easily eliminate anyone who presented a danger. The curved bow featured a golden mermaid riding a wave. The ship was beautiful. Molly believed it called to her. It pulled at her. However, the flag flying at the back of the ship concerned her.

"It is an East Indiaman ship?" Molly asked Séamus urgently.

"The men did not say so but the flag would say yes." Séamus replied grimly.

"What is an Indiaman ship? What about the flag?" Kate whispered urgently.

Molly swung around and moved close to Kate. "Kate, you don't have to do this with us. This is going to be dangerous. We have a greater chance of death and torture than of success!"

"Why?" Kate asked again.

Séamus answered Kate with a sigh. "This ship belongs to the East India Trading Company. They are the largest trading company in the world. They have their own military and they don't look kindly on pirates. By taking this ship, we will very likely be the focus of that military. The flag is Dutch. It means that people who have wealth and influence in society back this ship and its captain. The East India Company would not take losing this ship lightly. Molly's telling you the bold, honest truth. We have a greater chance of not living through this than living."

Molly gripped Kate's arm. "Kate, you do not have to board that ship. We will give you coin. You can go find that cousin, find employment, and have a proper life. Meet a man. Fall in love. Have babies. Even if we survive, pirates are not fit for polite society."

Kate's body jerked, her brow furrowed. Polite society. The same words Owen used to tell her that because of her tattoos, it would be impossible to live as they did. She would never fit into ordinary life. He was right, of course. Everything she did to attempt to become part of the town her parents loved didn't work. In their minds, she would forever be a savage slave that should have chosen death instead of allowing them to mark her. She still had the letter from Owen. She could try again to make the life she thought her mother and father would approve of. Kate sighed. No. Polite society was not for her. That dream hadn't worked for her. It was time to try something different, no matter the outcome.

Kate took a deep breath and let it out slowly. "Fuck polite society."

"You're certain? Once we board that ship, there is no going back."

Kate answered by turning and walking toward the ship with Maurice in tow. Séamus looked at Molly, shrugged, and followed in Kate's wake. Molly laughed to herself, "Fuck polite society indeed."

The four boarded the ship. The quartermaster introduced himself and took their money for passage when the captain noticed the four unlikely passengers: a man, two women, and a young negro boy. As he got closer, he realized they were even more curious than he'd first thought. One woman was missing an eye, and the other had tattoos on her face. What would bring these four to his ship? He had to introduce himself and find out. He rushed toward them.

He held out his hand to Séamus, "Welcome aboard, good sir. I am captain of this vessel. Captain Noah Clark."

Séamus gripped the captain's hand. "Pleasure to meet you, Captain Clark. I am Séamus Flanagan and this is my wife, Molly. These two are our servants. I see you are flying a Dutch flag but your accent and your name are British," Séamus remarked.

"My mother, who is Dutch, fell in love with a British naval officer. They married and she moved to England with him. I was born there. Her Dutch family is fabulously well off and arranged for this ship and my captain's papers. How could I say no to such a generous gift from family?"

"I am sure I would not!" Séamus laughed.

Séamus glanced at Molly, trying to gauge her reaction to all of this. Molly was staring directly behind the captain at another man. Molly's eye was wide with surprise. They all had to tilt their heads back just to look him in the eye. This was the largest man any of them had ever seen.

Captain Clark laughed. "This is my man, Mukanda. Do not be alarmed. He looks a lot more menacing than he is. Unless, of course, you intend me harm. Then, I cannot say if you will come out of that encounter dead or very dead."

Molly glanced at Séamus. He hadn't mentioned this extremely large black man in his story. Mukanda was wearing pants that seemed as long as Molly was tall. His arms were as large as some masts on the ship. Mukanda glowered at the four of them, silently warning them not to try anything.

Captain Clark laughed at all of their reactions. "What brings you to my ship?"

Séamus ignored Molly's glare. "My lovely wife and I are headed to Columbia. I have a cousin who owns a tobacco plantation there. He offered me work and lodging. I think the warm weather would be good for the pain in my knees."

"Quite right it will," the captain agreed.

Molly walked past the group and stood in the middle of the deck. She closed her eyes and listened to the ship speaking to her. Every movement and sound of the sails, ropes, and wood floated through Molly and sang to her. Molly was sure the ship was seducing her. Wooing her. Convincing her she was home. This ship wanted her to be the new captain. Molly tuned out every human-made sound. She wanted to stay in the moment soaking in the sun, the sounds, and the smells. In the distance, she heard a bird calling out to the other birds. Her body moved in rhythm with the ship's gentle rocking as each wave came in, caressing the hull. The sails and netting swaying in the slight breeze were a lullaby to her troubled soul. Molly was at peace. She wished she could stay this way forever. Just her and her ship.

Without opening her eyes, she called out, "Captain, what is the name of your ship?"

The captain looked at Séamus and raised an eyebrow. "She is the *Dousa*."

Molly didn't hear the name Clark stated. Her soul said the *Fortune's Revenge*. "Perfect," she whispered.

Captain Noah Clark snorted and looked at Séamus with a condescending gaze. "Your woman is not running with a full sail, is she?"

Séamus looked at Molly lovingly. The black dress dotted with large, bright orange flowers and a flat bonnet covering her wild hair made her seem feminine and vulnerable. Her red hair, never to be contained, was already escaping the pins she used to make her appear more woman than pirate. Séamus saw small curls floating in the breeze. A small twitch in the corner of his mouth.

"I wouldn't underestimate my Molly, Captain. What she lacks in sanity, she more than makes up for in enthusiasm and determination."

The captain looked at Séamus, unsure of what he meant by that, and motioned to a deckhand. "Mr. Jacobs will show you to your cabins."

Séamus nodded. "Thank you, Captain Clark."

Mr. Jacobs motioned for the four passengers to follow him across the deck to the aft of the ship. He led the group into a wide hallway with two rooms on each side and a large set of double doors at the end. The doors were ornate with gold and glass inlays. Molly fought the urge to rush to the doors and fling them open. She wanted the ship to know her intentions.

"Mr. Flanagan, this is your cabin, and this cabin is for your servants." Mr. Jacobs motioned to the doors on the left side of the hall. "My cabin is across from yours. This is Mukanda's cabin. If you need anything at all, please let one of us know."

Séamus thanked the first mate and the four settled into their cabins.

Early the next morning, the ship set sail. "There is no going back now, Molly Malone..." Séamus muttered before falling back asleep. Molly jumped out of the bunk and began getting dressed. She was eager to get on deck. Before Molly could finish putting on the layers of female clothing, there was a small knock at the door. She cracked the door open to see Maurice.

"Maurice? What is it?"

He pointed toward his cabin door, a concerned expression on his face. Molly threw a dressing gown on over her undergarments and went with Maurice into the cabin he shared with Kate. Kate was kneeling over a bucket, heaving. Molly rushed to her side and held her hair back as she wretched into the bucket.

"Maurice, bring me some water," Molly ordered, pointing to the pitcher of water.

Maurice poured water into a porcelain cup and brought it to Molly. She gently wiped Kate's face with a small cloth that lay near the bucket.

"Kate, drink some water. It will help."

Kate softly moaned and shook her head no. Molly put the cup to Kate's mouth. Reluctantly, Kate took a small sip.

"I fear this is going to be a long voyage for you, Kate. We have only just set sail," Molly said, concerned.

"Perhaps, you should kill me now. End my suffering and save yourself the money for my passage."

Molly stroked Kate's hair and laughed softly. "Let us see how you fare in the next few days before we feed you to the creatures of the sea."

Kate slightly smiled. "I did not realize how cruel you are, Molly. You will make me suffer before sending me to my end?"

"My friend, this won't last. It's your first time onboard a ship. Your body and your mind will come to accept their shared fate, and they will bend to your will. You'll see. This sickness won't last long."

"I hope you are correct. Now, please let me sleep."

Molly and Maurice helped Kate into bed. Maurice looked worried and Molly hugged him.

"Kate will be fine. I promise."

Maurice did not look convinced.

"Stay here and watch over her. I will be back to empty the bucket. Are you hungry?" Maurice bobbed his head up and down. "I'll bring some food for you, as well." Maurice's stomach growled loudly. Molly laughed and rubbed his head playfully. "Oh! You are hungry! I will be back shortly."

Molly went to the cabin that she and Séamus shared. Séamus was awake and dressed. He helped Molly finish dressing as Molly told him about Kate's sickness.

"I didn't consider that Kate would become ill on this voyage. My first time on a ship at sea, I was green for two weeks. I thought death would be better than the sickness at sea," Séamus mused.

"Let us hope she recovers sooner than two weeks from now. I'm going to empty her bucket and have more water brought to her. Maurice needs food. Can you take him with you to the galley to break his fast?"

"Yes. The poor boy must be hungrier than a bear after a long winter's sleep."

Molly gave him a side glance and shook her head. *What the hell is he talking about?*

She and Séamus parted ways to take care of their wards. A crew member brought water and bread to Kate's cabin. Molly sat with Kate until early afternoon. Maurice returned to watch over Kate. Molly was happy to leave the small cabin and take in the fresh air on deck.

By the fourth day, Kate was leaving the cabin to walk on deck. One afternoon, Kate was at the rail emptying her bucket but quickly dropped it and began heaving over the side. She looked down at the water and contemplated throwing herself overboard. Ending her misery was sounding more and more to her liking. Kate heaved once more over the side of the ship. She was leaning on the railing, her forehead resting on the cool wood when she realized a person was standing next to her. She stood up and found a tall young man looking down at her.

"Are you unwell, miss?" he asked, taking in the sweat on her face and the paleness of her skin.

Kate frowned. *Why would someone talk to me at a time like this?* She used a soft cloth to wipe her mouth and face. Before she could answer, she heaved once again over the railing.

"You have the sickness. I can help." He took the cloth from her, gently wiped her face, and put his arm around her to help her walk to the center of the ship. He pointed to the horizon. "Look out there. To where the sky meets the water. Keep your eyes to the horizon. It will help." Kate looked skeptical. He smiled. "I give you my promise. It will help. Stay here, I need to fetch a few things, then I'll return."

The man hurried off and returned a short time later with a blanket, rum, and bread. He laid the blanket down midship and brought Kate to it. He handed her the rum and bread. "Eat this bread and drink this rum. If nothing else, it will give you something to heave up."

Kate did as instructed. She drank the rum and ate the bread and felt slightly better.

"Lie down here. This spot on the ship moves the least. If you do as I say, you will be yourself soon enough."

Kate nodded as the man placed a cool, wet cloth across her eyes. She drifted off to sleep feeling better than she had in days.

It was dark when Kate awoke. For the moment, she didn't feel sick. She lay on the deck, listening to the ship move through the water. She relished the cool breeze caressing her skin. Kate was afraid to move. She had not been this well since the ship left New Orleans. Kate heard a male voice speaking to her.

"How are you? Any better?"

Kate removed the cloth, slowly opening her eyes, and found the same young man sitting on a barrel near her.

"Have you been watching me sleep?" she asked.

"It was less watching you sleep and more keeping the crew away from you," the man said with a smile.

"Thank you. I feel more like myself. I'm almost afraid to move from this spot."

"Each time the sickness looms, come to the center of the ship and keep your eyes on the horizon. Also, you must eat and have rum daily."

"How did you come by this knowledge?"

"I have been on a ship most of my life but one time I went out with my father and I became very ill. He's the one who passed on his cure for the sickness. It's my duty to pass on the knowledge to others who suffer from the same sickness."

"I'm Katherine Ersland."

"James Barlow. I'm happy to meet you, Miss Ersland."

"Call me Kate. All of my friends call me Kate."

"Very well, Kate."

Séamus, Molly, Kate, and Maurice settled into their daily routine as passengers making their way to Columbia. Séamus and Molly played their parts as a newly married couple, traveling to start a new life as tobacco farmers at a cousin's plantation. Kate and Maurice were servants to the wealthy couple. Their only job was to see to the day-to-day needs of their employers. Kate and Maurice were happy to play servants and not attract the attention of the captain and his crew. Kate passed the time with Maurice in their cabin, teaching Maurice English. Every day Maurice learned a new word and every day he seemed to understand her more and more. These long days with Maurice reminded her of the days when she'd taught her Indian brother how to speak the English tongue. Her heart ached as she thought of him.

Kate and Maurice would take a walk around the ship in the evenings when there were fewer crew members on deck. It was also the time that James Barlow began his shift as a night watchman. James taught Kate and Maurice to play a card game called One-and-Thirty. The object of the game was to draw cards until the cards totaled thirty-one or as close as possible without going over. This took a while for Kate and Maurice to master, as neither one had ever learned to play card games or learned to add numbers. James didn't mind. It kept Kate coming back to visit him night after night.

One such evening, Kate beat James at the game again and again. Finally,

James laughed and slammed down his cards. "I surrender! Katherine Ersland, you are too good at this game! It is a rare woman indeed that is as beautiful as you are and can beat men at their own games."

Kate looked at James, bewildered. *He's teasing me,* Kate thought. His bright blue eyes sparkled with humor as he gazed at her. *Does he mean it? Does he think I'm beautiful?* "You are making fun of me, sir?" she finally asked. She couldn't meet eyes to his in that moment. James reached across the barrel that held their card game. With a gentle hand, he placed a finger below Kate's chin and gently lifted until her eyes met his.

"I assure you, I am not making fun of you, Kate. You are the most beautiful creature I have ever laid eyes on."

Now that Kate was looking at him, she really saw him. She could not take her eyes away from him. He was handsome and large. Larger than most men she had ever encountered. His body and facial features were strong and seemed to be carved from solid wood. But those eyes. His eyes were so blue, they almost seemed unnatural. Perhaps his mother and father had made special offerings to their gods or to the little people to make their son so strong and fetching.

"Well, you are the most beautiful creature I have ever laid eyes on." Kate's own blue eyes matched the glow of the new love she saw reflected in the man's eyes across from her.

Those long days with Maurice and the evenings with James gave Kate a hopeful idea. A future for her. *Could I become a teacher?* Surely, there were children in the Caribbean that needed to learn English and Kate remembered her lessons from her childhood. She was learning the basics of arithmetic from James. She could teach history from books. Maybe teaching was how she could become accepted. Kate didn't need to become a pirate. Being a teacher was everything she wanted in life. She would talk to Séamus and ask him to talk to the captain. Captain Clark was a learned man. As an educated English man of privilege, he must have books on board that Kate could read to expand her knowledge. Kate paced in her small cabin. She couldn't sit still. She was excited about thoughts of her possible future. It had been a long time since she had a small spark of hope that her life may turn out like she wanted.

To keep Captain Clark and his crew at ease with their passengers,

Séamus had befriended the captain. Every evening they drank Irish whiskey, played chess, and discussed their lives at sea. Each night, their stories became more outlandish, with each trying to outdo the other. In the quiet of the evenings, the two laughed loudly. The sound floated out of the captain's cabin, filling the ship, and drifted over the water. Molly had never experienced this Séamus. Since she had met him, he always carried himself with quiet concern. He never relaxed and he never laughed. As Molly stood on the deck listening to the two swap stories, she was filled with deep regret. It was because of her reckless decisions that Séamus had became her protector. Always on guard. Always vigilant. Never able to just be a man without a care in this world.

On one such night, Molly stood outside the door listening to Captain Clark and Séamus out-English and out-Irish each other. Their accents became thicker and their stories of home became more outrageous the more they drank. Molly knocked on the cabin door. A male voice barked out a sharp, "Enter!"

Molly put on her best demure face and pushed open the doors. She walked to Séamus and laid a hand on his shoulder. "My darling, are you coming to bed?" Séamus looked up to study Molly's face. She looked fine. Her hair was piled high on her head and she had a swath of lace covering her missing eye. Nothing seemed amiss. Why was she interrupting them? Molly caressed his cheek. "I'm lonely without my husband in my bed. I cannot sleep unless he's lying beside me to keep me warm." She glanced at the captain with a slight smile. "I am very sorry, Captain but surely you must understand a wife's needs."

The captain laughed loudly. "Séamus, you have your hands full with this one! It's a shame she only has one eye on that pretty face of her's. Even with that grotesque scar, I would still invite a roll with her. What say you, Séamus? Care to share with your new friend? I would gladly pay you for the night with her."

Séamus stood up abruptly. "I appreciate the kind offer, my friend. However, my wife has stirred up my own longing and I will need her in my bed tonight. Perhaps we can continue our discussions on tomorrow's eve?"

The captain lazily raised his glass to Séamus. "As you wish."

Séamus gripped Molly's upper arm and forced her out of the captain's cabin and straight to their small room. Once inside, Séamus turned on Molly. "What were you thinking? Why did you interrupt us? Now we have a fresh problem to deal with! Somehow I have to keep this man away from you!" Séamus stood exasperated, with his hand on his hips. "Molly! Answer me!"

Molly sank to the floor of their cabin. She put her head in her hands and sobbed. "I'm sorry. I'm so sorry that I've pulled you into the wreck that is my life. I haven't seen or heard you laugh since you met me. This life with me has brought nothing but worry and strife to you! We should go to Columbia and we should part ways. I want you to be free of me and my black curse."

Séamus paused, concerned. Looking down at Molly, he sighed. Someday this girl was going to be the death of him, he was sure. He sat beside her, putting his arm around her shoulders and pulling her to him. He cradled her as she sobbed and he gently rocked her until she quieted. "Molly Malone, I want you to listen to me and listen well. I have never once regretted meeting you or regretted anything that has transpired from that day since. You and I have a bond that I've never had with anyone else. Sadly, not even with my own wife and daughter. The fates brought us together. Do I worry over you? Yes, as any protector would. That is my burden and I gladly carry it."

Molly straightened and wiped her face with her dress. "Tomorrow night, we do this. Tomorrow night, we take the ship."

Séamus cocked his head and raised his eyebrows. "Do we now? Why tomorrow night?"

"Tomorrow, after you two have drunk deeply from the captain's store of whiskey, you will offer me up for the night to your new friend. Captain Clark's night with Molly Malone will end in him failing to see another sunrise."

Séamus contemplated for a moment. "Agreed. The only way he would dismiss Mukanda was if there was a female in his cabin. We are thirteen days on the water, I believe now is as good a time as any. Tomorrow is a new moon, the only light on the ship will be the lit lanterns. I've been talking with our fellow conspirators and they are still with us."

"Good." Molly looked Séamus squarely in the eye. "We could change the plan slightly. The captain doesn't have to die. We can leave the captain, and any men who are in his support, ashore somewhere."

Séamus thought for a moment. He did really enjoy Captain Clark's company. The captain was a good man, despite being English. "No. He needs to die. We cannot risk his men having a change of heart and freeing him from his prison to take back the ship. You must kill him, and the men and I will try and kill Mukanda."

Molly nodded. "Then we are in agreement. Tomorrow night we take the ship."

First A Sailor, Now A Pirate
The Dousa

Séamus, Molly, and Kate went about their normal routine. Their casual demeanor hid the nervous energy rushing through their bodies. They couldn't tip the captain to their plan. Molly watched the crew through the day. Which of these men would back their captain? Who would stay out of the fray? Who would follow her? She hoped they wouldn't be forced to kill too many men. They needed as many crewmembers as they could keep. There was the added worry that the men who survived would not support Molly as captain. She was a woman and redhead. Two strong marks against her.

The captain emerged from his cabin late into the morning. One by one, the crew greeted him as he made his rounds. Séamus stood portside, his arms resting on the railing, studying the water beyond. Eventually, the captain made his way to Séamus. "Good morning, my friend."

"Good morning, Captain. I trust that your night was satisfactory." The captain smiled slyly, thinking he knew exactly what his friend's night entailed.

Séamus clapped the captain hard on the back. "I'm surprised that our fun didn't keep you and your crew awake last night." Séamus leaned close to the captain and said in a low, quiet voice, "My Molly was like a wild animal. I could hardly contain her desire for me."

The captain laughed. "Well, my friend, maybe you're too old for your wife. Perhaps you need another man to take over for a night."

Séamus smiled. "Perhaps. Perhaps." The captain watched Séamus walk across the deck back to his cabin. A small bit of hope settled into Noah Clark's loins. Maybe his new friend would allow him to enjoy his wife for at least one night.

Molly riffled through her clothing. She needed something that showed her assets and hid her scars. She finally chose a white shift with nothing underneath. The wide neck draped off one shoulder. *Perfect,* Molly thought. To hide her missing eye and scars, she changed out the cloth to match her dress with a piece of white cloth and lace. She tied the cloth and hid the ends in her hair. Her hair. She could do nothing with her hair. It was always going to be a wild, curly mess. At least she could pull it forward and hide her scar and missing eye. Her red hair had always been a curse. Maybe tonight it would add to her mystique? Molly laughed at herself. Mystique? Molly didn't consider herself to be some mysterious beauty. Plus, she wasn't actually seducing Captain Clark. She was going to his cabin to assassinate him. She tried to see herself in her small hand mirror that had been a gift from her mother. With the shift dropping off her shoulder, would he see her scars? Yes, he probably could. She would have to keep him in front of her. She didn't want him to abandon his lust for her before Molly could kill him.

Séamus knocked on the door. "Enter!" He walked in and stopped dead, staring at her. The scowl Molly saw on his face surprised her.

"Séamus?" Molly self-consciously smoothed her hair and shift. She frowned and picked up the small mirror, trying to smooth her wild hair. "Do you think I'm not pleasing enough for our dear Captain Clark?"

Séamus finally moved toward her. "No! You are too pleasing. I am worried, Molly. You're a beautiful woman and in this small... dress... obviously with nothing on underneath..." Séamus looked away, ashamed that he was viewing this girl as a woman for the first time. "I'm worried that his lust will be stronger than your will to kill him."

Molly hugged Séamus. "I appreciate your fatherly concern for my well-being. I promise you, Captain Clark will not see any more of my bare skin than you are seeing right now. Séamus, this is my ship. The *Fortune's Revenge* whispers to me. She wants me to be her captain. She cries each day because I'm not at her helm caring for her. She encourages me to gird my bravery, kill Clark, and make her mine. This is my ship. There is nothing stronger than my will to be her captain." Séamus didn't notice that as she spoke, Molly was slowly inching her shift up. He was only half listening to her because he was trying to reassure himself that this plan wasn't an unnecessarily risking to her life. Quickly Molly pulled the dirk from the wrap, holding it in place on her thigh and held the blade under his chin, pressing ever so gently, just enough so Séamus could feel his skin giving way under the pressure. The tip of the dirk under his chin broke him out of his reverie.

He held up his hands with a careful laugh. "Okay. I'm sorry I doubted the great pirate, Molly Malone. Now, put that blade back and let us get this unsavory deed done. Wait." Séamus stopped her and pulled her hand, holding the dirk toward him so he could see it. "You chose my father's dirk as your weapon?"

"I did." Molly admired the knife, rolling it in her hand to see the carved handle. The intricately carved weapon was a dark wood and had silver inlay with the Flanagan crest stamped in the center. Both sides of the long-tapered blade were sharpened to a deadly edge.

Séamus took the dirk from Molly. "My father left this with my mother when he left us. I carried it proudly when I was a young boy. Other boys had small daggers attached to their belts. I had this. The Scotsmen developed this blade for hand-to-hand combat. They weren't satisfied with the small size of a dagger and a long sword isn't practical for close combat with your opponent. They came up with something in-between. A wee sword that hurts like hell if they stab you with it."

"Did you ever see your father again?" Molly asked.

"No. All I have is this dirk that holds his crest." Séamus handed the knife back to Molly.

"This is a beautiful but deadly weapon. It has the energy of you and your father living inside of it. I will need both of you on my side tonight."

"You do, Molly. You have the blood of the Irish and the Scots fighting with you tonight."

Molly carefully slid the dirk into the wrap on her leg. "Did you take care of the night's watch?"

"Yes. They are men that are with us. One is enchanted by Kate. The others have no love for the captain. They should be of help tonight. I hope…"

"Enchanted by Kate? Who?" Molly asked, surprised. Kate hadn't mentioned a possible suitor.

"His name is James. A young, strapping lad. I'm counting on him to be a big help in dealing with Mukanda."

"You and those men must deal with the captain's man quickly and quietly. It won't be easy. Mukanda is more mountain than man."

"We can do it. Molly, don't worry about me. You have a big job to do. Worry about that."

Molly wrapped herself in a blanket and walked to the door. "All is going to go as planned tonight, Séamus. It has to. If it doesn't, then we're done for." Molly and Séamus left their cabin and made their way to the captain's quarters.

Séamus knocked on the door. Molly stood beside him with a blanket wrapped tightly around her. She looked up at him and smiled. Séamus absently patted her back. He was fighting down the acid hitting the back of his throat.

What happened to me? Séamus thought. He used to handle difficult situations better than this. He really was getting old. The stress of the situation was overpowering, and he was almost ready to call it off when the captain called out, "Come on in, my friend!"

Séamus walked in with Molly close behind him. The captain's face lit up when he saw Molly enter with Séamus. He jumped out of his chair and rushed over to them. Captain Clark enthusiastically clapped Séamus on the shoulder and then gently took Molly's hand and kissed it. He could barely contain himself when she giggled and demurely lowered her head.

"Would either of you care for some rum or whiskey?" Molly nodded and smiled at Séamus.

Séamus looked down at her. "Are you sure, my love? You know you cannot drink much. It goes straight to your head."

Molly shot a quick look at the captain and nodded to Séamus. "Yes, thank you. I would greatly appreciate a glass of rum."

The captain rushed to pour them a glass of rum each. His imagination was running wild. He wanted his friend to leave so he could have time alone with Molly. Séamus sat in a chair, looking relaxed despite the tension and stress he was feeling. Molly sat next to him, sipping her rum. She let the blanket slip so the captain could see how little she was wearing underneath.

The longer Séamus lingered, the more Captain Clark squirmed in his chair. He could barely take his eyes off Molly's cleavage. It was obvious why the captain couldn't sit still. His desire for Molly was straining the front of his pants. Finally, Molly gave Séamus a quick, exasperated look. She flicked her eyes toward the door. He gave in, downed the rest of his rum, and stood up.

Clark jumped up. "My friend, are you leaving so soon? Mukanda, please accompany my friend to the deck. It is a clear night. You two can gaze at the stars." He practically sprinted to the door and opened it for the two men.

Séamus kissed Molly on the forehead. "Have a fun night, my dear. Do try to leave something of Captain Clark for the morrow."

She smiled, "I won't make any promises, my love."

Mukanda lingered in the cabin. He didn't want to leave his captain alone with Molly. Captain Clark gave Mukanda a push. "I will see you in the morning when we break our fast." Mukanda looked unsure, but he did as his captain ordered.

Once Séamus left, the captain closed and locked the door. He turned to see Molly standing in the middle of the cabin dressed only in a short white shift that left nothing to the imagination. Captain Clark instinctively rubbed the front of his trousers. He needed to get these clothes off. They were uncomfortably restricting him. Molly motioned for him to come to her. He rushed over. No longer was he the wealthy captain with a family and a large social circle. Tonight he was a man with the most basic animal needs. He grabbed Molly and roughly kissed her before pushing her back and looking her over. She had a moment of hesitation. He looked like a person possessed and she didn't know him at that moment. Before she could react, he grabbed her clothing and ripped her shift down the front. He opened both sides of her shift and took her all in.

Fear welled in Molly's belly as the captain pulled her close, forcefully touching her bare skin. This was happening too fast. She hadn't anticipated that the good captain would assert himself so quickly. Molly tried to remain calm. She couldn't overreact and she absolutely could not let panic cloud her judgment and instincts. She was trying to meet him halfway, but his lips were harsh on her mouth. Each time he slightly lifted his head, she sucked in a deep breath. She realized he was pushing her backward toward the bulkhead. She gasped as he grabbed her by the neck and pinned her against the wall. Captain Clark's face was red, and he was panting from the effort of his attack.

Shit! Molly screamed in her head. *What in the hell is he doing?* Was he actually going to choke her until she passed out, or worse? Blackness clouded the edges of her vision. Molly knew she had to get control of this situation. His free hand wildly roamed her body as she reached for her dirk. He must have realized she was reaching for something. Looking down at the cloth wrapped around her upper thigh, he paused. Confused, he looked Molly in the face and, for a moment, loosened his grip on her neck.

"What is that? What are you hiding?"

Her instinct was to run, but she was acutely aware that now was the time to act before he saw the dirk and tried to overpower her and take it away. She had to finish this. She had to kill the captain in order to take his ship.

Now! Do it now! her brain screamed.

Molly fumbled with her shift and finally pulled out her dirk. With all of her strength, she wrenched her arm around and drove the knife deep into the side of his head at the temple. He looked surprised for a moment, then he dropped into a heap at Molly's feet.

Molly froze. The only thing she could hear was her breath coming in gasps. She looked at Captain Clark on the floor, blood spilling out of his wound. Molly roused herself. She had to act. She couldn't just stand here and stare at what she had done. She ran over to the captain's bed and grabbed a blanket, put it under his head, and pulled out her dirk. She hoped the blanket would soak up most of the blood. Molly wrapped the blanket around his head so the blood wouldn't flow so freely. She turned the lantern down until the flame was extinguished. She wanted the crew to think their captain was asleep so they wouldn't bother him. Then she quietly opened the door and crept down the hall, but she didn't see anyone right away. Her eyes adjusted to the near darkness of the deck. Finally, she spied Séamus and waved to get his attention. He saw the flash of white fabric and knew it was Molly. He made his way back to the captain's cabin.

Séamus and Molly quietly re-entered the cabin. Séamus noticed Molly's torn shift but said nothing. They emptied Noah Clark's pockets and wrapped his head and the top half of his body with another blanket. With that done, Séamus pulled the torn fronts of Molly's shift together. "Go to our cabin and change your clothes. Get into bed and pretend to be asleep."

Molly vehemently shook her head. "No! I won't leave you to deal with this on your own! What if the wrong person spies what you are about?"

"Yes, Molly. What if I get caught? I can accept what they will do to me but I could never watch you suffer. That is a pain I do not wish to experience."

Molly protested, "Please, Séamus. If we do this together, there's less of a chance anyone will catch us in the act."

Séamus sighed forcefully. "Molly, for once in your stubborn life, can you please just do as I ask?"

Molly paused. "What about Mukanda?"

"He is with Davy Jones now." Séamus decided Molly didn't need to know the details surrounding the fight he and four men had gotten into with Mukanda on deck. He still wasn't sure how they had won that battle. Mukanda had the strength of ten men and the ferocity of a pride of lions. Séamus was sure that he and the others would be feeling their bruises for weeks.

Molly turned and raced to the door. Without looking at him, she whispered, "Thank you for everything, Séamus. The moment I found you, it gave me hope the gods did not hate me as wholly as I thought." With that, she slipped out of the cabin and into the dark.

Séamus leaned over the captain. He felt a sense of loss and regret. He really did like this man and had considered him a friend. It had been a long time since he had felt completely relaxed, smoking a cigar, drinking rum, and telling sea stories. With stoic resolve, Séamus retrieved a few things from Captain Clark's desk. He placed Clark's pocket watch, his favorite glass, and a cigar on the captain's chest, then wrapped the captain and the trinkets in an additional blanket to keep it all close to his body.

"May these things make it with you into the next life, my friend. I am regretful that you had to be sacrificed for this pirate life I have been dragged into." Séamus dropped his head and wiped his eyes with his hand. "No. Now is not the time for untruths. I ran headlong into this life and I could have left at any time but I haven't. I found your men with mutiny on their minds and encouraged them to that end. Now, here we are. You are dead and I am going to bury your body at sea. Tomorrow I will help fix Molly as captain of this vessel in your stead. For that, I'm sorry… and yet not. May you have safe travels, my friend."

Séamus stood up and went to the deck. There were several men waiting there. He motioned to them and turned to go back into the cabin. The four men joined him there and stood around the captain. Each man gazed down at their former captain, caps in hand. The youngest wiped away a tear rolling down his cheek.

Séamus spoke up. "The time for contrition has passed. We need to finish this job and face what is coming next."

The men lifted the captain as Séamus led them to the door at the back of the cabin and he opened the door that led to the small balcony at the back of the ship. He looked above and below but didn't think any crew members could see them throwing their captain into the water. They quickly made their way to the balcony with the captain's body. With only a slight hesitation, the men sent their captain into the dark depths. The four turned to Séamus, wondering what was next. He sent each man back to their posts. He had no answers for them yet. Tomorrow will come soon enough. Tomorrow they would need to face the rest of the crew. Would they succeed in taking the ship? If they didn't, what would happen to them? Death was a certainty, but how would that death come? Hanging? Shooting? Sword? Would they spare Maurice and Kate? He shook off those negative thoughts and made his way to Molly.

Early the next morning, Molly and Séamus emerged from their cabin. Molly was dressed in her pirate clothing. She was thrilled beyond measure to be out of that cumbersome dress and all the undergarments that women were required to wear. Her outfit, tight breeches, knee-high boots, and white ruffled shirt was complete with a long, black vest. The vest was held closed by a thick black belt at her waist. Her customary silver rose belt was slung across her hips along with the black leather sheath that held her jeweled scabbard and sword. The black hat she had purchased at the shop in New Orleans sat firmly on her head. The left side rode low, hiding much of her eye patch and scar.

The men gathered on the deck. The captain and his man Mukanda couldn't be found. One group of men glared at the others, accusations on the tips of their tongues. It was no secret that some of the men hated the captain and his penchant for spending their hard-earned pay. Hated his drunken tirades against them. Hated the abuse he unleashed on the younger sailors. The men turned to see Molly and Séamus approach them. Their mouths were agape as they stared at her. Molly bounded up the stairs to the helm. Séamus and the men loyal to both him and Molly flanked her on the two sets of stairs leading to the upper deck. The rest, loyal to the hopeful new captain, kept their places behind their fellow sailors on the main deck.

One man stepped forward. "What the hell is going on here? What have you done with our captain?"

"Your former captain is dead! You and your ship have a new captain!" Séamus called out.

The men below Molly burst into a chaotic chorus of curses and denials. Molly held up her hand, "Silence! You and this ship are now in the brotherhood of pirates. No longer will you be slave to a captain of privilege and status. You are now part of a crew that works together for the profit of us all!"

The first mate stepped forward with his sword drawn. "Pirates?! You want us to accept a woman pirate—a redhead, no less—to be our captain?" He spat on the deck and glared at Molly. "I will never be a cursed pirate! I will bloody well kill you, bitch, before that ever happens on this ship!" Some of the men shouted in agreement while others backed away slightly. Having a share in the profits didn't sound like a bad thing.

Molly could see the crowd of men parting. It looked to be about forty that were standing with the first mate. Others might join in the fray once the fighting started. That was for Séamus and the others to think about. Molly had only one member to deal with.

She slowly took a breath to steady her nerves, pulled a cigar from her pocket, and strolled to a low-hanging lantern. She opened the side and put the tip of the cigar into the flame. After the end caught, Molly took in a long drag and released the smoke. It drifted from her mouth and dissipated in the sea breeze. She used the cigar as a reason to take another moment before heading into a fight. Once she steadied her hands and her nerves, she drew her sword from its sheath. The gold inlay set ablaze in the strong Caribbean sun.

Molly walked deliberately down the stairs, keeping her eye on the first mate. The ship was quiet as all eyes locked on her. Her red hair, wild and free, was blowing in the breeze, kept only slightly under control beneath her black hat. Her long vest fanned out gently behind her, showing the black pants that hugged her body. The white, ruffled shirt peeking out from underneath the vest softened the stark look of black and metal that covered Molly. The belts slung on her hips to hold her sword and dirk shifted gently with each step.

All eyes were on her. The only sound that hung in the air was her boots hitting each wooden step as she gradually descended the stairs to make her way toward the first mate. Molly knew this wouldn't be an easy fight. He was a large man. He looked accustomed to the sword he was holding. Not the typical merchant sailor. This man had military training. Molly paused and whispered something to Séamus; only taking her eye off the first mate for a moment. When she returned her focus on him, she had a slight smile. She was ready. In the next few moments, either she will be captain or she will be dead.

Molly stepped onto the ship's deck and dropped her cigar, casually crushing the lit end with her boot. Facing the first mate with her sword at the ready, she motioned for him to come to her. With a loud growl, the first mate rushed her. Their swords met with a violent clang. The reverberation of the metal rang out. Molly kicked him in the stomach to get him to back off. Her strength surprised him but he rebounded quickly and charged her again. The first mate was strong and savvy. She wouldn't catch him off guard again. He slashed at her with his short sword and caught her side. The sharp pain was not new to Molly. She knew it was a cut she would live through.

Midship, one man let out a battle cry and dove into the midst of the crew standing against Molly, his sword hacking down everyone it came near. Chaos followed. Man against man. Sword against sword. Crew member against crew member. The deck became slick with spilt blood. Men screamed in agony as weapons landed deep within bodies.

Molly kept her focus on the first mate. She had to best him or the men would never follow her. Molly was beginning to tire. She hadn't been physically training or had any strenuous activity in a couple of weeks. Her muscles screamed in pain but her mind kept her sharply focused on the task at hand. The first mate wasn't only strong but he also had stamina. He wasn't tiring. He was well versed in the use of a sword. He easily deflected most of Molly's thrusts. His advances were disciplined and purposeful. She staggered a few steps back after receiving a punch to the face. The side of her head throbbed. As she cautiously stepped back into attacking range, Molly noticed that he wasn't protecting his right side as well as he protected his left. She slowed her attacks slightly, wanting him to think she was losing her will and tiring of the fight. He smiled

Good, she thought, *He thinks he is winning.*

"Is our new captain losing her strength? I knew a woman could never beat a man in battle. Give up now, Molly, and maybe I will let you live. You might serve to satisfy me in my new captain's chamber as my whore." His eyes gleamed. He was already planning his next move as captain. His focus on Molly wasn't as acute. His mind was drifting.

Molly lunged forward, slicing him from his shoulder to his mid-chest. Then she whirled and dropped low to slice across his thighs. He screamed in pain and backed away from Molly, slipping in his own blood. Molly went for another slice across his chest. The first mate was able to block her sword. Using his sword as a fulcrum, Molly flipped her sword and stabbed it down into his other shoulder. Slice after slice into his body was weakening her foe. This is where Molly's curved sword was her best ally in a fight. With all of the cuts, the overpowering first mate was struggling just to stand. He was hemorrhaging blood onto the deck. Ready to end this fight, Molly pulled her dirk with her left hand swept it across his face. Cutting him from right cheek to across his nose to his forehead. He cried out and grabbed at his face as the blood gushed from the wound. Molly pulled her arm back and rammed her dirk in just below his ribs and up into his chest. With her knife buried deep in his body, he dropped to his knees.

Molly leaned down and pulled her blade out. "You made a mistake, dear sir. Molly Malone is no-one's whore. This ship is mine. I will be her captain and you will be food for the beasts of the seas." Molly kicked him over, and he landed hard on the deck of the ship. The fighting ceased as the men realized that the biggest and strongest among them was lying dead on the deck in a large pool of blood. Swords began dropping around the ship. Men dropped to their knees, hands in the air in a signal of surrender.

Molly looked around for Séamus. Finally, she saw him. He was wounded but alive. He was bloody but standing. Molly let out a sigh of relief. She locked eyes with Séamus and smiled. They had done it. The ship was theirs.

The Captain And Her Crew
The Dousa

Molly ordered the wounded to be cared for and the dead to be sent to the depths of the sea. The men cleared the decks of bodies, weapons, and blood. As the crew worked under the watchful eye of their new captain, they sent each other quick glances. Was this happening? Were they going to allow a female pirate to take over their ship? None of them were willing to take Molly and her men on. They were still in shock that the two most powerful men on the ship died at the hands of this woman. If she could do that, what else was she capable of?

One of the crew members emerged from the cabins with Kate and Maurice. Maurice ran to Molly and hugged her leg. He held tight, his head pressed against her and his small body spasming with sobs. Molly lay her hand on his head. She was sitting on a barrel as the surgeon was stitching up her side. The surgeon glanced at her, eyebrows drawn tight in obvious confusion. Molly wasn't sure that was the best way for her new crew to view her.

Kate saw Molly's discomfort and gently extracted Maurice from her person. Molly took a deep breath and smiled at Kate, grateful that she understood. Molly looked down and saw how upset Maurice was. His head was bowed and his fist covered his mouth as he tried to catch his breath and stop his tears. Molly took pity on him and motioned for Maurice to come back to her. He climbed onto her lap. While the surgeon finished, Molly hugged him. When his sobs subsided, she gently wiped away his tears.

"What is this, then? You are okay, little man." Maurice kept his eyes down and wouldn't look at her. Molly glanced at Kate. Kate rubbed Maurice's head sympathetically. Molly tried again. "You were never in any danger. I had a man guarding you and Kate. You two were safe." Still, he seemed upset with Molly. She hugged him close. Sometimes she forgot just how much this boy had been through in his very young life.

The surgeon finished stitching up her wound but he lingered. Molly stood and spoke to Kate. "You two are probably hungry. Go to the captain's quarters and I'll have food brought to you."

Kate nodded. She took Maurice by the hand and urged him to the captain's cabin. Molly's cabin. Molly watched them go. As soon as she could manage it, those two had to start training. If they didn't show promise, she would need to find another life for them. She couldn't worry about them each time there was a battle.

Molly directed her attention to the surgeon. "How is my crew?"

"Those that are still alive will continue to live and serve."

"Good. Make sure it stays that way. I am sure surgeons are difficult to find in this part of the world. I would hate to search for someone else to take your place."

"Threatening your surgeon is not a good way to keep your crew healthy... Captain."

Molly ignored the snide way he forced the term captain past his lips. "Yes. That is a true enough statement. What's your name?"

The surgeon straightened. "I am Stanley Prescott. I followed my father's trade and developed my skills under his strict tutelage in the most elite hospitals of London. You are lucky to have me on this ship. You won't find another as proficient as me anywhere."

"I stand corrected, Mr. Prescott. Please, freely come to me with any of your needs. I am most appreciative to have someone of your ability on this ship seeing to my men."

Mr. Prescott just let out an artificial, "Much appreciated, Captain" as he rushed off to help the wounded men.

Séamus emerged from below deck with the help of a large, handsome man. The young man was tall, by any standard. He had a number of tattoos on his well-muscled arms. His sandy-blond hair was gathered at the back of his head in a knot. His bright blue eyes made him look almost inhuman. He seemed to be something from a heroic poem about the old gods. How had Molly never seen him before? The man and Séamus stopped in front of Molly, their approach shaking her from her thoughts.

"Molly... Captain, this is James Barlow. He is a trusted member of our new crew. He was a deckhand and night watchman because of his station in life but, if you would permit me, I would like to recommend him for boatswain. Mr. Barlow would be replacing the former boatswain who is now with Davy Jones."

Molly looked the young man dead in the face. "What's your experience?"

"I've been a sailor since I was nine years of age. I have had many jobs on a ship but I've been a deckhand on this ship for three years. I know this ship and what she needs. I know how she feels and I know how she should sound. I know the men and I know how to task them to their jobs."

"How she should sound." Molly understood that. She could hear her ship. She knew when her ship was happy and when it wasn't. "Will you have a problem with taking orders from a woman, Mr. Barlow?"

James hesitated. "Will you be a good captain to your crew? Will you do as you say and make a profit for all of us?"

"I will."

"Then yes, I will gladly take orders from a woman."

Molly smiled. "One last question. Are you willing to become a pirate?"

James laughed out loud. "I relish the idea of being a pirate, Captain."

"Well then, congratulations on your new post, Mr. Barlow. Get your men together as we prepare to make way."

James Barlow hurried off to start his new life as the boatswain of a pirate ship.

Molly turned to Séamus. "Unless we are in desperate need, I don't want to make any additional changes in ship duties. We need to go to Tendaji first."

Séamus looked down at the deck, seemingly deep in thought.

Molly frowned, concerned with his silence. "Séamus? Do you disagree?"

"No. I agree we need to go. You go get some rest. I'll put us on course." Séamus made his way to the helm. Molly watched him go. From his gait, he was in pain from his wounds. He was the one that should go rest but he was proud. Séamus would never take that suggestion. Molly understood his reluctance to go to Tendaji but she had some unfinished business there. They had to go. They needed additional crew that were familiar with the pirate life. Tendaji was where she hoped to gain that crew.

Molly went to the galley to find some food for herself, Kate, and Maurice. They ate the food with relish. The three of them were so hungry. Molly told them the tale of her night with the captain and her morning of becoming the new captain. She jumped up, "Then, the giant first mate slashed at me with his pathetically small sword. What should have been a mortal wound was so tiny that I just laughed it off. Hah! You poor fool," she raised both of her fists in triumph, "you cannot best the great Molly Malone!" She tried to make her fight that morning funny and full of adventure so poor Maurice would no longer be so worried. He finally laughed at Molly's funny faces and her enthusiasm in telling the tale of her rise to the captain of the *Fortune's Revenge*.

STORY 4
THE NEW QUARTER MASTER

Ikemba Kamara
Tendaji, A Settlement on a Caribbean Island

Séamus put the *Dousa* on course for Tendaji. He knew Molly was determined to go and he knew why. Ikemba Kamara. Séamus had hoped she was done with that man and the Vodu of his mother, Nicole. He shook his head. Nicole and her practices were what brought Molly back from the brink. He owed them. She owed them. Still, their ways were strange and frightening to him. Molly wanted them to bless this ship and get the blessing of their spirits for her to become captain of this vessel. He wasn't looking forward to seeing what that would look like.

A shout went up. "Land!"

Séamus began yelling out orders. The last time he and Molly were here, their ship had dropped anchor in a bay and they took longboats to shore. Finally, he spotted the bay. He and the men maneuvered the ship into the bay and then he ordered the men to drop anchor.

Molly and Kate went through the ship's hold to find gifts for the people of Tendaji and offerings for their spirits. Molly needed them on her side. She needed the people to ask the spirits of the sea to bless her as captain of this ship. They found a large barrel and filled it with food, cloth, wine, weapons, and a crate of chickens. Molly studied the contents critically. She hoped it would be enough.

"What is worrying you, Molly?" Kate asked.

"I need help from some old friends. I'm hoping this offering will entice their gods to bless me and bless my ship."

Kate nodded. She remembered the many rituals the Indians performed asking for help with a hunt or a raid against a neighboring tribe. Whoever these friends of Molly's were, Kate was sure their ways wouldn't be too different from what she was used to. Kate grabbed Molly's hand and waited for Molly to meet her gaze.

"You are meant to be the captain of the *Fortune's Revenge*. I don't know who their gods are, but I'm sure they will be very happy to bless a warrior such as you."

Molly hugged Kate. "Thank you, Kate. Are you ready to go ashore?"

Molly, Maurice, and Kate stood ready as the men dropped the longboats. They left James Barlow in charge of the ship. Séamus had chosen a few men to accompany them to the island. It had been a while since they had been there. They needed to be prepared for any dangers—known or otherwise.

The men rowed to shore in silence. Molly and Séamus exchanged knowing glances. These men were merchants. They hadn't been trained to fight. They were frightened and would probably run at the first sign of trouble.

The boats hit the beach and a few men jumped out to pull the boats ashore. Molly stepped out of the boat and onto the sand. She smiled. It had been too long since her last visit here. She turned to Séamus.

"I think everyone should stay here. Let me go see if our friends are still here before we unload everything and... everyone."

Séamus jumped onto the beach. He drew his sword. "We will stay here, just give a shout if you need us."

Molly turned to walk up the beach she turned quickly when she heard Kate yell out. Maurice was running toward Molly and Séamus went after him. Molly raised her hand and waited for Maurice. She knelt down when Maurice reached her. "Your captain told you to wait in the boat. We need to have a serious talk about your constant disobedience of my orders." Maurice hugged her and smiled. Molly let out an exasperated sigh. How could this small creature get through all of her defenses and defy her without any consequences whatsoever? Molly stood and held out her hand to him. He took her hand and together they made their way toward the tree line.

Molly took in a deep breath, remembering the smells and sounds of this place. All stress left her body and she felt at ease. This island and its people were family to her. The last time she was here, they had saved her life. Now, she was here for one of their own and for a favor. She hoped what she brought was enough for all of that.

Maurice stopped with his feet planted in the sand, his eyes on the trees. Molly looked up and saw a dark-skinned woman dressed in white. Around her was a group of people. Molly's gaze went back to the woman. She was exceptionally tall and her white headwrap gave her even more height. She looked imposing with her hands on her hips and her dark eyes were narrowed as she watched Molly and Maurice's progress up the beach. Molly gently pulled Maurice's hand, trying to urge him forward. He shook his head no emphatically.

The woman and the people around her slowly walked toward them. The woman towered over Molly. She slowly took in Molly and Maurice. Molly stood her ground. Finally, the woman laughed out loud, "Molly Malone!"

With that, chaos ensued. The people rushed to Molly and Maurice, hugging Molly and welcoming her home. There were so many people around them. Maurice pressed closer to Molly's leg. After a bit, the woman shooed the people away. She hugged Molly, enveloping her with long arms. "I am very glad to see you again, child, but why are you here?" Molly could listen to her talk all day. Her lilting accent had authority and compassion. The woman let Molly go, stepped back, and looked down at Maurice. "Who is this?" Her gaze darted past them to the boats and the men in them. "Who are those men?" Her gaze stopped on Kate's blonde hair gleaming in the sun. She narrowed her eyes. "Again, I ask what are you doing here?"

"I have brought gifts to the family who once saved my life."

The woman cocked her head, waiting for the real reason Molly was there.

"I need your help Mambo Nicole… and… I've come for one of your men."

Mambo Nicole didn't take her gaze off of Molly. "You are here for Ikemba." Nicole said with certainty. "As for the rest, we will speak of that over food." Nicole yelled out an order. The young men broke off and went to unload the goods and the people from the boats. Séamus, Kate, and the rest of the men joined Molly and Maurice. Nicole smiled widely and squeezed them in welcoming hugs when she greeted Séamus and Kate.

Nicole and Molly walked arm and arm up the beach. Molly couldn't help but tear up a little. Nicole wasn't her mother but Molly felt safe and content with this woman. She was reflecting on the Nicole's impact on her life when she heard a loud call.

"Molly Malone, the most beautiful pirate ever known! She will either kiss you or kill you depending on her mood that day!"

Ikemba was wearing nothing but a colorful wrap that went from his waist to his knees. His dark skin was glistened in the hot sun. Molly had forgotten how much she admired his body. He was tall and muscular with a wide chest, narrow waist, and long legs.

Nicole looked down at Molly. "Well, go girl. He has been waiting every day since the day you left for your return."

Molly gave Nicole a quick squeeze, then ran to Ikemba. They met halfway with laughter and a tight hug, both were overjoyed to see the other. Ikemba put his hands on both sides of her head and kissed her. "I was not sure you were ever going to return. I thought you forgot about me."

Molly took his hands and stepped back so they could see each other. "I could never forget you. You have a piece of my heart. I am not whole without you."

Ikemba hugged Molly tightly.

"I'm surprised you're here. Why aren't you on the *Serpent's Return*?" Molly asked.

"A few of us have come back here to help Mambo Nicole. There was a large storm that damaged the village. I've been here for a few weeks."

"Fortunate timing for me, I guess. I hope the village wasn't too damaged. Was anyone hurt?"

"No. The village is fine. As are its people. I have missed you, Molly. I too feel that my heart is not whole when I am away from you."

"I am ready to have that missing piece with me every day."

Ikemba looked puzzled but hopeful. "What are you saying to me, Molly?"

Mambo Nicole walked to Ikemba and laid a hand on his shoulder, "She wants you to be a crew member on her ship."

Molly rushed to explain. "Not just a member of the crew. I want you to be our quartermaster. My men are merchant sailors. Not pirates. I need you to help Séamus get them ready to fight. And... they will need you to be their voice to their new captain. You and Séamus are the only two people I will listen to or, at the very least, not kill when I am angry."

Ikemba hid his disappointment. He thought Molly was here to be his.

He knew he should be grateful. This was probably as close as any person could be with Molly.

"Well?" Molly broke into his thoughts. He looked at her face. The face he loved. Her scar and eyepatch did nothing to diminish her beauty. Her wild red hair was longer than when he last saw her. His heart broke when he saw her smile. "Well? Are you ready to set sail with Captain Molly Malone?"

"*Bo nan bouch, men pè dan.* As usual with Molly Malone."

"What does that mean?"

"Kiss the mouth, but fear the teeth."

"Kem..."

He pulled her close and held her. "I will speak with Mambo Nicole. Yes?" Molly nodded. "Yes."

Maurice ran to Molly and grabbed her leg. Ikemba's mouth opened in surprise. "Who is this? How do you come to have a negro boy with you?"

Molly knelt down to gather Maurice close. "I bought him. I found him in a slave market in New Orleans and I couldn't leave him to whatever fate was waiting for him on a plantation."

"You own a slave?" Ikemba's voice was tight. "I am surprised by you, Molly. I did not think you had that evil within you."

Molly stood and faced Ikemba. "Yes, I own him. For now. It is not safe for such a young child to be a freed slave. As my property, no one would dare take him and claim ownership of him. Until such time there is no slavery or he can communicate his freedom to a court of law, I will own him."

Ikemba knelt down on one knee in front of Maurice and said something to him in a language unfamiliar to Molly. Maurice gasped and smiled. He jumped into Ikemba's arms and whispered to him. Ikemba hugged the boy and stood up with Maurice in his arms.

Molly laughed. "He likes you. That smile is a rare commodity." Ikemba took Molly's hand and the three of them made their way to the camp.

That night, Molly, Séamus, Kate, Maurice, and the few crew members that came to shore ate a lively meal of iguana, wild pig, and fruit. The girls and boys of the camp entertained them with dancing and drumming. Kate and the crew sat around the outer edge of the crowd, their eyes wide. None of them had ever witnessed the frenzied performance of African dancing and drumming before. Molly took in the joy on Maurice's face. He was finally among others who looked like him. Some spoke a language that was familiar. He seemed to enjoy the drumming and dancing. Molly guessed he remembered this from his home. Maurice was not so young and had not been gone so long that he would forget his home and his people.

Ikemba asked Maurice if he wanted to drum with the other boys. Maurice emphatically nodded, and ran to catch up with Ikemba. Ikemba found a drum and got Maurice situated among the other drummers. Molly's heart broke as Maurice played the drum. He had done this before. *Should I leave him here?*

She hadn't seen him this alive since she had found him, starving and dirty in that slave market. Those large, dark eyes had been so full of sadness. When Molly found him, he had no hair because the slavers had shaved his head. It was finally growing out. He was gaining weight. His clothes were clean and fit him well. He was learning English. None of that seemed to be of any consequence to him. Tonight, he was happily playing the drum, singing and watching the dancers.

Séamus sat between Kate and Molly, remembering his last visit here. Kate noticed Séamus was deep in thought. "What are you thinking about? You seem to be somewhere else," she whispered to him.

He nodded. "The last time we were here, I watched these people dance like this as Molly was knocking on death's door. They sacrificed goats and chickens and danced in the blood of the animals to beg their spirits to bring her back to the living. The entire village drummed and danced for days. I remember thinking that their gods must be very strong to give them the ability to stay awake and plead for Molly's life with such passion for so long. I owe them a lot. They are the reason Molly is alive today."

"Has Molly known them for long?"

"No. Our former captain dropped us here. He wanted Molly off of his ship and these were the closest humans he knew of. They could have just as easily killed us. In fact, it would have been a lot easier to kill us. Molly was nearly dead, and I was—am—an old man. They could have killed us and taken that sword of hers. If they sold it or traded it... it could have fed the village for a year. Instead, they sacrificed their animals, their blood, and their bodies for her. I still don't understand why."

Kate contemplated why this village would do such powerful magic for a stranger. Maybe there was more to Molly than she realized.

Mambo Nicole stood and motioned for Molly to follow. She pointed to Kate and waved for her to join them. Kate hesitated for a moment, but then she stood up and trailed behind Molly and Nicole. Molly looked back at Séamus and Maurice. Ikemba had found another drum and was sitting next to Maurice, playing. The young boy was enthralled with Ikemba. Again, Molly wondered if Maurice would be better here than with her. She spied a young woman with ample breasts coaxing Séamus to join her. He gave in and followed her out of the crowd into the dark. Sometimes Molly forgot that Séamus was a man with male needs.

Mambo Nicole waited in the doorway for Molly and Kate. They walked into the hut. In one corner, there was a rough-hewn bed. Not tall or wide but long to fit Mambo Nicole's sizable body. The bed was covered in all sorts of patterned blankets. It was colorful and stood out in the sparsely furnished dwelling. Next to the bed, a large tree branch was planted in the ground. All the leaves were stripped off and a large snake lounged on the bare branches. In the middle, there was a fire ring with small blankets to sit on each side of the fire ring. Looking past the fire ring, there was a statue. From Molly's previous visit here, she knew that the mound of mud, candle wax, blood, feathers, and flowers was Legba.

Legba, the deity that served as an intermediary between the Lwa and the people. He stood at the crossroads and either granted or denied permission to speak with the spirits. Molly recalled they would beseech Legba for permission to speak with the spirit world before a ceremony. That was why they had him on a movable alter. The village would move him from Mambo Nicole's hut to their ceremonial circle in the jungle when they came together for celebrations or rituals. The wooden base where Legba rested was painted red with white symbols drawn in each corner and on the handles. Perhaps protection for those moving Legba?

Molly asked permission to give a gift to Legba. Mambo Nicole gestured to him. It was okay. Molly pulled a necklace from her pocket and draped it around Legba. It was thick, braided leather with a piece of eight attached. Molly had made this necklace for Legba months ago. She had hoped she would be back here to thank him for her life.

Molly turned to see Kate taking in the surroundings. Molly remembered the first time she had seen all of this. For Molly, it had been overwhelming. Mambo Nicole watched Kate's reaction to her home. There was very little. Kate had grown up in an Indian tribe, after all. There wasn't a lot that would shock her.

Mambo Nicole sat opposite of Legba on a thick mat of braided reeds and motioned for Kate and Molly to sit. Molly removed her sword and sat on Nicole's left. She motioned for Kate to sit at her right. Molly squirmed a little. The small rug kept her off of the dirt but it provided little comfort. Kate laughed. This felt like home to her.

"Mambo Nicole, would it be okay for me to remove my boots? They are not comfortable and I would love to be free of them for a short while."

"Whatever you wish, child."

Kate shed her boots and sat cross-legged on the mat. This felt familiar and warmed her with thoughts of her Indian family. She breathed deeply, closed her eyes, and took in the smells. The dirt. The fire. She was right back in the tipi with her family, her father telling stories of great buffalo hunts, her mother sewing colorful beads onto clothing pieces, and her brother bragging that he was going to be a great warrior someday. Kate felt the usual sharp pain in the pit of her stomach. As always, she recognized the deep feelings of guilt, pain, and love. It seemed these emotions were destined to be a part of her life until her dying day. On the day of her death, which of the great spirits would greet her? Those of her blood ancestors or those of the Native tribes?

Kate opened her eyes and realized Molly and Mambo Nicole were watching her.

Molly asked Kate, "Are you okay? If being here is too much, I can have you taken back to the ship."

"No. I'm okay. Just, painful memories."

Mambo Nicole waited for Kate to look at her. Once she did, Nicole smiled. She leaned over to grasp Kate's hand and gave it a squeeze. No wonder Molly came to Mambo Nicole. One touch and Kate felt better. As if Mambo Nicole had taken the pain from her. Kate looked closer. Nicole's deep brown eyes sparkled. She had removed the white head covering from her hair and it rested on her wide shoulders. Her hair was long but it wasn't free. Almost like long ropes, she had it wrapped at the top of her head. Fragrant and colorful flowers were pushed into her locks. To Kate, this woman looked ethereal.

Mambo Nicole slid her eyes from Kate to Molly. "So, you found her."

Mambo Nicole
The Tendaji Encampment

Molly looked at Kate and nodded. "Yes, I found her. As you said I would."

Mambo Nicole cocked her head and smiled as if to say *was there any doubt?* "Besides taking my son with you when you leave, why are you here, Molly?"

"I have a ship and I need the blessing of Mami Wata so I may be captain. I want my ship and my men to accept me. If Mami Wata gives her blessing, then I will be in favor with the seas. With that favor, I believe the ship and the men will follow me as captain."

Mambo Nicole looked at Kate. "And what have you to say about this? Do you support Molly as captain?"

The question surprised Kate. Her eyes flicked between Mambo Nicole and Molly. Molly didn't seem upset by the question. Why would she ask Kate her opinion? She didn't know these people, and they didn't know her.

Mambo Nicole waited patiently for Kate to answer. Finally, Kate found her voice.

"Molly should be captain. She will lead well and if the men follow, she will be good to them."

"And if they do not follow?"

"Then they will pay for that mistake. Probably with their lives." Kate nodded as she spoke. Yes, she was certain of this.

Mambo Nicole thought for a moment. "Tomorrow, I will give you my answer. I must consult with the spirits and ask if they are willing. Agreed?"

Molly nodded. She wasn't worried about the spirits landing in favor of her. They had saved her very life once before. Giving their blessing for this should be easier to gain than a life.

Mambo Nicole suspected Molly didn't know the tale behind Kate's tattoos so she dove right in and asked, "Tell me, Kate, how did you come to have those markings on your face?"

Kate sat a little straighter and looked Mambo Nicole straight on, surprised by the direct question. She took a breath, glanced at Molly, and began her tale. "I was captured by Indians. My entire family was killed and one of the Indian men took me back to their camp. When we arrived, everyone came out to see me. They wanted to touch my hair and my skin. They seemed afraid of me, and yet, curious. I don't think they had ever seen a person with my hair and skin color before.

My captor tried to take me to his tipi but the chief and elders stopped him. There was much arguing between them. A woman and a boy about my age broke through the crowd and stood next to the man. He motioned to me and to what was obviously his family."

Kate paused. Her hands were shaking. She had not thought of that day in a long time.

Molly could see that Kate was tense and sad. Kate didn't talk about her time with the Natives. Molly wasn't sure she wanted Kate pushed into those painful memories and she looked at Mambo Nicole, her expression unsure. Mambo Nicole gestured to Molly to keep silent.

"The man pushed me in front of him and his family. He pointed to the eagle feather in my braid and to the eagle feather that was sticking straight up in his hair. The woman and the boy stood proudly in support of the man. I think they accepted his decision to bring me there because of the eagle feather. It was a good omen for them, maybe? A sign that I should be one of them. The crowd began to calm as my captor told them the story of how he found me. One man, who I later found out was the medicine man of the village, stepped forward. He came to me. He was chanting and shaking a gourd full of something. It was very loud and frightening. I would not cry though. I wanted to be brave. I was only eight years of age but if my family was looking down on me, I wanted make them proud of me."

At this point, the tears fell freely down Kate's cheeks. Mambo Nicole got up and yelled out of her doorway. "Asha! We need water." As Mambo Nicole returned to her seat, a young woman rushed in with water for them. Asha gave each of them a small container made from shells. Kate sipped the water and cradled the shell in her hands. The shell momentarily distracted Kate. The outside was a rough, dull color. The inside was smooth and pink. She watched the water move gently as her body moved with each breath. Finally, Kate began her story once again.

"The medicine man finally stopped chanting and was still for a moment. All of a sudden, his eyes rolled in the back of his head and he began moaning loudly. Then, he stopped. His eyes flew open and he announced something. My new captors clutched me to them, shouting. As I looked around, the rest of the tribe seemed shocked into silence. None of them moved or spoke. The chief clapped his hands and must have called for the man and his wife to be silent. They stopped speaking and no longer held me tightly. The medicine man and the chief had made a decision. A group of men rushed forward and grabbed me. Would they kill me? I had seen my family killed that morning. Their screams were still ringing in my ears. I was so frightened. My world was fading to black because of that fear. I wanted to stay awake for my death so my family would be proud. My mind... my mind had other ideas though."

Kate wiped the tears from her face and continued.

"I faded from awake to asleep and awake again as the men carried me to furs laid out by a fire. They held me down by my arms and legs. The medicine man crouched beside me with a stick that had what looked like my mother's sewing needle through it. He dipped it in something black and began hitting me around the mouth with it."

Kate drew in a deep breath and began talking faster and faster. The story spilled out of her.

"It hurt. It was a pain I had never felt before. I couldn't be brave any longer. I became a wild animal and started screaming and fought the men. My captor, his wife, and son tried to calm me. The woman was crying, and the boy seemed as frightened as I was. The four men tightened their hold on me. They were bigger and stronger, but I was an Ersland. I descended from a strong, proud people. They would have to kill me before I allowed whatever it was that they had planned." Kate paused. Shaking, she took another sip of water.

Molly realized her own hands were in tight fists. She felt ill. The poor child that Kate was. Molly could only imagine the fear that girl felt amongst people she didn't know and spoke a language she didn't understand.

"An old woman broke through the crowd. She spoke softly and clucked to me. Moving the medicine man out of the way, she motioned for the four men holding my arms and legs to let me go. I grabbed her arm and begged for help. She smoothed my hair back and sang softly. She encouraged me to drink a liquid she had. It did not taste good, but she was being so kind I didn't want to upset her, so I drank it. I drank from it three times. By the third drink, her voice seemed to float away from me. I couldn't see anyone clearly. She continued to smooth my hair and sing to me. Soon I was free from the pain and fear. The world went black. When I woke, I was in a tipi and my face felt as if it was on fire. I was wearing different clothing... My new family looking over me."

Kate smiled slightly.

"That morning, I had found an eagle feather. When I picked it up, I knew. I knew I needed it. I had to keep it with me. It would protect me. I had a small bit of string in my pocket and I tied it into my braid. Mother would have hated it. She wanted me to be pretty and proper. I rarely was." Kate shook her head and laughed sadly. "If I had left that feather where I found it, what might have been? Would I be dead and buried next to my family? Would that have been better? Once I returned, many thought I had shamed myself. That it would have been more honorable to die."

Kate kept her eyes trained on her hands. She couldn't look at Molly and Mambo Nicole. What if they agreed? What if they thought death was better than living as a savage? She continued without looking up.

"I spent the next nine summers as a member of the tribe. My new family loved me. The rest of the Indians never fully gave up their fear of me. Every year on the day I arrived, the medicine man added to my tattoos. It was something I accepted. In truth, insisted on. It was a way for me to show them my strength, and the markings helped them accept me and ease their fear of me living in the village. It was a better way to live."

"How did you come to leave them?" Molly asked.

Kate didn't look up. She stared at her hands and considered her answer. "My brother. My brother woke me one night. I still slept in my mother and father's tipi. He quietly took me out. We sat next to the stream under the moonlight. He held my hand and said I had to go. That I was long past marriageable age. The elders were deciding what to do about me. He overheard them talking. They did not want me to bear any children. They could marry me to an old man past his time to make children or they could sell me to another tribe as a slave. In the end, they had decided they would need to kill me even though my mother and father would fight them. The elders decided it would be best."

"I didn't want to leave. I had already lost one family and didn't think I could lose another. I cried and begged him to help me find another way. He told me there was no other way. Once the elders had decided, there was no changing that decision. I knew I had to leave or die."

"As we sat by the stream, he told me, 'White Eagle Feather, you are my sister. My mother and father are your mother and father. My ancestors are your ancestors. It is time for you to go back to your white world. The tribe has protected you from evil with the marks on your face, but now, you need a new mark. One that will help you remember me, mother, and father. The Great Spirit has shown me that you and I will be together again. I have seen a strange settlement on the water. We will meet there when it is time.'

"He took out his knife and cut two Xs into my right hand just under my second finger." Kate absently rubbed the marks on her hand as she talked. "The two Xs touched as if they were one. He carved a circle above each X and closed the bottom of one. He wiped the blood away so I could see. It was my brother and me. He was one X, and I was the other X with the bottom closed—like I'm wearing a dress." Kate opened her right hand and showed Molly and Nicole the marks. "He did the same on his left hand. He rubbed soot, bear fat, and something else into the marks so, like the markings on my face, they wouldn't fade away."

Kate held her hand to her face, remembering that night.

"Then, I left. I walked away from another family. My brother made a sling with food and a blanket. He gave me his favorite knife, hugged me, and sent me away. I walked for days until I found the cabin of my childhood. Every footstep was heavy with grief and longing to go back to the village and my family. What kept me going was the thought of returning to the white world of the Ersland family. I thought... I thought, that I could go back to the settlement. That the people who were my family's friends would welcome me back. There was also the small hope that my family had survived the attack. But... here I am sitting around a fire with a pirate and a Vodu Mambo in an ex-slave encampment."

Mambo Nicole stood up and walked over to Kate. She knelt down and hugged her tight. "You are going to be just fine, child. You are meant to be here. Your face tattoos were a gift from the Lwa. We needed a marker so we could find you. And here you are! The Lwa always know what is best for us. Yes, Kate, you are exactly where you are supposed to be." Kate leaned against her and openly sobbed. Even Molly couldn't stop her tears.

Molly stood and quietly exited the hut. Mambo Nicole knew exactly where Molly was headed. To her son. Ikemba could not think clearly when it came to Molly. He would follow her to the ends of the Earth and back if she asked him to. And she probably would. Isn't that why she was here?

Molly stepped out into the tropical night and breathed in the air. She stood quietly, listening. The drumming and dancing had stopped. Now the night was now filled with the sounds of the jungle and of the people enjoying each other in the most primal way. Her need to find Ikemba was growing. She turned to go find him and stopped short. There he was. His beautiful smile made her catch her breath. Molly would never again be tied to one person, but Ikemba tested her resolve. She smiled back and strolled up to him.

Face to face, they took each other in. Every detail. He reached out and touched Molly's face, gently tracing her lips with his fingers. A need burned inside of Molly. She took a deep breath to steady herself. Instead, her breath came in quick gasps. Her entire body was warming. Ikemba ran his fingers down her arms and took Molly's hands in his own. He raised her hand to his mouth and kissed each of her fingers. Slowly, one by one. Molly watched him kiss her fingers. His eyes were closed. With each kiss, he was breathing in the smell of her. With each touch of his lips, Molly's need for him intensified. When she could take no more, she lowered their hands, pulling both of their hands behind her, drawing him closer to her. Molly lifted her face to his and kissed his full lips. A soft moan escaped her. She very much missed this man.

The Fortune's Revenge
The Tendaji Encampment

Ikemba and Molly awoke the next morning with Mambo Nicole standing over them, arms crossed. She did not look pleased.

"Mother, did you need me for something?" Ikemba flashed his best smile at Nicole.

"You cannot use that smile to charm me, boy! Both of you up! The spirits have spoken." Nicole left the hut without another word.

Molly jumped up and got dressed. She was shaking so hard she could barely manage her clothing. Ikemba laughed and helped her.

As he buttoned her shirt, he asked, "Why are you nervous? The spirits brought you back from death's door for a reason. Why would they not grant this for you?"

"Mambo Nicole is not happy about you and me. She knows I want to take you with me. If the ship is not blessed, maybe I won't leave. You stay."

"Molly Malone, first, I have not said I would go with you. Second, the Mambo does not say whether or not the spirits give their blessing. They decide on their own. Now, stop this worry. Let us go see what will happen next."

Ikemba and Molly exited Ikemba's hut and found the entire camp assembled, as well as Séamus, Kate, Maurice, and the rest of her men. Molly noticed Séamus wore the same disapproving look that Nicole did. His disapproval annoyed Molly. She didn't like Séamus to be upset with her but in this case, he could mind himself. Molly's relationship with Ikemba was hers and hers alone. She did not need his approval. Kate, on the other hand, could barely contain her smile and was clearly choking down laughter at Molly's annoyance.

Mambo Nicole called the two over to stand on each side of her. She stepped forward and spoke loudly. "Molly Malone has come to our island to take one of our own and to beseech the spirits for their blessing on her behalf as captain of the ship sitting in our bay. I have spent the night talking to Legba, Mami Wata, and our Lwa. They are willing to bless Molly Malone and her ship. They agree they saved her life for a greater purpose and believe she will make a fine captain. They say that the ship has accepted her. Molly and her ship will make an excellent pair in whatever quest they choose." Mambo Nicole paused.

Now for the bad news.

"The Lwa are in favor and not in favor of Ikemba joining Captain Malone's crew. They say that Ikemba will be happy with either choice. As Mambo and his adoptive mother, I say that Ikemba may not go. He will stay here and begin training to be Houngan."

With that declaration hanging in the air, Mambo Nicole gave members of the encampment different duties to get the ritual ready. They would begin when the sun was at the highest point. Molly couldn't move. Her heart was breaking but she was relieved. She tried to tell herself it was for the best. It wasn't fair for her to keep Ikemba for herself, knowing she would never fully give herself to him. Mambo Nicole had conveyed the more important message—she had the blessings she needed to be captain of her ship. Ikemba's voice shook from her thoughts.

"Mambo Nicole, I need some time to talk with you about the decision you made for me."

"As you wish. Come to my hut." Mambo Nicole knew this would not be a simple talk. Ikemba was very headstrong, and he loved Molly.

Molly watched the two of them walk to Mambo Nicole's hut. Mambo Nicole walked with calm purpose while Ikemba was angry and tense. Kate and Séamus made their way to Molly.

"I have the blessings I came for. The rest is up to them." She nodded her head in the direction Ikemba and his mother had gone. "They are going to do the ritual this afternoon. I want to leave on the morrow. Get every man back on the ship except for two. The five of us will spend one more night on shore. I have one more decision I need to make. I don't think I can make it until after the ritual is complete." Molly's gaze was on Maurice who was playing with other children from the camp. He was no longer wearing the clothes she had purchased for him. Dressed like the rest of the children, a colorful wrap tied around his waist that fell just below his knees, Molly had never seen him look happier. How could she take him from this place?

Séamus placed his hand on Molly's shoulder. "He may do better here."

"I agree."

"Maurice has grown very attached to you, Molly. If you decide to keep him with you, I think he would be just as happy." Kate was trying to shake Molly from her grim thoughts. First, she lost Ikemba. Now she was losing Maurice. She knew little about Molly Malone but it was obvious she had lost many people in her life. Kate wasn't sure Molly could lose both Ikemba and Maurice at the same time.

"Séamus, go back to the ship. Take the men with you but leave two of your choosing here. You and the rest of the men help James get the ship ready to sail at dawn. Make it quick. I want you back here for the ritual at noon. Kate, you are with me. We will help gather everything for today. Whichever two men are staying behind, I want provisions gathered for the ship. I'm sure the men on board would appreciate eating some fresh food. At least one or two wild pigs and some fruit. If need be, some iguanas. Maybe the cook can make a stew with it and the men wouldn't notice that they are eating lizard." They all laughed and split up to carry out Molly's orders.

At noon, when the sun was at its highest point in the sky, Mambo Nicole and her people gathered in a circle of trees. The Legba statue was at the southernmost point in the circle. There was one entrance and exit in this stand of trees. Molly remembered this place. She marveled once again at the perfect circle of trees blocking out the world beyond. Molly's crew and the villagers trailed behind Mambo Nicole. Nicole stopped on one side of the Legba altar with Ikemba on the other side. Everyone else filled in the circle. Two drummers sat in the middle, pounding out a solemn, steady beat. On either side of Mambo Nicole and Ikemba, there were younger men and women dressed in all white. They were carrying bowls filled with offerings. The rest of the villagers were dressed in colorful skirts, wraps, and headscarves. They wore necklaces made of shell and bone. The women had beautiful tropical flowers in their hair.

It was hot even under the shade of the trees. Molly was dressed in thick, gray and black-striped breeches. She wore her white shirt with the sleeves rolled up without her black vest. She also wore her usual silver belts on her hips but she left her sword and sheath in Ikemba's hut. Molly glanced at the lightweight dresses and skirts the other women were wearing and wished she had dressed like them. She was sweating in these clothes. They served her onboard a ship but weren't practical in a tropical jungle.

The drummers kept the steady beat and the women in white began singing a slow, deep song. It was difficult to hear over the drumming. The entire circle of people moved to the rhythm. The energy was building in the circle. It became thick and almost oppressive. It didn't feel unpleasant but a person not accustomed to feeling the wild energy would find it foreign and heavy.

Maurice squirmed a little, brushing at his arms and face. Molly knelt down. "Easy little man. Don't fight it. Listen to the drums. Let those sounds seep into your heart." Molly patted his chest in rhythm with the drumbeats.

"Relax and allow the energy of these people to flow around you and through you." Maurice exhaled and began to breathe naturally. His body took over, and he swayed with the beats. "Better?" He didn't answer, but Molly could see that he was accepting what was going on around him instead of trying to push it away.

Mambo Nicole took a long stick and drew an intricate symbol in the sand. Her ancestors had passed each element of the symbol down to her. This beautiful, and intricate drawing told the story of her Vodu heritage. As Mambo Nicole drew the complex symbol, the others sang softly in honor of Nicole and her line. When she finished her drawing, she stood and opened her arms wide.

"Legba! We call on you and ask that you open the way to the land of spirit and ancestor! We come to you on behalf of our sister, Molly Malone. Legba! We ask that you open the door! Lead us to the world of mist and bone. The place of earth and water. I am Mambo Nicole, daughter descended from a long line of Vodu Mambos. Here is my mark for you to consider."

Mambo Nicole gestured proudly to the symbol in the sand. This design was uniquely hers. No other person on earth would have this exact symbol.

"He is coming..." she whispered.

Suddenly, one of the old men in the village cried out, "My children! My children, it is good to see you again! Your numbers have grown! I am happy to see you are doing well. Now, bring me my drink and let us walk together through sand and sky, water and earth, ash and wood." Mambo Nicole motioned to one of the young girls to bring a coconut filled with liquid to Legba.

The old man took the coconut and drank deeply. He handed the coconut back to the girl and called out, "Another!"

This time, a young boy ran to Legba with a coconut. The old man patted the boy on the head with a laugh. He gulped the liquid down. When he handed the coconut back, he didn't call for another. Instead, his gaze searched the circle until he found who he was looking for. The old man stood tall and made his way to Molly. Molly shot Mambo Nicole a slightly panicked look. The mambo motioned for her to be calm. Molly was not sure she could stay calm under the circumstances. The man walking toward her was not the old man. He looked like the old man but his body and his walk was one of a younger man. It convinced Molly this was Legba.

Legba stopped close to Molly. "So, we are here again for you?"

Molly couldn't speak. She could only nod yes.

Legba turned to Mambo Nicole. "You call on me for this girl who is not a Vodu. She does not follow our ways. She does not look like us. Tell me why I should speak to the spirits for this, *blan fanm!*"

Mambo Nicole motioned for another child to bring Legba a coconut. As Legba drank, she answered him. "Molly is a sister to our village. She is a lover to my son. She is a daughter to me. Molly is one of us. I ask as Mambo to this village that you accept Molly as one of us, Legba, for I am her family and she is mine."

Legba turned to Molly. "Do you feel the same as she does? Is she mother and Mambo to you?"

Molly found her voice. "Yes. Yes, she is mother and Mambo to me. The people of this place are family to me."

Without warning, Legba grabbed Molly's arm and slashed it with a large knife. Blood began spilling from her arm. Legba caught some with the coconut and poured it over his head. With the blood on his hand, he marked Molly's forehead with a wavy, almost snake-like line. He dragged Molly to the Legba statue and held her arm over it so her blood flowed over the statue. Molly was bleeding a lot. The entire village was not sure what was going to happen.

"What is it that you want from us?" Legba demanded.

"I wish to be captain of a ship. My ship. I wish for the spirits to bless my ship and bless me as I become Captain Molly Malone and the ship which is now called the *Dousa* will become the *Fortune's Revenge*. I wish for the waters of the Earth to accept us and reveal to us the treasures they hold. I wish for me and my crew to have great luck and great fortune."

As Molly spoke, blood flowed from her arm onto the statue. Séamus was in a frenzy. Should he stop this? Was this so-called Legba going to let Molly bleed out? Would Nicole step in? Molly would be angry if he stopped the ritual prematurely. At what point was this no longer a ritual offering and become a sacrifice? Séamus put his hand on his sword, ready to take Molly from this place, when Legba shouted, "I accept Molly as one of you! I accept her offering to me and our Lwa. I will speak to the spirits on her behalf! To the water!"

The entire village cheered. The procession followed Legba and Molly to the beach. They drummed and sang as they moved through the jungle to the water's edge.

Kate locked eyes with Séamus as they fell in behind the others, making their way to the water. "I thought he was going to kill her!" Kate whispered harshly. Séamus nodded. This was his second time watching Molly go down an unfamiliar road with these people. It wasn't any easier this time.

Séamus and Kate stood at the edge of the beach, watching the chaos below them. Legba, Molly, Mambo Nicole, and Ikemba were standing around the Mami Wata statue. The rest of the village spread across the sand, dancing, and drumming. One at a time, a person approached Mami Wata and placed an offering. Shells, coconuts, flowers, dolls made of hair, snakes, and lizards—all laid lovingly at Mami Wata's feet.

Legba called out, and men rushed to pull a hidden canoe from the trees to the water's edge. Legba, Molly, and Mambo Nicole boarded the longboat. The same men rowed them to the *Dousa*. The sound of singing and drumming coming from the beach was deafening. Séamus and Kate watched the boat stop at the bow of the ship. Mambo Nicole dipped something in the blood from Molly's arm and drew a symbol on the ship. The men rowed to the stern and did the same thing. They rowed to the other side and did the same on the aft. The crew on the ship were leaning over the side to watch their captain and those with her. Most hadn't seen anything like this before.

Séamus chuckled. He could just imagine what the men were thinking. If nothing else, they would follow Molly for fear of angering the spirits of these people.

They rowed the longboat back to the beach. Legba shouted to everyone on the beach, "It is done! Mami Wata and the Lwa have given their blessings to Captain Molly Malone and her vessel, the *Fortune's Revenge*. The waters of this earthly place will allow safe passage to them both. As long as Molly and her ship are one, they will be safe and successful!"

The villagers shouted their praises to Mami Wata and their Lwa. When Molly stepped ashore, the villagers rushed to her. The throng became overwhelming as they cheered her accomplishment. They wanted to touch her. The spirits had accepted her request. The spirits had blessed her. Ikemba was suddenly at her side. He put his powerful arms around her and hugged her to his body. He made his way through the crowd over to Kate and

Séamus. The four of them walked back to the quiet of the village. Before Molly could sit down, she ran to a stand of trees and began throwing up. When she threw up all she could, she collapsed against a tall palm tree. She couldn't move. She was weak from blood loss and the overwhelming energy that had entered her body and then suddenly left when her part of the ritual was over.

Ikemba carried her to the fire and cradled her in his lap. Kate brought her water to drink and Séamus gave her meat to eat. Mambo Nicole found them. She needed to check on Molly. Mambo Nicole picked up Molly's arm to look at the wound. She smiled at Molly, "You will be fine, child. I've seen you survive much worse than this."

Molly weakly laughed. "Yes, you have. Still, this one burns like a hell's fire has taken up residence in my arm."

Mambo Nicole left and then returned with liquid and cloth strips. She poured the liquid on Molly's arm. Molly cried out in pain. Ikemba held her tight. He hated seeing her like this. Nicole put a paste in the wound and bandaged it up.

"She needs sleep. Take her to your hut and let her rest. Tomorrow she will be herself again." Mambo Nicole stood and made her way back to her people on the beach. She needed Legba to return to the spirit world. Depending on Legba's mood on this day, it could happen quickly or it could take hours.

Ikemba carried Molly to his bed. He stroked her head until she finally relaxed and fell asleep. Safe in his arms, Molly slept deeply until the morning.

STORY 5
CAPTAIN MOLLY MALONE

From Sailors to Pirates
The Fortune's Revenge

The next morning, Molly woke with the rising sun. She was ready to embark on her new journey as captain of the *Fortune's Revenge*. There was a lot to do to get the men ready for their new life. It would be even more difficult without Ikemba. He was an experienced sailor and warrior. She and Séamus would just have to make do. Molly hastily got dressed and, for the first time in a few days, strapped her sword on. It was heavy and she couldn't be happier to have it back on her person.

Molly walked out of the hut where she had slept the past few nights to feel the warm Caribbean breeze on her face. She loved the sound as it moved through the trees. With her eyes closed, she savored the feeling. Molly wanted to remember everything about this island so she could carry it with her while she was on the water. Molly opened her eyes when she heard someone approach. It was Ikemba. He looked solemn. She would have preferred to not say goodbye. She wanted to leave the island quietly to avoid an emotional departure.

Seeing the look on Molly's face, Ikemba asked, "You were planning on leaving without saying goodbye?"

"I thought it would be better for all of us if I did." She looked down and saw Maurice standing next to Ikemba. Dammit! Molly did not want to do this. She wanted to get back to her ship and drown her sorrow and the pain of missing these two by getting her ship and crew ready for a life of piracy.

"Well, you were wrong. Besides, Maurice and I have come to a decision." He paused.

"And, what is that?" Molly was getting impatient. She needed off this island.

"We have decided that a life without Molly Malone is no life at all."

Molly looked from Ikemba to Maurice and back. "Meaning?"

"We are coming with you. We do not wish to be anywhere that you are not. Is that right, Maurice?" Maurice nodded his head yes.

"What about Mambo Nicole? She said no to you coming with me. I wouldn't want to hurt her or upset her. She is a mother to me as well, Kem."

"We talked all night. Even little Maurice here made a plea for us to go with you."

"She gave her approval?"

"Yes, she did…"

Molly swung around to see Mambo Nicole. As usual, she was beautiful in her white dress and her beautiful hair piled high on her head with tropical flowers placed almost like a crown.

"What made you change your mind?"

"Why you, Molly Malone. The Lwa reminded me you are more in need of Ikemba and Maurice than I am. They say that you are starting a dangerous new life and you will need them by your side."

Molly hugged Mambo Nicole tight and whispered to her, "Thank you, Mother. Thank you." Molly could not stop the tears from trailing down her cheeks. Nicole was very important to Molly. She felt as close to Nicole as she had to her birth mother.

Nicole let a tear slip and hugged Molly, rocking her slightly, wondering if she should she tell her what was waiting for her. Was it better not to know? She looked past Molly to Ikemba. He was safe. It was Molly that had danger waiting for her. Nicole and Ikemba locked eyes. He nodded. He understood what was needed of him.

Mambo Nicole stepped back suddenly and put Molly at arm's length. "That is enough of that! A fearsome pirate cannot be crying like a small babe!" She handed Molly a thick package wrapped in bright cloth. "This is for you, Captain Malone. Open it on your ship. Now, off with you! The world awaits."

Molly turned back to Ikemba and Maurice. It was only then that she noticed they had changed their clothes. Maurice was wearing his shirt and breeches while Ikemba was dressed in a red shirt and black breeches. He had a sword hanging from his side and a bandolier of small knives hanging from his shoulder. It draped across his chest and ended at the opposite hip. Molly took a deep breath. Maurice and Ikemba were coming with her after all.

Molly and Ikemba gathered the supplies and her men. Waiting on the beach beside the longboat were twenty men from the village. Molly's stomach tightened. Were they here to stop Ikemba from leaving? Ikemba felt Molly tense beside him. She slowly reached for her dirk. Laughing, Ikemba put his hand on her arm.

"No need to shed blood today, Captain. These men would like to join your crew. They are good men and well-trained to fight. I have taken many ships with these men."

"Damn you to hell and back, Ikemba! I thought we were having to fight to get you off this island!" Molly put her hand to her chest. Her heart was pounding. "If you say they are good men for our crew, then yes, of course, they may join. We need experienced men on the ship. Captain Khalfani won't come looking for his lost crew members, will he?"

"I asked Mambo Nicole to give him a message from me and the men when he returns to the island. He always liked you, Molly. He knows how I feel about you. Besides, I do not think he will want to cross you for the likes of these sorry sailors."

Molly looked at the men who were laughing and nodding in agreement. She hoped they were right. She wouldn't want to be on the wrong side of Captain Khalfani. He was a boisterous man with a booming laugh but he was also a strict captain with a quick temper. Molly herself had almost fallen under the lash on his ship more than once. She shook off those dark memories. It was time to get back to her ship. Her ship. Molly smiled slightly at that thought.

They loaded everything onto the longboat and got ready to shove off. Ikemba stopped to take one last look at his mother and the island he had called home for so long. Maurice, growing impatient, ran to him and grabbed his hand, pulling him to the longboat. The men and Molly laughed.

Ikemba swept him up in his arms and set him in the boat beside Molly. Ikemba pushed them off and jumped into the boat while the men rowed them toward the ship.

Molly grinned at the giant smile on Maurice's face. "Mambo Nicole isn't fooling anyone. She doesn't differ from me or anyone else. Look at those eyes and that smile. How could anyone say no to this boy?" She ruffled his hair and hugged him. As the men rowed toward her ship, Molly's excitement grew. This was it. This was the beginning.

The longboat bumped into the ship and Molly shouted, "Crew ho! Your captain has returned!"

James looked over the side. "Captain! Welcome back!" He disappeared for a moment and returned with a rope and a wooden ladder. He attached it to the side of the ship with the hooks and let the rest unfurl toward the longboat and its occupants.

Maurice was the first to clamber up the ladder. Then Molly, Ikemba, and five of the new crew. When everyone was on board, the two sailors positioned the ropes around the longboat, and hoisted it out of the water, and stored it on the side of the ship. The crew gathered around to see what supplies were being brought on board. They cheered when James picked up one of the roasted pigs and held it over his head.

"We eat like kings tonight!" he shouted.

Another picked up the crate of live iguanas and grimaced. "Any of you scabrous dogs disobey the new captain and you'll find yourself locked in the hold with nothing to eat but these tiny, green monsters!"

Molly laughed with the crew. They were in a fine mood.

They had lowered a second boat to go ashore and retrieve the new crew. The last of the men arrived and climbed over the ship's edge and stood on the deck, taking in their new home. The crew quieted at seeing them.

"Men! I would like to introduce our newest crew members. This is Mr. Kamara. He is here at my invitation to sign on as the quartermaster of the *Revenge*. Mr. Kamara is an experienced sailor and he's walking death in a fight. He will be in charge of getting all of you sorry excuse for pirates fixed for a fight. If you listen well to Mr. Kamara, there will be no stopping this ship and crew. Next time you step foot on dry land, you will have coin enough in your pocket for whatever your black hearts desire. I'll leave it to

Mr. Kamara to make introductions of the others." The crew rushed forward to greet Ikemba and the other men.

Molly made her way to her cabin. Séamus was standing at her desk, going over a map so intently that he didn't notice her entering the room.

"Where are we headed, first mate?" Séamus didn't seem to hear her. "Mr. Flanagan! Do you have a heading in mind? I would like to get the ship underway."

Séamus jumped. "Oh, Molly... Captain... Yes, I was considering sailing around Cuba, past the colonies, and over to the group of islands here." He pointed to the Bahamian islands. "If we head this direction and take the long way, it's a less-traveled passage. We would have time to work with the crew. We might come across a smaller ship or two that are trying to avoid other ships because of what they are carrying or they cannot defend against larger ships. Might be a good way for our new pirate crew to shed their merchant-sailor skin and find out what they're truly made of. For us as well. We need to know how they're going to fare in a fight before we attempt to take larger ships with more men and guns. What say you, Captain?"

"Agreed, Mr. Flanagan. Please put the helm on the correct course. Have Ikemba begin sword training. You will train the men on boarding other ships. Do this in shifts. Make sure each man trains once a day on each skill. I'll check with James. If we are in a fight and don't come out on top, do we have everything we need to patch the ship long enough for us to make it to a port for repairs? If you see Mr. Barlow, send him in."

Molly sat at the desk. Her desk. She smiled and placing both hands, palms down, on the surface, rubbed the top of the desk. She saw a pipe and tobacco neatly placed on a stand that looked to be made just for that pipe. Molly frowned and stood abruptly. She paced around the cabin looking for anything that had once belonged to Captain Clark. There were drawers and a wardrobe in a large built-in cabinet on the entire side of one wall. Molly opened the drawers and the door to the dark wooden wardrobe. It was empty of everything that belonged to Clark. Someone had moved Molly's things into the cabin while she was on shore. She placed her forehead on the smooth wood. Good. She didn't need any more reminders of that man and that night.

Molly heard a knock at her door. "Enter!" she called out. Kate and Maurice came in. Maurice was carrying a tray with tea and biscuits on it, looking very proud as he carried the silver tray. Kate helped him set it on the desk.

"Captain, I am sure you are hungry. Your steward demanded that the cook prepare tea and sweet treats for you." Kate's eyes creased from the smile she was trying to hide as she watched Maurice stand on a short wooden step, attempting to pour tea for Molly. The tea sloshed out of the cup and landed on the biscuits. Maurice growled and set the teapot down firmly, picking up a cloth from the tray, trying to dry them off.

Kate stopped him. "Remember, growling is not talking. Use the words that you have been learning."

Maurice stood tall on the step. "I am sorry, Captain."

Molly's mouth dropped open. She had never heard him speak before. He talked with Ikemba but he only whispered and Molly wasn't privy to their conversations. She resisted the urge to grab him in a tight hug to reassure him. Instead, she responded in her best captain's voice, "You are doing a fine job. I like my biscuits with a little tea on them. It makes them a bit easier to eat. The cook always makes them too hard for my taste."

Maurice stood tall, clearly proud of his accomplishment. "Permission to leave, Captain?"

"Permission granted."

The minute the door closed, Molly clapped her hands together in excitement. "Kate! Did you teach him all of that?"

Kate laughed. "Yes! I've been waiting for him to get brave enough to use the words he's been learning. He is very stubborn. I don't think he wanted to talk in front of you until he was sure he would get it right. I think it was okay to push him."

Molly hugged her. "Yes, it was okay. Thank you! Thank you!"

"I'm teaching him to read. He is quickly learning new words every day. He reminds me of my brother. I taught him to read and write in English too. We would speak English together and the rest of the tribe would be angry because they couldn't understand what we were saying. They punished us for it more than once!" Kate's eyes sparkled as she thought of the memory. "The punishments were worth it." It seemed like a wonderful memory.

Molly hugged her once again. "You are clearly good at teaching. Maybe, if the men want to learn, you could teach them?"

"Maybe, or maybe if we find an island that has a school in need of a teacher, I could stay and teach there?" Kate posed the question hesitantly, not sure how Molly would take it.

Molly didn't show any change in expression as she sat down to drink her tea. She bit a biscuit that was soaked in tea. *It actually is better,* Molly mused. "So, you haven't given up hope of having an ordinary life?"

Kate shook her head no.

Molly understood the need. "Kate, you can travel to the ends of this earth and you will still be you. They will still be them. You won't look any different and they won't look at you any differently. But, since I cannot convince you of this, next port we make, or any port thereafter, you are free to leave the ship and attempt to find your own way. Agreed?"

"Agreed. Thank you, Molly."

"Until then, I would like you to continue sword training with the men. I'll feel better setting you loose if you can defend yourself."

"Thank you, Captain. I will do so."

Molly watched Kate leave her cabin and sighed. Kate needed to find her strength. Even if Kate found a community that would accept her, would she be content with that life? Molly doubted it. She and Kate were similar. They both had lived extraordinary lives. How does one go back and live in society after that? Molly leaned back in her chair, put her booted feet on her desk, and sipped her tea. There was no going back for Molly Malone and she doubted there was any going back for Kate, either.

For the next three weeks, Molly and her crew worked together to prepare the ship for battle. The crew learned to fight and unlearn the accepted rules of engagement. They were pirates. They needed to win and they needed to do that in any way possible. One afternoon, Kate watched Ikemba try to teach the crew how to be intimidating. It would be to their advantage to frighten the other crew long before the fight even began. They couldn't seem to grasp the concept, and he was getting frustrated.

"Were none of you ever on a ship attacked by pirates?"

They all turned and looked at Molly and Séamus. "They are the only pirates I have ever seen!" one sailor called out. The rest murmured in agreement.

Ikemba turned to Molly. "I give up. I cannot teach this crew to be fearsome."

Kate stepped forward. "Let me try?"

The entire crew looked her way. Ikemba did not look convinced that this quiet blonde in her severe blue dress was going to teach what he could not? He stepped aside and swept his hand toward the crew in an invitation.

Kate pointed at one man. "You there, go and fetch some black powder." She jabbed a finger at another, "You, go get fat from the cook!" The men hesitated and looked at Ikemba. "Go! Now!" Kate shouted. The men rushed to do as she ordered. "When natives are going to fight another tribe, they have a ceremony to ask the great spirits to bless them. They prepare for death and victory. They are prepared to either win or to die. Whichever way it goes for them is great medicine as long as they live or die well."

The men looked confused, but Kate continued on.

"One way to let the spirits know they are going into battle is to shout it to the Sky Father and Earth Mother. The louder the shouts, the easier it is for them to hear the warriors. It is also a warning to the other tribe that they are ready for the fight and whatever end that may bring. They are ready to give everything they have in battle, even their lives. Who is more frightening in a fight? A person who is afraid to fight because they might die or a person who is prepared to die because that will give them power in the spirit world?" A few of the men were nodding. They were starting to understand.

The two men came back with the fat and powder and Kate mixed both items together. She motioned for one man to come forward. She dipped three fingers into the mixture and spread it down his face, starting on his forehead, slashing down over his eye, and ending near the side of his mouth. She also slashed her three fingers over both wrists. "Now, when you turn around, you want the other men to know you are fierce! You are there to kill them and take everything from them. You want them to be afraid to face you. If you die, it is good medicine because you are a warrior. They are not. Turn around and scream your power at them."

The sailor took a moment, then turned and howled a deep, guttural cry. He used his entire body. He was leaning into it with his weapons raised. His expression had turned dark and dangerous. The crew jumped at the difference in their mate. They gathered around the pot of black mix, eager to try it for themselves.

Ikemba clapped Kate on the back. "Let me know when you are ready to become a warrior yourself. Even if you are only half as cutthroat as Molly, you could do some serious damage to our victims."

Kate grimaced. She wasn't a pirate. Molly had already approved of her leaving the ship to find a town where she could teach. She couldn't do that if she was a pirate. Kate backed up slowly. She needed to get back to her cabin and her books. She looked down and noticed some of the black paste had smudged on her blue dress. *No! No! I need this dress.* It made her look more acceptable. People didn't see her tattoos in this dress. They saw Katherine Ersland, not the girl who was marked by Indians.

She rushed to her cabin to clean her dress and was desperately trying to clean it when she heard a knock at the door. She was sure it was Molly. *Molly will try and convince me that it would be fine. That I don't need this dress.* Kate didn't want to answer. She was not in the mood to be talked out of being upset. The person knocked again more urgently. Reluctantly, she opened the door and found not Molly, but James Barlow.

"May I come in?" he asked.

"Yes, of course." Kate blushed. She turned to walk back to the water bowl, keeping her head down so he wouldn't see her reaction. She picked up the cloth and began rubbing water into the black stain. It wasn't fading. It was getting worse. Tears of panic and frustration welled in her eyes. *What is wrong with me?* She was acting like a young girl!

James took the cloth from her and set it on the small table that held the water bowl. He then put both hands on either side of her face. "Kate. Kate, look at me." Kate finally met his eyes. They were blue. Not bright blue like Kate's, but deep blue like the sea.

"Are you okay?" he asked.

Kate nodded. She was blushing again. Damn her pale face that showed every emotion!

James was concerned for Kate, but he decided not to push the subject with her. "You were great with the men. They're finally understanding what Ikemba wanted." James laughed. "I was sure at least one of the men was going to be thrown overboard if they didn't figure it out. So, thank you. You saved some crew members a visit to the deep blue."

Kate laughed. "I'm happy I could help."

James took a seat in the only chair in Kate's cabin. "Ikemba is right, you know. You would make a fearsome pirate. You just need to put aside the crazy notion of being a teacher on an island somewhere."

"It's not a crazy notion!" Kate protested.

"It is. It is, Kate. You will never make a life as exciting as you will have on this ship."

"Who says I want an exciting life? Maybe I want to live in a small house making my wages teaching people how to read and write."

James stood up. He swallowed the extra space in Kate's cabin with his height. "I say you want more than that life can offer you. The Kate I've come to know would hate every minute of that life."

"The sooner you accept that you are a pirate, the sooner you will find out your true power. You're more than a blonde beauty with eyes of blue and marks on your face. I see a strong will in you. I see an uncommon strength. You can do a lot with that strength. Would you use these things to be a teacher and have a quiet life or will you use them to take on the world by Molly's side... and mine. It's up to you."

James turned to leave the cabin, but Kate stopped him just as his hand slid the lock open. "Where are you from? Most of the crew are English. You are not."

"No, I'm from the colonies. My family lived in the Massachusetts Commonwealth. My father, brother, and uncles were all fishermen. I used to go out and fish with them. It was a good life. One day, my mother asked me to stay behind to help her. She needed to patch the roof of our small house before the rains started. On that day, a sudden storm came up and capsized the boat. All were lost at sea, my father, my brother, and my two uncles. All gone in one day. It was too much for my mother. She took ill a month later and died. With almost my entire family gone, I found a merchant ship and joined. I've been on the sea ever since. I knew I couldn't stay in that place. It was no longer the same. I was no longer the same."

"I'm so sorry, James."

"That was long ago, and I was happy with my sailor's life. Then you and Molly boarded this ship. I had another choice to make. Accept the terms our pirate captain put forth or die. I chose. I chose to become a pirate. Mostly, I chose you." With that, James opened the door and left Kate to her thoughts.

Kate tossed and turned that night in her bunk. The next morning she rose with the sun. She dressed quickly and went to find the mate in charge of repairing the sails. She found him sleeping in his hammock below decks.

"Mr. Poole, wake up."

"Leave me alone, I'm trying to sleep." The man grumbled as Kate tried to shake him awake.

"I need your sail mending kit. That's all. Give it to me and you can go back to sleep."

"Fine. Just so ya know, miss, this is not how a man likes to be roused in the morning." To make her go away, he got up to find what she was looking for. It was the only way he would get back to sleep.

Kate excitedly returned to her cabin and pulled out the brown skirt that Bertha had sent her to New Orleans in. She quickly went to work altering it with the kit Mr. Poole had loaned her. After an hour of cutting and sewing, Kate was happy with the results. She slipped on the skirt that she had converted to wide-legged pants. Perfect. She found the men's shirt that Molly had purchased for her in New Orleans, put it on, and tucked the hem into the pants. She added a wide brown belt to cinch the waist and keep everything in place. Kate sat on her bunk and sighed.

Is this it? Am I really making this choice?

She slowly combed her hair, deep in thought. Without thinking, Kate braided her hair into two long braids. The eagle feather was waiting for her. The feather sat on her small writing table. It called to her. It begged her to make the choice to become the wild and free pirate she seemed destined to be.

Kate stepped out onto the main deck, her blue dress in hand. Molly and Séamus were on the deck as well. Molly was practicing with her sword and Séamus was assigning tasks. Kate ignored them and hurried to the side of the ship. She looked down at the waves splashing against the *Revenge*. She hesitated, holding the dress to her face. This dress... it was her last hope. Her last hope of living the life her mother, Birgitta, would have wanted her to have. Bertha knew her mother as well as anyone else. She had made this dress for Kate. Bertha must have felt that Birgitta would want a certain life for her daughter. Kate hugged the dress to her chest as a tear slipped down her face and landed on the field of blue scattered with pink flowers. She didn't want to disappoint her mother. Maybe she was giving up too easily? Kate thought back on what Mambo Nicole had said. She said Kate belonged with them. With Molly. What would Small Snow Fox, her native mother, think?

Kate shook her head, confused by her internal conflict. *What am I doing? This is my decision.* She had to live with the outcome of the choice. There were a lot of gods looking down on her. Kate was sure they would all agree. Standing strong and being brave came first. The rest would fall into place. Kate sighed. She felt at peace. For the first time in a long time, she was at peace. Kate was about to throw her dress into the water when she heard someone call her name.

"Kate!"

Kate turned to see Molly heading toward her, a look of concern on her face.

Molly took in her unfamiliar clothing and the blue dress in her hands. "What are you doing?"

"I'm choosing."

"Choosing?"

"I've been hanging on to the thought that I could live in a town, have a simple life, make my living as a teacher. Maybe marry and have children. Have the life my mother would want me to have. I've allowed that thought to anchor me to this blue dress. This dress that did the best it could to hide my face. To hide my shame. To hide me. In my life, I have had two families who loved me. I have lived in two different worlds and fit into neither one! It's time to choose the path where I will fit in. A choice that will accept all of me. I am choosing a life that will allow me to see just how strong I am and find out everything that I can do."

Molly smiled, "I like this Kate. You are no longer the frightened rabbit I found in New Orleans. You will be a pirate that all sane men will fear."

"Maybe insane men as well?" Kate laughed.

"All kinds of people will see you and assume that because you're a woman, you're weak. That would be their greatest and possibly their last mistake."

Kate realized Molly was being serious. "Thank you, Molly. Thank you for believing that I can do this. That I can become a pirate."

Kate turned and flung the blue dress overboard. Molly slipped her arm through Kate's. Arm in arm, Kate and Molly watched the blue dress float down to the water and rest on top of the waves. The waves pushed it down the side of the ship. Soon it sank down into the depths and took with it the last of Kate's old life. She hugged Molly.

"Thank you for being a good friend to me Molly."

Molly smiled and hugged her tightly.

A crew member called out for Molly. Molly hurried off to take care of business. Kate took one last look overboard. She already felt better. *How could a dress bring so much stress and confusion to a life?* Now that it was gone, Kate could move on with her new life. Unencumbered. Freer. Happier. She turned and saw James watching her. His slight smile told her he was happy. Molly interrupted them before they could speak to each other.

"Mr. Barlow! Perfect. I want to speak with you. Where is Ikemba? Kate, go and fetch Ikemba. James, you will walk us through the ship. We want to be assured this ship can withstand a fight."

"A fight? Are you planning on going into battle?"

"Yes. Perhaps, with luck, today or on the morrow. The men are ready. If the ship is ready, we will start hunting our first prey."

Kate The White
The Fortune's Revenge

"So soon?"

Molly tilted her head and raised her eyebrow. "You are questioning me, Mr. Barlow? Or, are you questioning your fellow crewmates?"

"Neither, Captain. I'm questioning me. I'm not sure I'm ready for what is to come."

Molly gripped James by the shoulder. "The only way to know if you can do something is to do it, Mr. Barlow. It's my goal to understand what this crew can stand up against by this day's end. I have all confidence in your abilities and I'm counting on you to step to and prove that my confidence in you is sound. Soon enough, we will truly know what kind of man you are. I'm betting my ship that you will lead and fight like the menacing pirate I know you to be."

James sighed as he watched Molly walk away. Soon enough indeed. James hoped he wouldn't let her or the crew down.

Molly, Séamus, Ikemba, and James walked around the ship from top to bottom with James showing them the extra materials they had on hand and introduced them to the ship's crew that would be in charge of making any repairs needed during battle.

"Well done, Mr. Barlow." Séamus complimented James. "What say you, Captain? Is the ship ready?"

"It is. Get lookouts into the crow's nests. Find me a ship."

The three men exchanged smiles. It was time. Séamus ordered men to the lookouts and then stood on deck with a spyglass, scanning the horizon for any glimpse of a rival sail.

Three hours later, a shout rang out from the top of the ship. "Sails ho!"

Molly rushed out of her cabin. Séamus was still looking through the spyglass. "Mr. Flanagan, have we a ship?"

"Aye, Captain! It's a merchant vessel and she is running low in the water!"

"Mr. Kamara, outfit the men! Helm, steady as she goes!"

Ikemba and the men rushed to the weapons locker. After Ikemba issued the men weapons, they hid below deck and painted their faces with many hideous markings meant to frighten their prey. The men had also made clothing and other accessories to appear more frightening. Sharpened teeth carved from whalebone. Caps with a long strip of hair down the center, spiked straight with pine pitch. They ripped the sleeves off of their shirts to show the black markings on their arms. Molly went below to check on them and stopped short as soon as she saw them. The men waited for her to respond.

"You are the finest bunch of pirates I've ever laid eyes on! You are frightening. When you're on the deck of that merchant ship, take care where you walk. You don't want to step in shite. Plenty of those men that won't be able to control their bodies when they see this crew coming at them." The men laughed. Molly's smile faded. "Today is a test for us all. Do I have what it takes to captain you and this ship into battle. Do you have what it takes to kill another man for what he possesses? Together, do we have what it takes to be pirates, vicious in nature, ruthlessly taking bounty, yet skilled enough not to lose too many of our own? Whatever happens today, we are in this together. Whatever happens today, good or bad, we're learning together. Whatever happens today, I am proud to be the captain of the *Fortune's Revenge* and I am very proud to be your captain."

The men were quiet for a moment, then one called out. "Captain Malone! We will follow you to the ends of the earth and back again!" The other men shouted in agreement.

"Get ready, men, and listen for our signal!"

They were closing in on the vessel. Her stomach was churning. She casually wiped her sweat palms on her coat. As she walked across the deck and made her way up the stairs to the helm, her legs were shaking so badly she wasn't sure how she made it to Séamus. He glanced at her and quickly turned his eyes to the raised spyglass. *Good,* Molly thought. He didn't seem to notice that her nerves were threatening to send her to the side of the ship to be sick.

"Mr. Flanagan, who did you put in charge of the cannon crew?"

"That would be Mr. O'Shea." Molly shook her head. She didn't know him. Séamus went on, "Conlan O'Shea." Molly smiled and raised a brow. "I know what you're thinking. No, I didn't put him in charge of the cannons because he's the most Irish person I've crossed paths with since leaving Ireland. I put him in charge because the men like and respect him. The man knows the cannons. I'm thinking a little too well. I've never known a person who can talk at such length on cannons. A word of warning, Captain. Do not enter a conversation with him unless you have a lot of time to spend with him."

"Understood. Thank you, Mr. Flanagan. I'm certain, that I will avoid Mr. O'Shea like I avoid walking over fire with bootless feet."

Séamus laughed and once again brought the spyglass to his eye. Men were gathering on the aft deck. They finally noticed a flagless ship tracking them across the water. They were close. Close enough that it was obvious to the merchant ship that the ship trailing them probably had ill intentions.

Molly heard shouts over the water. Prepare as they may, they couldn't outrun the *Revenge.* She was a fast ship. The cannon ports on the starboard side were flung open. A few moments later, the cannons on the port side were readied.

"Helm track to the port side. That crew is not as ready as the other."

"Aye, Captain. Headed to the port side."

The helmsman steered toward the port side. Molly hoped she was correct about the port side crew being less likely to reload quickly.

Séamus lowered his spyglass, "Are you ready to raise your colors, Captain?"

"Raise the flag."

Séamus shouted, "Raise the captain's flag!"

Two of the crew ran over to the flag mast and tied a flag to a line. They pulled the line until the flag reached the top and unfurled. It was the flag that Mambo Nicole had given Molly. It was a white skull with a single red rose running down through the left eye socket and the stem came out through the jaw behind the teeth. In the other eye socket there was a single four-leaf clover. Molly loved her flag. Mambo Nicole knew her well. The skull represented the death she would bring as a pirate. The single rose represented her mother Rosaleen and the clover represented her Irish heritage. Molly was intently admiring her flag when she realized Kate was standing next to her.

Kate had on breeches and short boots. Her shirt was more like a long tunic with the sleeves removed. The wide belt kept her shirt tight to her body and her hair was in two messy braids with an eagle feather tied into one. She painted her a diamond on her forehead and a straight line extending from the bottom of the diamond, down her nose, over her lips, and it met with the other tattoos on her chin. On her arms, she had painted a diamond on each with a thick line leading down to the three stripes on her wrists. She was holding a sword in one hand and a knife in the other.

"Are you certain you're ready for this, Kate?"

"Whether it be life or it be death. I am ready."

"Then go below and wait with the rest of the men for our signal."

"Kate."

Kate stopped and turned to face Molly.

"I hope it's life."

"For us both, Captain." Kate hurried below to wait with the men.

"Did you know the men are calling her Kate the White?" Séamus asked.

"No."

"They are impressed with her. She has come a long way from the frightened rabbit you found in the streets."

"She has." Molly's brow furrowed. It was times like this that she wondered if she did right by Kate. Was bringing her into this life a path to an early grave? She shook herself from her dark thoughts. It was too late to turn back now. They were all committed at this point.

The ship they were chasing began firing rifles at them but they were still far enough that the bullets didn't pose any danger. The captain was clearly trying to warn them off.

"Mr. Flanagan, the ship is yours. Keep her steady until we are either victorious or defeated. The crew and I are in your capable hands."

"Thank you, Captain. I'll see you after, Molly."

Molly nodded and rushed to her cabin to prep for battle. She entered her cabin to find Maurice huddled in the corner. Molly went to him and knelt down beside him. She hugged him.

"Everything is going to be fine. Don't you trust your captain?" Maurice nodded.

"This is what we do. Pirates take ships and that can be messy or easy. Either way, there will always be someone left to take care of you. Séamus isn't leaving the ship, if you need anything he will help you. Just wait until the battle is over. Okay?" He hugged her tightly, fighting hard to keep the tears from streaming down his face.

Molly stood. "Will you help me get ready?"

Maurice nodded and wiped the tears from his eyes. Molly tied a portion of her wild red hair back from her face. He helped her remove her coat so she was in a shirt with a tight, buttoned vest. The shirt was tucked into her breeches. Molly liked wearing little clothing when she fought. What she did wear fit well and moved with her flawlessly. She drew a thick, red line across her face, below her eyes, and across her nose. She also made sure it dripped down below her eyes so it looked like she was weeping blood. She put on her wide belt and checked to make sure her two push daggers were securely placed at the small of her back. Her trusty scimitar and dirk were always at her sides. She heard Séamus shout.

"Maurice, lock yourself in this cabin and do not come out for anyone except me, Ikemba, Séamus, or Kate. Understood?"

"Yes, Captain," he whispered.

"I will see you soon." Molly paused. "But, if I don't... you must be strong. Whatever life gives you in my absence, you must meet it head on with every ounce of bravery you can muster. Do you understand, Maurice? No matter what, you can survive it. You are a brave lad. You are strong and no matter the circumstance, you will be okay."

He nodded solemnly and locked the door behind Molly. He laid down on her bed, wrapping himself in her coat. He closed his eyes tightly, trying to be brave.

Molly and the rest of the crew rushed to the deck. They were just meters from the ship.

"Grappling hooks at the ready!" Séamus yelled.

The crew from the merchant ship were shooting at them with rifles. One of Molly's men dropped from a bullet wound. Two other crew members dragged him to the side.

Ikemba yelled out, "Hold steady men!"

Neither ship had fired its cannons. Maybe they had the same thought Molly did. They didn't want her ship and possible bounty destroyed.

As they came alongside the enemy ship. Kate stepped forward and screamed out her battle cry. The men followed her lead. The crew of the merchant ship stood shocked by the frighting vision of pirates on the other ship. Chaos broke out on the merchant ship, many of the men dropped their weapon and tried to run below deck. "Hold your position, men. We need to defend this ship!" the merchant captain was shouting.

"Loose the grapples!" Ikemba yelled. One the grapples were thrown, the men pulled until the ships crashed together. The deafening sound of wood tearing and splintering followed a jolt as the ships shivered and slowed. The pirates threw planks across to span the gap between the two ships. Ikemba and James were the first across with men following directly behind them. "You men, once you are on the other ship, go below to the cannon ports and kill anyone preparing the cannons to fire." Molly shouted. With that, Molly made her way to the merchant ship. As soon as her feet hit the deck, she was in a fight. Two sailors came at her with swords. She quickly killed one with a slash to his neck. The other began backing away. She pursued him and, pulling out her dirk, stabbed him in the stomach.

Molly looked around for her crew. Ikemba, Kate, and James were in the thick of the fighting and doing just fine. Gun smoke hung over the ship's deck causing her eyes to burn. The metallic smell of spilt blood permeated the air. Men were crying out in pain and surrender. Molly could not get distracted by any of these things, she needed to find the captain. He had to be captured. She found him by the helm with several armed men standing around him. Molly grabbed a few of her men and fought their way to the captain. One of the merchant ship's crew shot a rifle. The bullet grazed Molly's arm and hit one of her men. Molly and the men rushed up the stairs and took the fight to them. Her arm was throbbing with pain but Molly ignored it. Her focus was on the captain. Each man that stepped forward, she or her men cut them down. Soon, it was just the captain standing with a group of dead men at his feet.

The captain of the merchant vessel took a pistol from his pocket and held it to his head. Molly rushed him and knocked the gun from his hand with her sword. She elbowed the captain in the face and kicked his legs so he landed hard on his knees. Molly leaned in close. "You would take your life and leave your men in my hands?"

Molly and her men stood him at the helm railing and watched the fighting below them.

"Stop!" Molly bellowed. The fighting slowed as both crews realized the pirates had captured the merchant captain.

"Put down your weapons or I will kill your captain." Molly whispered to the captain, "Tell them to surrender and maybe you and crew will live through this day."

"Lay down your arms, men. Let these black-hearted pirates have their bounty and we will have our lives."

The crew did as their captain commanded. Ikemba, James, and Kate set about ransacking the ship and transporting the goods to their ship.

"Now, captain. How about you and I go to your quarters?"

Molly, the captain, and two of her men went to the captain's cabin. The lavish space impressed her. This captain obviously came from wealth and stature. She cleared his cabin of maps, some books she thought Kate and Séamus would like, and fine liquors in crystal decanters. She sat at his desk, and went through the drawers. Most she deemed useless to her until she came across a box with a small pocket pistol and several bullets. It was beautiful. It was made with walnut wood and had silver workings and flowers stamped in a feminine pattern. Clearly, it was either a gift for a woman or a gift from a woman.

"Is this yours or is it a gift?"

The captain glared at Molly without speaking. Molly shrugged. She snapped the box closed and took it with her.

Molly arrived back on deck to see the last of the goods being loaded onto the *Revenge*. "How are we doing, Mr. Kamara?"

"We have everything, Captain. We're ready to shove off."

"Mr. Barlow! Get the men back on the ship!"

James shouted for everyone to get back across to the *Revenge*. Molly, Ikemba, and Kate stood guard over the merchant captain and crew until the rest of the men were back onboard their ship. All planks except for one were pulled across and stored away.

Molly called out to the rival crew. "Molly Malone and her crew thank you for your contribution to our welfare. I am sorry for the men you lost. I hope they are few. If we ever meet again, do not put up a fight. I may not be so generous with your lives next time."

As Molly, Ikemba, and Kate made their way to the *Fortune's Revenge*, they cut the grappling hook ropes and pushed the ships apart with long poles. Séamus was yelling out orders to get the ship under way. Molly and the rest of the crew stood watch on the deck to make sure the merchant ship didn't retaliate. There was no chance that the merchant ship could follow them. James had sabotaged the merchant vessel's sails before he left. It would take them some time to make the repairs. The *Revenge* and her crew would be long gone before the merchant ship could make way and give chase.

Once they were far out of gun and cannon range, the crew set about storing the goods they had collected. Molly returned to her cabin and knocked.

"Maurice! It's Molly. Open the door."

The door flung open and Maurice launched himself at Molly. She laughed and hugged him.

"Were you really that concerned I wouldn't return? I'm not sure I'm happy with your lack of faith in my ability to stay alive."

Maurice answered by hugging her tighter.

Molly handed the box containing the small pistol to him. "I have a gift for you."

He opened the box and gasped. He tried to grab the gun, but Molly stopped him. "You must wait for Séamus to teach you about this gun. I cannot have you accidentally shooting me or one of my crew. Agreed?"

"Yes." Maurice whispered. "Thank you, Captain."

"You are most welcome, little man. Soon, you will stand next to me and Ikemba taking down our enemies with the rest of the crew."

Maurice couldn't take his eyes off the gun. Molly entered her cabin and took off her bloody clothes. Maurice followed her in and brought her fresh water and clean clothing. Molly could hear the ship quieting down. She needed to assess their gains and their losses. Maurice helped her put her coat on.

"Let us go see after the crew and bounty."

Maurice followed Molly to the deck where she found Ikemba, James, and Séamus. "Tell me, how did we do?"

Ikemba spoke first. "We took a fine haul, Captain. The goods will fetch a nice payment when we make port. We lost two men and ten more were wounded but not severely. The surgeon is looking after them."

"Very good. Did we take any rum or wine?"

"We did," James answered. "Three barrels of rum."

"Order the cook to give an extra ration of rum to each of the men."

"Aye, Captain." James hurried off to relay the orders to the cook.

"How did the men perform? Did all do their jobs? Did we have any run from their duties?"

Séamus nodded gravely. "We had two that hid in the hold. We found them when we were storing the goods."

Ikemba nodded. "They are in the brig until you are ready to deal with them."

"We will do so on the morrow. Tonight, let the men bask in their victory and their rum."

Molly was not looking forward to dealing with those men. She had to be careful. She couldn't be too harsh but she also couldn't allow cowards on her ship. Tomorrow would tell the men more about her as a captain than a hundred battles combined.

Molly looked down at Maurice. "Shall we check on Kate?"

He nodded and raced to Kate's cabin. He knocked, and they heard, "Enter!"

Maurice opened the door, and they found Kate sitting on the floor of her cabin. She still had blood on her face, hands, and clothing. Maurice hurried to her side, a concerned look on his face.

"Kate? Are you feeling ill?" Molly asked softly as she closed the door behind them.

"I killed at least two men and wounded many others. Am I feeling ill?

Yes, I am. I did not believe that I could do it until the fighting began. When I killed the first man, I was stunned. It was easier than I thought it would be. I ran the man through and then I just kept fighting without pause. He was standing there holding his wound, blood flowing between his fingers and spilling onto the deck. He had a shocked look on his face. As though he could not believe that I had plunged my sword deep within his body, and now he was going to die. But for me... it was as though I had just killed a bug and not taken a man's life. I felt only surprise that it was so easy. Nothing else. No remorse. No regret. I just moved on to the next poor soul. I really don't know how many men I killed today, Molly. How is that possible?"

"Kate..."

"Molly, I'm fine. I am. Death has been by my side for most of my life. This won't be the last time Death and I walk side by side. I'm only feeling these deaths much deeper in my spirit because today, I was Death."

"Maurice will stay with you and help you clean yourself. If you don't want to eat with the crew, Maurice can bring your dinner to you here. Can you do that, Maurice?"

"Yes, I will stay with Kate."

"Good man. If either of you needs me, I will be in my cabin."

Maurice helped Kate change out of her clothing and wash the blood from her skin. They were both quiet while Kate tried to remove all traces of blood from her arms and hands. Maurice used a wet cloth and cleaned the blood from her hair. Kate sat on her bed and Maurice brushed her hair. He helped Kate braid her hair and make sure there was no blood to be seen.

"You need to sleep, Kate. Sleep always helps me feel better." Kate and Maurice laid together on her small bed and they slept. Maurice kept his small hand on Kate's head, patting her occasionally. His way of reassuring her all would be well.

They were awoken by the dinner bell. Maurice's stomach growled loudly and Kate's stomach answered almost as loud. They both laughed.

"I think we should go eat with the men. Will you join me?"

Maurice nodded. As they entered the crew's eating area, the men all stood. One sailor raised his cup. "To Kate the White! A pirate I will fight beside any time and any place!"

"To Kate the White!" the crew chimed in.

Their show of support overwhelmed her. *Kate the White? Is that what they are calling me now?*

"Thank you! It was a proud day for me to stand shoulder to shoulder with this pirate crew. Let us hope the captain is in favor of doing it again soon!"

"Hear! Hear!"

Kate and Maurice sat next to James Barlow. He had been worried when Kate disappeared after the fight. He should have known she was okay. The men were right to give her a pirate name. She had been fierce today. He needed to remember that in case he fell out of favor with her or upset her unduly. He chuckled and downed his rum.

The men were in high spirits. They drank and sang and danced the night away. Molly went to bed at an early hour. She had a long day ahead of her tomorrow. The new captain of the *Fortune's Revenge* drifted off to sleep with sounds of laughter and music floating around the ship. She was right to let the men have tonight. The looming unpleasantness could wait.

Molly and the Flogging
The Fortune's Revenge

"Mr. Kamara! Bring forth the accused!"

Molly waited while Ikemba and two other crew members went to the brig to fetch the two crew members who had hidden in the hold during the fight. She scanned the crew gathered on deck. Clearly, some knew of the transgressors but others did not. They shifted nervously as they stood under the morning sun. This was Molly's first time disciplining the crew. They didn't know what to expect from her.

Ikemba led the two men up the stairs and they stood beside Molly at the railing. Séamus and James were on Molly's opposite side.

"We found these men hiding in the hold while the rest of you fought on the merchant ship! This is a pirate ship! We need men who will fight. Men who are willing to fight beside me and willing to fight beside you! If we cannot count on every man on this ship, we leave ourselves open for more of us to be wounded or killed. I, for one, would not want any one of you to lose your life because the man that was supposed to fight with you ran! Ran away and hid! I am angry that we were missing two swords in yesterday's fight. We lost two good men and ten others were wounded. That is to be expected in this pirate life we lead but, what if those two swords could have saved even one life? What if those two swords could have spared even one wound?"

Molly paused and ran her gaze over the men, trying to see if they were with her or if they had sympathy for these cowards.

"State your name, then answer to your crewmates. Answer to your fellow pirates. Why were you not in the fray with the rest of us?"

The younger of the two called out, "My name is Palmer Brinley, and I am new to this ship. I boarded this ship in New Orleans with Captain Malone and her lot. I have never fought before. I have never even been in a fight as a boy. I came to the ship to be a merchant sailor. If I knew of things to come, I would not have joined this crew. In my cowardice, I ran to the hold when I should have held fast with the rest of you and I am ashamed. I make this solemn promise. If I live to see the sun set on this night, I will never again run from a fight."

Molly took in his appearance as he spoke. He was young. Sixteen, maybe? He had shaggy blond hair and wide blue eyes. As he addressed the crew, the breeze moved his hair. Molly thought he would be better suited for a schoolyard than a pirate ship.

The other man was short and stocky compared to the thin, lanky build of Palmer Brinley. He was bald and had dark eyes. His face had scars and the weathered look of a sailor that had been at sea most of his life. He glared at Molly. "I am Calvert Harden. I didn't fight because I won't be accepting a woman as a captain. You sorry sots have forgotten our ways. A woman—a redhead, no less—as our captain? I will not be a part of this witch's crew. You can cast your spell on the rest of these men, but I see you for who you really are!" He turned and spat at Molly.

Molly stood fast, her head tilted and an eyebrow raised. With a calm voice she called out, "Each man is to receive a twenty-lash flogging. After, Mr. Brinley will be elevated to weapon's steward and will assist Mr. Kamara in training the men further on swordsmanship and the firing of pistols. Mr. Harden will be given his wish and will be set adrift in a boat to find his way to a crew that better fits his needs."

Calvert screamed and lunged at Molly. "You bitch! You redheaded whore! I 'm going to kill you!"

Ikemba grabbed him and pulled him away from Molly. They dragged both men down to the main deck. Calvert fought Ikemba the entire way to the mast where the floggings would take place. Palmer followed quietly, his head bowed. Molly could hear him faintly crying as he walked past. She followed the group and took her place on the deck. She hated this. She knew exactly how the lash felt but she couldn't show weakness. The men would never follow a weak captain. She stood tall, ready to bear witness to the punishments she had ordered.

Once on the deck, Palmer Brinley stepped forward. "Captain, I ask to be the first to take my punishment." He was trying to be brave, but Molly could see he was violently shaking. His eyes were red and his face was streaked with tears. She motioned to Ikemba. He took Palmer by the arm and led him to the mast.

"Strip off your shirt, Mr. Brinley."

Palmer tried to take his shirt off, "I'm sorry sir but I'm shaking so badly I can't seem to get it off." Two of his fellow crewmates came forward and helped him. They placed his hands on spikes protruding from the mast.

"Hold here. If you must cry out, know that most men would do the same." They patted his blond head and stepped back.

Ikemba picked up the flog and looked at Molly. She hesitated for a moment. She could stop this boy's flogging. He seemed so young and innocent. It was not his choice to become a pirate, after all. How could she blame him for hiding from the fight? She remembered her first fight. She was scared to death but she did do it. She did join the fight. No, this boy had to learn. Maybe a flogging will toughen him and make him a stronger man.

"When you are ready, Mr. Kamara."

The crew stood quietly as Ikemba flogged the young man. The only sound was Séamus counting out loud. Young Mr. Brinley only cried out a few times.

"Twenty and done!" Séamus yelled after what felt like forever. Molly finally exhaled. She didn't realize that she had been holding her breath until that moment. Several others in the crew exhaled loudly. She wasn't the only one that felt terrible for the young sailor.

"You two, take Mr. Brinley below to see the surgeon. Let Mr. Prescott know I expect this man to be fit as a fiddle as soon as possible. He has a new job to do."

"Yes, Captain," they both chimed in. One grabbed Palmer's shirt and the other helped him release the spikes. He was gripping them so hard his knuckles were white.

As he carefully walked past Molly, he stopped. He faced her and tipped a bent finger to his forehead saluting her. "Thank you, Captain, for allowing me to make things right with you and the crew."

"Carry on, Mr. Brinley. The surgeon will see to your back."

He nodded and slowly made his way below to find the surgeon.

Molly glanced at Séamus. He was as impressed as she was with this young man. They would make certain he was well looked after.

Mr. Calvert Harden, on the other hand, was still trying to curse Molly. The crew had stuffed a kerchief in his mouth to shut him up.

"Remove the gag from this man's mouth." Molly ordered.

Séamus ripped the piece of cloth out of Calvert's mouth.

"You go to hell, you one-eyed, cursed trollop! I will not be flogged by the likes of you and your boys! I accept you're kicking me off the ship. I am ready to leave this godforsaken hellhole but I demand that you set me adrift without the flogging."

"Mr. Harden, the flogging is punishment for your actions against your fellow crew members. The flogging is meant to square your misdeeds with them. The boat we are to send you away on is in response to your request not to be a member of my crew. Think of it as my gift to you."

"Gift?" Calvert screamed.

"Yes, a gift. Replacing that boat will cost me coin. As for your request to be set free without a flogging, the answer is no. Before we set you on your merry way and while you are still a member of this crew, you must pay for your transgressions. You will make that payment, Mr. Harden, with pain. Your pain."

He was dragged forward and his hands were tied around the mast. Ikemba lifted Calvert's shirt over his head and out of the way.

Again, Ikemba delivered twenty lashes as Séamus counted them out. After the flogging was done, the men put some food and water along with Calvert Harden into a small boat and lowered him down to the water.

Molly called out to him as he pushed away from the ship using an oar. "Good luck, Mr. Harden. I certainly hope your next captain is more to your liking."

For a moment, Molly watched Calvert Harden attempt to row away from the *Revenge*. Was this the right decision? She couldn't have such a strong detractor on the ship. Eventually, his venom could spill over to the other crew members. Yes, Molly thought. This had to be done. Kate leaned over the edge of the ship to watch Calvert Harden's attempts to row the small boat he was in.

"He is going to be a problem for you later, Molly. You should have killed him," Kate whispered.

"That seems like a long shot, Kate. The chances of him living through this are slim. Unless the gods owe him a large bounty, then perhaps a passing merchant or pirate ship will find him and bring him on board... but I wouldn't bet on that happening."

"You will meet him again..."

"If that's to be, then so be it." Molly left the side of the ship and made her way to her cabin. She called out, "Mr. Flanagan and Mr. Ikemba, please see me in my quarters. The rest of you best be about your business. We have a ship to repair before we come across another quarry!"

Molly listened contently as the men hurried back to work. In a few minutes, the sails would catch the wind once again. She wanted to be underway, leaving this morning behind them. Molly entered her cabin and sat behind her desk. She was suddenly very tired. Punishment was a part of the job as captain. She needed to take it less to heart, otherwise each punishment she ordered would continue to feel like a thousand knives to her soul. That was too heavy a burden for any captain to bear. Ikemba and Séamus found her slumped in her chair with her head in her hands. They both paused. This morning had taken more of a toll on her than they thought it would.

"Molly?" Séamus walked around her desk and leaned down beside her. "What you did was as good for the crew as it was for you as captain. The men won't likely challenge you going forward."

"I know how it feels to be beaten, Séamus. It's a hard thing to give the same sentence to another human. Every lash they took, I felt it on my own back."

"Molly, this differed from what your husband did to you. This was punishment for a man's actions against his captain and the crew. You were a young girl at the mercy of a monster."

"Yes, but it doesn't seem to feel any better in the pit of my soul."

Ikemba stood at the front of her desk and placed both hands flat. He leaned forward and said in a soothing tone meant to reassure her, "If you want the men to respect you and do their jobs, then punishment is required. Nothing says that you have to feel good about it. I believe if you enjoyed seeing your men flogged, then you aren't right and shouldn't be walking this Earth. It's good that you are in pain along with your crew. It shows you to be a fine person, Molly Malone. A person deserving of being captain. A person deserving of being my captain."

Molly looked up at Ikemba and Séamus. "Thank you, both of you. Thank you. I would not want to walk this path without either of you. I am the person I am with your help."

Molly took a deep breath and slowly let it out. "On to ship's business. Our raid on the merchant ship was a success. I cannot wait to do it again!" Molly smiled. The heaviness lifted as the three of them relived the raid and planned the next.

The Pirate Ship, Fortune's Revenge
Atlantic Ocean

The ship fell into a routine. The men performed their ship's duties and attended sword training with Ikemba and Palmer during the day. Séamus and James also set the men to work building boarding ladders and weaving long ropes to hold the grappling hooks. The men practiced throwing the hooks perfecting their ability to catch a ship's lines. Palmer took on his new job as weapon's mate with joyful zeal. It pleased Molly that Palmer Brinley was thriving on the ship. At night, the crew filled the ship with music and laughter.

Molly stood at the helm, watching the men below her. Maurice, as usual, was Ikemba's shadow. The only time Maurice left Ikemba's side was to help Molly or to resume his schooling with Kate. He was growing up fast. Kate came to Molly's side and followed her gaze. It was clearly on Maurice. Kate nodded, understanding. Maurice was so young, but he was being raised by pirates. It wouldn't be long before he would want to be part of the boarding crew.

"As captain, you have the final say in who joins the fight. If you don't want Maurice in danger, order him to take up a new skill. Maybe he could learn to cook or fix the sails or anything that doesn't require a sword."

"To what end? He is Ikemba's shadow. Maurice looks at him like he is a god come to earth. He will want to follow Ikemba to hell and back. No, if I didn't want Maurice to become a pirate, I should have left him on Tendaji with Mambo Nicole. In truth, I sealed his fate the moment I purchased him. I seem to drag every poor soul I meet into this pirate life. Seamus, you, Maurice... I pity anyone who crosses my path."

Kate considered her words for a moment. Molly wasn't wrong. She brought all three of them into this life. "Séamus and I chose to follow you to a life of piracy. You forced neither one of us to stay on this ship. In fact, if you remember, you tried to discourage me the day we boarded. You shouldn't carry the weight of our willingness to join this life in your heart. As for Maurice, if he is fated to be a pirate, who better to teach him than you, Ikemba, and Séamus?"

Kate leaned closer to Molly and bumped her. "Well? Are there any three people better to teach him the pirate life? Look at me... look at this crew. What we have done and what we will do. I was not sure these men could have stood toes facing an enemy and win. I would have bet my soul against their success but they did it. Not only did they run headlong into battle, but they also came out victorious. That's a feat I would never have expected. You, Molly Malone, did that. You made sure your men were ready. Maurice will be no different."

Molly slipped her arm through Kate's arm. "Thank you. I was about to run screaming down to the deck and drag Maurice back to my cabin." Kate and Molly laughed at the image of Molly's motherly instincts kicking in and her dragging Maurice away from harm.

"Truly, Kate. I'm grateful you are here."

Kate leaned closer to Molly. "I too am grateful I am here."

Ikemba looked up and saw Molly and Kate watching them. "Kate Ersland! Are you so proficient with a sword that you can stand around watching us? After your last lesson, I'm thinking no."

Kate's face turned red with embarrassment. "Pirates are boorish."

"Yes, they are. However, I believe he has a point. Your sword skills are about as good as my sewing skills," Molly joked. "If 'Kate The White' is going to strike fear in a fight, she best be able to easily run a man through."

Kate nodded with a wide smile. "Yes Captain!"

Palmer Brinley saw Molly watching them and waved to her. He briefly spoke with Ikemba, then raced across the deck and up the stairs to where Molly was standing. He crooked a finger and lifted it to his forehead, saluting her before he spoke.

Molly smiled, "Mr. Brinley. We are not a merchant ship or a military ship. Do not salute me."

"So—Sorry, Captain." He stammered.

Molly waited for him to tell her what he wanted.

He was blushing deeply and couldn't look at Molly. Whatever he wanted to talk to her about was weighing heavily on him.

"Would you like to adjourn to my cabin? Maybe you would have an easier time talking in a more private location."

He nodded. "Yes. Thank you, Captain."

He and Molly went to her cabin. She poured herself a glass of rum and offered him some. Again, he just nodded. Molly handed Palmer the glass. She forgot how young he looked up close. His sandy blond hair and blue eyes did not help. Palmer held the glass with both hands and admired the etching. It was heavy, fine crystal. Molly guessed he had held nothing of such quality before. She patiently waited while he appreciated the beauty of the crystal and the golden liquid within. Eventually, he gulped down the rum and set the glass on Molly's desk.

"I want to apologize for the name the men have assigned you after my lashing. I have desperately begged them to drop it, but they will not. They said that it fits you." Molly's eyebrows came together in confusion. Palmer raced on. "I have offered many other names. I have reminded the crew that I am the one that deserved my punishment. That was not to do with you. You were just doing what a captain should. But..." He let out a deep sigh. "But, the men are persisting with the name. There is nothing I can do to talk them away from it. For that, Captain, I am sorry."

Molly debated. Did she want to know the name? She would find out eventually. "Mr. Brinley, what is the name that the men have committed to me?"

All color drained from Palmer's face. She didn't know. He wiped his sweaty hands down his pant legs. One of his legs was bobbing up and down rapidly. He grabbed his knee with his hand and pushed his foot flat to the floor.

Exasperated, Molly barked, "Mr. Brinley, the name if you please."

His hung his head and whispered, "Red Rose."

"Red Rose? That's the name you don't approve of?" Molly asked.

"It is not so much the name, Captain, as it is the rhyme that goes with the name."

"What is it?" Molly was growing impatient with young Mr. Brinley.

The lad cleared his throat and recited the poem. "Molly Malone is a beautiful rose. The reddest rose you ever did see. *Unalike* another rose that will only prick your thumb, This rose will flog your back and be happy to watch you bleed."

Molly sat stunned for a moment. She couldn't find her voice. Finally, she said, "You may go."

Palmer jumped up and ran from Molly's cabin. Molly couldn't move. *That was what the men thought of her?* She poured herself another splash of rum and downed it. She poured another and returned to her chair behind her desk. That was how Ikemba found her. Lost in thought and toying with the glass of rum sitting on her desk.

"Palmer told you." Ikemba was stating the obvious but was not sure how else to broach the subject with her.

"Yes. The red rose that happily watches her men bleed is how my men see me. The men think I am a cruel captain."

"Cruel? No. A captain above all else? Yes. That name was given out of fear and respect. The men know you will give punishment to those that do not hold their own for you, the ship, or the crew. The men know you are not a weak woman that cannot do a man's job. Molly Malone, the red rose who will see her men flogged for not doing their jobs, is a leader, a captain, and a hard taskmaster who requires everything from the crew that they have to give. Captain Malone demands that the crew fall in line. She demands that every person on this ship hold their own. Now they know if they do not, they will face punishment. They know they will pay for their lack of focus on the tasks assigned to them. If that is a problem for you, you should never have become a captain."

Still lost in thought, Molly didn't answer.

"Well? Are you a woman that should be in her husband's home cooking for him and bearing his children or are you Molly Malone, captain of a pirate ship?"

Molly locked eyes with Ikemba. Slowly, she stood up and walked around her desk. She kept her eyes on his while she made the quick journey. He was enthralled with her and didn't notice that she was pulling her short push dagger from behind her back. When she reached his chair, she leaned down, bringing her face ever closer to his. He felt the dagger under his chin, pressing into the soft flesh. His eyes widened.

"Molly..." he growled.

"Do not—I repeat—do not ever suggest that a woman is not fit to be captain of a pirate ship. I am Captain Malone. I am the Red Rose and most of all, I am a woman. The next time you dare challenge my ability as a woman will be your last. Do you understand me, quartermaster?"

Ikemba remained rigid, attempting to keep the blade from penetrating his skin. He wasn't happy that Molly was making this point with him. He, above anyone else, supported Molly. He narrowed his eyes and in a stiff voice replied, "Yes, Captain. I understand."

Molly stood up and swiftly stashed the blade back in the sheath at the small of her back. "Good. Now get out."

Ikemba left Molly's cabin without another word.

Molly sipped the rum pondering her new name and Ikemba's words. He was right, of course. No man would question disciplining the crew. Molly had never considered herself to be soft, but the name the crew had given her had cut her to the core. She swallowed the last of her rum and slammed the glass down. This was nonsense. So what if the men didn't name her for her ferocity in battle, her skill with a sword, or even her red hair, for god's sake? The flogging was the event they chose to commemorate her. What was done was done. She had a crew to keep on task and bounty to find. Molly shook her head and laughed. Ikemba really was a brave man to confront her as he did. Her reaction surprised him. She would have to make it up to him later and smiled at the thought.

STORY 6
THE QUEEN'S HEART

K&M.

The Crew Needs Shore Leave
Tortuga, Pirate Stronghold in the Caribbean

After a few months at sea, the men were getting restless. Molly had relentlessly captured ship after ship. Their hold was full of bounty and treasures. The men were ready for time ashore to spend their earnings on women and drink. As quartermaster, Ikemba Kamara was in charge of making their case to the captain. Ikemba looked up at Molly, standing tall at the helm. She was keeping a sharp eye out for merchant ships. He marveled at her focused drive and resolve to earn a profit for the crew. He thought back to when he had first met her. Wounded after losing her eye in a fight, she had seemed so weak and helpless. No-one thought she would or could survive. She had proved them all wrong. Not only did she survive, she seemed to have been bedeviled by a warrior spirit that wouldn't let her or her men have peace.

Ikemba sighed. He might as well get this done. He climbed the stairs to face his captain. She did not turn to look at him. He stood next to her, arms crossed over his chest, looking out at the sea. "The men want to go ashore and they have sent you with the request," Molly stated without taking her eye from the scene before her.

"Yes. They have fought like pirates. Now they want to spend their earnings like pirates. They have earned some fun." Ikemba paused. "I'm not sure how much longer you can keep the men aboard this ship without the grumblings becoming a problem." He turned to Molly. "Captain, the men are asking for time on land to enjoy the bounty that you and this crew have seized. They have earned that."

Molly looked down at the men working on deck. They were clearly interested in the conversation happening at the helm, though they were trying to act as if they weren't. Molly knew he was right. The men had followed her to into many skirmishes. They had done well. Molly was proud to be captain of this crew. She knew they needed time to be men and spend their coin. "Where would the men like to make land?"

"Tortuga, Captain."

"As you will, Mr. Kamara." With that, Molly strode down the stairs toward her cabin.

Ikemba spent the time working with the ship's accounting, making sure the men would leave the ship with their correct earnings. He also spent time with the cook and the boatswain. It was difficult to get Molly and the ship to land. He needed to take advantage of this time with the ship's resupply and repairs. Before they made land, Ikemba assigned watch shifts to the men. Even after paying the men, the ship still had a lot of treasure that needed to be protected. As he told the men about their watch shifts, he heard some complaining.

"Who would dare moan about taking their turn protecting our ship? Which of you is willing to miss their watch and risk the looting of our ship? Step forward if you would like to explain to our captain that this ship is not worthy of your protection!"

As Ikemba suspected, the complaining stopped.

Molly, Kate, and Séamus left Ikemba to handle the crew. Molly decided it was time for Kate to purchase clothing of her own. She glanced over at Kate and secretly smiled. Kate had modified some of her clothing, but it wasn't meant for a life at sea and had quickly worn out. The crew had given her some clothing, but pirates weren't really known for the quality of their clothes. They also weren't a tall lot, and since Kate was very tall for a woman or a man, everything was too short. Kate was getting better at using a sword, and she was an excellent shot. The last vessel they took, Kate had led the charge. She was a natural leader and fierce in battle. Molly knew it wouldn't be too long before she would want a ship of her own. It was time that she started looking like a ship captain instead of a shipwrecked sailor. Séamus quietly left them to go find some female company. As he walked away, the familiar feeling of vulnerability and loneliness crept into Molly's stomach. She shook it off. She and Kate had business to attend to and Séamus needed time to be a man and not Molly's protector.

Molly and Kate made their way to the seamstress that had made most of Molly's clothing. After spending hours with the seamstress and boot-maker fitting Kate for new clothes, Molly needed a drink. She and Kate headed to the Lusty Maiden. When they entered the tavern, Kate heard a shriek, "Molly Malone!" A young woman rushed to them and threw her arms around Molly. Molly hugged the woman back. She stood back, keeping her hands on the woman's arms, taking her in. "GraceAnn O'Connell, you are beautiful as ever!"

The woman laughed and hugged Molly again. She turned to see a bemused Kate standing next to Molly. GraceAnn looked from her to Molly, eyebrows raised. She looked pointedly at Molly. "Are you not going to introduce us?"

Molly smiled at GraceAnn, held her gaze as she caressed a long lock of GraceAnn's sun-streaked, brown hair. "GraceAnn, this is my friend Katherine Ersland."

Kate smiled. "Please, everyone calls me Kate." GraceAnn smiled at Kate. Kate took her in. Her clothing and attitude didn't say barmaid but more like owner of this tavern. She was thin but curvy. Her wide smile was bright and welcoming. She wasn't very tall, but she didn't feel like a small, fragile woman. Kate decided that GraceAnn carried herself like a woman who had grown up among men.

GraceAnn led them to a table. She called out an order for bread and rum to be brought over. "GraceAnn owns the Lusty Maiden. Her father lost an eye, an arm, and a leg from a single battle. Even with his grievous injuries, he still fought hard and saved several other crew members. For his loyalty and bravery, his pirate brethren wanted to make sure they rewarded him with the means to still earn for himself and his daughter. They helped him *acquire* this place," Molly said with a cocked head and a laugh. "He sent for GraceAnn and she's lived here since. When he died last year, she became The Maiden's owner."

"I'm impressed that you remembered all of that, Molly Malone."

"I listen."

GraceAnn laughed and kissed her on the cheek, "Of course you do."

Molly looked at Kate with feigned shock at the slight, "I do!"

"You grew up in this tavern?" Kate asked GraceAnn, noticing that the bar owner's two front teeth were slightly larger and more prominent than her other teeth. To Kate, it seemed to give her a more youthful appearance.

"I moved here when I was ten. So, yes, you could say I grew up here."

"You must have some stories to tell about this place!"

"Yes, I do! I'll be back with more food for you." As she walked away, she looked over her shoulder, a sparkle in her eyes as she looked back at Molly. Molly smiled back. Kate looked pointedly at Molly.

Molly frowned at Kate. "What's that look for?"

Kate smirked. "Not a thing."

GraceAnn came back with two mugs and plates of food. "Will you join us?" Kate asked.

Molly gave Kate a quick side glance. "Yes, please join us, Grann."

Kate noticed GraceAnn blushed. "Thank you, but I'm very busy today. I think every pirate in the Caribbean is on this island." With that, GraceAnn rushed off to help two loud patrons that were expressing their displeasure that they were not getting drinks fast enough.

Kate pressed Molly. "You two are close. How did that happen?"

Molly frowned at Kate. "Not that my friendships are any of your concern…" Molly paused. "The first pirate ship I was on was the *Hades Curse*. I escaped an inhuman husband by posing as a young man and joining the crew." Kate tried to hide her surprise. Molly had never told her how she became a pirate. "We made port here and while every other crew member looked for whores, I came here. I would sit in a booth and drink ale. I became a master at making a mug of ale last a long time." Molly laughed and shook her head at the memory. "That was when I met GraceAnn. She took pity on me and allowed me the time to hide from my shipmates. We began talking and quickly became friends. The other men noticed not only my avoidance of the whore houses, but my friendship with Grann. We had two more days in port and the men decided this unsullied boy needed to 'get his wee willie wet.' GraceAnn took pity on me and relented to being my first. Imagine her surprise when she discovered that I did not have a willie. She kept my secret. For that, I owe her a debt that I cannot repay. We have been close since. Now when I'm in port… we… catch up on each other's lives." Molly finished her story with a faraway look and a soft smile.

Kate sipped her rum and studied Molly. She had never met anyone like her. Just when Kate thought she knew everything about her, she found out something new. GraceAnn brought them food and Kate and Molly chatted about the ship's business while they ate.

As they were leaving, GraceAnn hugged them both. Kate first, then Molly. As she hugged Molly, she whispered something in her ear. Molly nodded, but she offered no explanation as they walked out into the strong Caribbean sun and headed back to the *Revenge*.

Back on the ship, Molly checked on the ship and the men. All the repairs and provisioning were going according to plan. Molly packed a small bag and was leaving when Kate stopped her. "Where are you going?"

"I have a room at the Lusty Maiden. I'm going to stay there for a few days. Will you watch over Maurice while I'm gone?"

"Of course." Kate watched Molly leave the safety of the ship and tried not to worry about her being alone in the wild town that was Tortuga.

Molly found Ikemba and Séamus in the galley, going over supplies. "I'm spending a few days ashore. Kate will watch over Maurice but if you two could help her with that, I would very much appreciate it."

"You have a room at the Lusty Maiden?" Ikemba asked.

"I do," Molly answered curtly.

"Be cautious, Captain. We don't want another pirate with a mind to be captain of the *Revenge* to kill you and come aboard to take your place. We might get a better captain but, then again, we might not. What is that people say?" Séamus pretended to ponder. "Oh yes! The devil you know... that's it! It's better to stick with the devil you know."

"Very amusing." Molly said, clearly not amused by her first mate's attempt at humor.

As she walked away, Séamus looked at Ikemba, watching for some signs of his feelings about Molly's time ashore and who she was spending it with.

Ikemba furrowed his brow. "What, old man? What are you looking at?"

Séamus chuckled. "Not a thing."

"Am I supposed to act like the jealous beau? Molly is not one to be caught in any one person's snare. I have no doubt that she cares for me. Deeply. That husband of hers broke her in ways we will never understand. We see the scars on her body, but not the damage done to her very soul. I'm happy to be near Molly... in any way she allows me."

Séamus thought about the dark day he found Molly. She was being beaten by her husband. He still felt that anger in the pit of his stomach. He patted Ikemba on the back. "You are a good man, Ikemba."

After being on the island for a week, Ikemba, Séamus, and Molly met at the Lusty Maiden to go over the ship's supply and repairs. Everything was nearly complete. In a few days, they could get back out to sea. Molly was ready. She was feeling anxious and felt vulnerable on land. On her ship, she was the captain. Her crew was loyal and she could let down her guard around them. Here in this hive of filth, one had to be ready to fight for their life at any moment. Most of the men here knew who Molly was and stayed very far from her infamous sword. Still, Molly was ready to get back on the water and away from this place.

GraceAnn came to their table. She smiled at them. "How do you like my rum? I purchased a slave who had worked as a rum maker at a small sugar plantation across the island. The husband became ill and the wife needed money. In one lot, I got everything I needed to distill rum for the Lusty Maiden."

Séamus asked Ikemba. "What do you think? Would the men enjoy this on the ship?"

Ikemba nodded, "Can you sell us a few jugs to take with us?"

"I'm sorry but I only have enough for my place. I will set some aside for your next visit to shore." She glanced at Molly, "I hope it's not as long between your visits."

Molly stood, ready to go back to her room on the second floor, when a young barman bumped into her. She grabbed his hand, which was clutching her coin pouch. Molly cocked her head and stared at the young man. Without releasing his hand, she gestured toward the door. Séamus and Ikemba flanked him. Séamus grabbed the young man's arm and clapped him on the back in a friendly gesture. He laughed as if the lad had said something funny and began walking him toward the open door. The young man was trying to object to leaving with the group when Ikemba pressed a knife into his side.

"You can surely die here or we can go outside and have a talk about your intentions with our captain's purse." The young man nodded and walked willingly to the door.

They walked around the corner until they were mostly out of sight of prying eyes. Molly leaned against the wall, arms crossed. "You have some stones, young lad. Trying to pick the pocket of a pirate captain in front of her men."

The young man wished he had never left the safety of the tavern. These three menacing people looked as though inflicting pain was second nature to them. His dark hair lifted in the breeze and his brown eyes were huge with fear. He looked young. Maybe fourteen? "Well, speak up! Why would you do something so ill-advised?"

Ikemba punched the lad in the stomach. "Our captain is talking to you! Answer her question!"

The boy would have collapsed if Séamus hadn't been holding him up. The boy wouldn't speak. Molly sighed, "It's not important that this wastrel explain himself to us. I will just cut off his hand so he won't be able to pick another person's pocket."

Molly drew her sword. Séamus looked at Molly, eyebrows raised.

She paused. "Too harsh?"

Ikemba intervened. "It will make it more difficult for him to earn an honest coin if you cut off a hand, Captain."

Molly shrugged. "There are many ways a lad can earn with only one hand. He's a handsome boy. I know many a pirate that would pay for time with him." She didn't think it was possible but against all odds, the boy's eyes got even bigger. All the color drained from his face. It looked like he was going to pass out or throw up.

She took pity on him.

"All right then, a finger. This slight cannot go without a punishment. I won't have him telling his thieving friends that Molly Malone is an easy mark."

Séamus nodded in agreement, dragged the boy to a barrel, and slapped his hand down. Ikemba held the boy so he couldn't run away as Molly took out her dirk. She stopped, contemplating which finger to cut off. Finally, she chose his middle finger. Molly grabbed it and lowered her dirk to cut off the digit. She hoped this went quick. She was already wasting time she didn't have dealing with this would-be thief. Molly turned to Ikemba. "Stuff something in his mouth so others won't hear his screams." Ikemba nodded, and pulled a handkerchief from his pocket, and moved to stuff it in the boy's mouth.

"Wait! Wait, wait, wait... I have information. Information that would be of much more use to you than my finger!" The boy desperately looked at Molly. "Please. Please, if you do me no harm, I can tell you where to find the Queen's Heart."

"The Queen's Heart. What is the Queen's Heart?" Molly's eye narrowed slightly in thought. It was probably just a story this boy was trying to trade for his finger.

"It's a necklace. A ruby necklace. Almost one week past, I heard some men in the tavern talking about it. They picked it up here and were taking it to their home in Cartagena for safekeeping until the Spanish Navy arrives in a few weeks to collect it along with the rest of the jewels for a dowry. They are taking it back to Spain in preparation for a royal wedding. It's why I tried to lift your purse. I need the pieces of eight to get to Cartagena so I can steal the necklace!"

Séamus let out a harsh laugh. "Why would you risk such a foolish endeavor, boy?"

The boy lowered his head, "*Una chica.*"

Séamus laughed out loud and clapped him on the back hard. His body jerked forward under the pressure. "Of course it was a girl! Why else would a young man attempt something so stupid?"

Molly frowned at Séamus. She grabbed the boy's chin and pulled his face toward her. She put her face close to his. "I don't believe you. Now, instead of just losing a hand or a finger, you are going to lose your life."

"I can prove it! Reach into my right pocket. I wrote the details. Please! Look at the paper. It proves I'm not lying to you."

Ikemba reached into the boy's pocket and pulled out a tightly folded paper and handed it to Molly. She unfolded it and spread it on the top of the barrel for all of them to see. The writing was hardly legible, some words were in Spanish, and most of it was impossible to make out, but Molly could pick out names of some people and the town of Cartagena. Molly, Séamus, and Ikemba exchanged glances. Either this boy pulled this deceit often, or the Queen's Heart really was waiting to be pilfered. Molly wouldn't take any chances with the boy giving this information to anyone else. "Séamus, take him back to the ship and hide him. Kem, when can we get the men back on the ship and set sail?"

"About two days, Captain."

"Good, two days it is. What's your name, boy?"

The boy muttered, "Domingo."

"Séamus, don't let anyone talk to this lad. I'll finish my business here and be back onboard by nightfall."

"Aye, Captain." Séamus responded.

"Domingo, you are one lucky boy. You will have the pleasure of sailing on the *Fortune's Revenge*. If, I find that you have lied to me…" Molly paused. She leaned close and said in a low voice, "You will wish you had never tried to pick my pocket and you will find yourself praying for death… for a long, long time."

Ikemba, Séamus, and Domingo swiftly made their way to the ship, staying in back alleys and keeping a low presence on the streets. They didn't want Domingo calling for help from anyone they encountered.

Molly headed to the blacksmith's shop. She was eager to pick up her purchase and get back to the ship.

The blacksmith stopped working when he spotted Molly. With a big smile, the large man greeted her. "Molly Malone! You finally made it back to the island!" Samuel dropped his tools, walked over to Molly, and grabbed her in a tight hug, lifting her off of her feet.

Laughing, Molly hugged Samuel back. "It's good to lay eyes on you, my friend." Molly stepped back and took in the mountain of a man before her. Samuel was an escaped slave whose skin was as dark as night and a smile as bright as the sun. It was hot in the barn where Samuel had his shop. He was dressed only in boots and pants. His large muscular chest was dripping with sweat. When he turned to walk to the back of the shop, Molly could see the scars left from his time on the plantations under cruel overseers. Once again, Molly pondered the depth of human cruelty.

Samuel returned with a beautiful, long wooden box in his hands. He opened the box with pride. His dark eyes waiting for Molly's reaction. She clapped her hands together in delight. Her green eye bright with joy, she smiled at Samuel.

"Samuel, you did a fine job. Maurice is going to love it." Molly reverently lifted the wooden practice sword out of the box. It was the perfect weight for Maurice. She put it back and picked up the metal sword. It was a perfect mirror of its wooden counterpart. It was stunning. The blade was thin and sharp. Samuel had inlaid the handle with gold leaves. Molly placed the sword back in the box. Samuel closed the lid, handed the box to her.

"Someday I hope you allow me to meet Maurice. I know you don't like him about town but maybe I could come to your ship and meet him?"

"Yes. Our very next visit. I think you two should meet. He should know the person who made such a beautiful gift for him."

Molly handed a bag of coins to Samuel. They hugged once more time and Molly set off to return to her ship. She was excited about this wonderful gift for Maurice and the possibility of a Spanish treasure. Molly was lost in her thoughts when she realized there were six men blocking her path. She stopped abruptly. The men said nothing at first but their swords were drawn and all eyes were on Molly. That said everything that Molly needed to know. The men stood evenly spaced out in order to block the alley. Molly could see that a few of the men were nervous. Their chests were heaving from their labored breaths. One man took a step back, his sword hand shaking. The leader turned and hissed something to his frightened companion.

The men were rough. Their clothes were tattered and dirty. They looked thin. Their swords were of poor quality. They stunk of desperation. *Maybe they just want to rob me,* Molly thought.

She waited for them to tell her what they wanted. Finally, the man in the forefront spoke up.

"You are Molly Malone? The captain of *Fortune's Revenge?*"

Molly raised an eyebrow and cocked her head in response. Were they seriously asking if she was Molly Malone? How many female captains were on this island?

"I say again… are you Molly Malone?" The man was growing impatient with Molly's silence.

"Why? Are you seeking Molly Malone because you are curious to see a redheaded pirate captain?" Molly kept her tone light despite knowing she was in real danger.

"No, our leader sent us to find you and demand the boy."

"The boy? What boy?" Molly feigned ignorance, though she suspected they were talking about Domingo.

"The Spanish boy that knows where a treasure is. Calvert saw you and your mates take him. We want him. If you don't give him to us, we will kill you."

The man smiled at the thought. Molly could see that he had only one rotten tooth in his mouth.

"Do you men serve on a ship? Who is your captain?" Molly demanded.

The man laughed and advanced a step toward her. His eyes narrowed as he growled, "No, we ain't on no ship. We are free men. We live as we please."

"Who is this Calvert you spoke of?" Molly asked.

"Calvert Harden. You remember the man you flogged and set adrift in a boat with no food or water? He remembers you, Captain Malone." The man said her name with sarcasm and disdain.

"I did not set him adrift with no food and water. Your leader was a coward and hid when it came time for battle. In fact, I don't see him here. Where is he? He sent you to face me while he is hiding."

The man looked like Molly gut punched him. Her jab hit the mark.

He shook his head. "No! You won't bewitch me with your vile words! We want that boy. A treasure would surely make our lives more gentlemanly."

"Gentlemanly? You could have all the coins in the Caribbean and your lot would still be the mangy street dogs that you are."

Proving Molly's point, the leader growled and advanced another step. "Give us the boy! I won't ask again!"

"Do you have a name? I like to know the names of people I'm going to kill," Molly stated casually.

With a wide grin, the man answered. "Remy. Remy is the name of the man that's going to kill you, you redheaded bitch, if you don't give us the boy."

The man took another step toward Molly. She could smell him now. Molly wasn't sure this was going to end well for her. She casually walked a few steps to set the box holding Maurice's swords on a dry spot on the ground. While she did so, she scanned for help or an escape. Neither seemed likely. She was ready to draw her sword and take on the men when she spied a man round the corner. He was wearing short boots, a sleeveless tunic, and cropped pants. He stopped when he saw the scene before him. Molly noticed the large knife tucked into the wide belt holding his tunic closed. She hoped he knew how to use it and would be willing to help her out.

The man set the canvas bag he had slung over his shoulder on the ground and slowly approached Molly. "Captain, Malone?" Molly nodded. "I have been looking for you." He looked past Molly to the group of thugs. "Are these friends of yours?"

"No. They most assuredly are not friends of mine." Molly replied.

Deliberately, the man slid the knife free from his belt and turned to face Molly's attackers. Molly fell in beside him, her sword drawn. She quickly glanced at her ally. He was thin but strong. He looked like a man who was used to hard work and a hard fight.

"Enough! Give us the boy or you both will die!" Remy screamed at them as he raised his sword and pointed it at them.

"I don't have what you are looking for. I only have a gift for my ward. A small practice sword fit for a child and not practical for men such as yourselves. I may have a few coins. Would you like those? I would hate for you to go away empty-handed." Molly smiled at them and pretended to pat her pockets looking for coins.

The man at her side snorted with suppressed laughter.

That was too much for Remy. He charged Molly and Molly's ally ran to meet him. He elbowed Remy in the nose. Remy stopped and bellowed, holding his nose as blood flowed from it. The man used Remy's distraction as a chance to ram his large blade deep into Remy's gut. He leaned in and forced the blade up through Remy's body. When he pulled out his knife and let go, Remy dropped to the ground.

One of the other men screamed, "Remy!" He looked at the man and Molly. His eyes were wild. "You killed my brother!" He gestured toward his compatriots. "Kill them!"

The five men rushed forward. Molly, and the man both stood their ground. "What is your name?" Molly asked the man.

"Jesse!" he shouted as the first swords connected with his knife and Molly's sword. Molly and Jesse stood side by side, fighting.

Molly slashed two of the men. With deep cuts to their bodies, they turned and ran away from the fight.

Jesse jabbed his blade deep into Remy's brother. When he pulled it out, the man crumpled to the ground. The final man standing dropped his sword, grabbed Remy's brother and dragged him away from Jesse and Molly. They quickly disappeared around a corner.

Molly and Jesse waited, ready for another fight if the men came back. They didn't.

Molly waited for Jesse to clean his blade with Remy's clothing. He placed the knife back in his belt and returned to Molly.

"Thank you. I am not sure I would have come out of this unscathed if you had not happened along." Molly said.

"I did not happen along. I was looking for you."

"Why? What do you want?"

"I want to join your crew, Captain Malone."

For the first time, Molly really got a good look at the man. He was not a young man. His hair was a dark gray and his long beard was a light gray. His eyes and cheeks were sunken and there didn't seem to be any extra meat on his body. Seeing his wiry frame, one might assume that he wasn't fit for life on a ship but his stance showed the underlying strength of a man who spent his life on the sea. Molly followed the lines of muscle and veins showing through the many tattoos on his arms.

"What is your full name, Jesse?" Molly asked.

"Reese. Jesse Reese. I've worked as a bosun... probably as long as you've been alive. My life is among the lines and ropes on ships."

Molly picked up the box. "Why do you want to be a part of my crew?"

"I want to go home and see my daughter. The last time I saw her, she was two. She must be about thirteen or fourteen years of age now. I want to see her at least once again."

"Why did you leave her?"

"It was't my choice. I worked in a shipyard running lines on ships. From there, a group of men that needed someone who could help them repair their ship's lines took me. I was pressed into service on that day and have been since. I've had enough. I want to earn enough coin to get me home. As I hear, your ship is the one that can get that done for me."

Molly nodded. "Come with me, Jesse Reese. I will introduce you to our crew. If they approve, you may join. Fair enough?"

"Fair enough." Jesse's thin lips seemed to raise in a tight smile.

Molly and Jesse made it back to the ship without further incident. Molly found Séamus and Ikemba and told them that Jesse had helped her out in a difficult situation. Mr. Reese wanted to join their crew and Molly wanted it done. Ikemba and Séamus both agreed. It was rare that Molly pressed her station as captain when it came to the crew. This man must have made a serious impression on her.

That night, as Molly lie in her bed, she was grateful that Jesse had came along when he did. Calvert Harden. Kate was right. He had survived and he was keeping tabs on her. Molly needed to sort that situation out the next time she came to Tortuga. She didn't want to be surprised again. Between Calvert's cowardice and Jesse Reese's help, she was sleeping in her own bed. If not for those two things, this day could have ended differently. Content to be safe back on her ship, Molly drifted off to sleep with the sound of the ocean coming through the open doors of her balcony.

The Race to Find the Queen's Heart
Tortuga to Cartagena

Two days later, the *Fortune's Revenge* was heading to Cartagena in all haste. The men were told that they were going after a treasure but the details weren't shared. They stashed Domingo in Kate's cabin where the men weren't welcome. Molly, Kate, Ikemba, Séamus, James, and few other trusted crew members who were familiar with Cartagena made plans to land and scout out the home where the Queen's Heart was being held.

After much discussion, James mentioned that there was one member of the crew who was familiar with Cartagena.

"Can we trust him? Are we certain that he knows the city?" Molly asked.

James shrugged, and the look on his face did little to answer Molly's questions. "I've heard him talk about Cartagena. He's been a member of the crew since a little before we arrived in New Orleans. He's a hard worker. That's all I know."

Kate spoke up. "I know him." All eyes in the captain's cabin turned toward Kate. "He is very nice. His father was a merchant sailor and so was he, before we took over this ship. He is teaching me how to navigate."

It was only then that everyone realized Kate wasn't in her usual second-hand clothing. Her hair was in the messy braids they always saw her in but the sleeveless cream-colored shirt and the gold vest fastened closed with brown ribbons was new. Her tan breeches fit her perfectly and her brown thigh-high boots were clearly made for her. Kate was blushing under her fellow crew members scrutiny.

Molly finally spoke up. "Kate, has he talked about Cartagena?"

"Yes. Yes, he has. I believe he has not only been there, but he has spent a lot of time in the city. His name is Charles Fisher."

"Maurice, please go fetch Mr. Fisher."

Maurice ran out of the cabin and re-appeared about five minutes later with Charles Fisher in tow. Charles entered the cabin, his sailor's cap in his hand. He was an older man with tanned skin that was wrinkled and rough from his time at sea. His dark hair was sprinkled with gray and his dark brown eyes were a dead giveaway to his apprehension about being summoned to Molly's cabin. His gaze desperately scanned the cabin, trying to gain some understanding of why he was there. Finally, his gazed stopped on Kate. He smiled slightly and his body relaxed.

Molly glanced at Kate. She was making more friends than Molly realized. Molly cocked one eyebrow and waited for Kate to look her way. Kate realized the room's eyes were shifting between her and Molly.

Molly spoke first. "Mr. Fisher, I understand that you served as navigator under the previous captain. Is that correct?"

"Aye, Captain, I did indeed," he answered in a deep, gravelly voice.

"I also understand that you may have spent some time in Cartagena."

"Yes. When I was a younger man, I served on a ship that made port there. I fell in love with a bar maiden, so I stayed to woo her and hopefully make her my wife. I lived in the city for two years."

James asked, "Did you marry the barmaid?"

Charles laughed and shook his head. "Turns out young girls don't favor old men with a taste for rum."

The crew collectively laughed at the truth held within his humor.

Molly motioned for Charles to join them around the table. He took his place around the table and noticed a map of Cartagena spread out. It was then that he noticed a nervous young man standing next to Ikemba. He looked at Molly. "It is my pleasure to meet you in person, Captain. I hope I can be of better service to you and to this ship."

Well, Molly thought, *it is no surprise why Kate enjoyed spending time with this old charmer.* "We have need of your knowledge. We are headed to Cartagena to acquire a treasure. Mr. Kamara, if you please."

Ikemba passed a wrinkled piece of paper to Charles. Charles scanned the paper. The writing was almost illegible scratch. There was, however, one name he could pick out—Iglesia de Santa Cruz. The Church of Santa Cruz. Charles looked at the unknown young man, "Is this your writing?" The boy nodded. Charles looked at Molly. "Captain, do you know the city is fortified? It's a jewel in the Spanish crown and an important port for trade. It's almost impossible to make landfall there and a full-force attack would not end well for us."

"Domingo, please relay to Mr. Fisher, in as much detail as you remember, what you overheard at the Lusty Maiden."

All eyes focused on Domingo. He was visibly shaking, head and eyes on the floor. He was shaking his head as if in denial over his predicament. He clenched and unclenched his fists. It wasn't hot in the captain's cabin, but the boy was sweating. Charles felt bad for this young man. Obviously, he had some important information that the pirates wanted. Charles made his way around the table and inserted himself between Domingo and Ikemba.

Charles draped his tanned arm around the boy's shoulders. "Your name is Domingo?" The boy nodded, keeping his eyes downcast. "Domingo, I'm Charles Fisher. I too was made a part of this crew not of my own free will." Charles quickly glanced in Molly's direction but immediately focused back on the boy. "Now I'm a trusted member of the crew. I could have left the crew at any time when we were at port, but I chose not to. I stayed on with the *Revenge* because I like the crew and I'm making more coin than I ever did as a merchant sailor. The captain is fair. I've never seen a man lashed who didn't deserve it. You and I will come to understand what they seek and we will do our best to make sure they can get it. Can you help me with that, Domingo?" Again, Domingo nodded. "Well then lad, out with it! Tell me your story."

Domingo slowly started telling Charles in a broken combination of Spanish and English how he had learned of the Queen's Heart. Once Domingo finished his tale, Charles asked him more questions and placed markers on the map after each question Domingo answered. Finally,

Charles looked around the table with a wide smile and his deep brown eyes sparkled. He stabbed a finger down at the map. "There! This is where you will find the Queen's Heart! And,I know exactly how we can get in and get out under the cover of night."

The Queen's Heart
Cartagena

"All hands more sail!" Molly shouted from the helm. The men rushed to follow her orders. Molly stood steady, feet apart, standing strong with the movement of the ship. The ship bucked and shook as the sails filled with the wind. Molly loved when the ship's sails were full and her ship was racing through the water. It filled her with deep gratitude and happiness. She wondered if the reason she was in awe of the full sails because of the size and number of sails on the ship. The *Revenge* was larger than most ships. It had three masts. Most ships had two. The sight and sounds of all those sails full of wind was amazing to behold.

"Captain, perhaps we are pushing the men and the ship too hard?" Séamus hated questioning Molly but he was sure both men and ship were almost at their limits.

"I won't miss that treasure, Séamus. The men and the ship can stand a bit more. I'm sure of it."

"Aye, Captain. As you say."

By sheer force of Molly's will and the stamina of the men, they made it to Cartagena ahead of the Spanish armada traveling to take possession of the dowry.

They made anchor behind a small island and waited until dark. Molly left Kate in charge of the ship and ordered Ikemba, Charles, James, Jesse, and three additional crew members to set out on a long boat.

"You are bringing our newest crew member on such an important landing?" Séamus asked.

"He helped me when I was in a tough situation, Séamus. I am confident in his skills as a fighter. He has led a long life. He can lend his wisdom to the younger crew members when we are separated in the city. We need to be cautious. We cannot have the men use unnecessary violence or draw attention to us with reckless behavior. I doubt any of us would survive a face-to-face fight with the military guarding Cartagena. The men will listen to Mr. Reese. He has experience and authority."

Séamus shrugged. He wasn't convinced but he wasn't willing to argue with Molly any further on the subject.

Once in the longboat, Charles directed them into a low waterway that led into the city. Once inside, they lit one lantern so they could navigate their way through the tunnel. They could see eyes in the water shining in the reflection of their small lantern.

"What are those creatures?" James asked Charles.

"Those are crocodiles. Do not put your hands outside of this boat. They will grab you and there will be nothing we can do to save you," Charles answered James grimly.

Molly and the rest of occupants of the boat kept a close watch on the eyes moving about in the water. Here and there, they could hear a low growl. Molly was wondering if the Queen's Heart was worth this risk.

They made it into the city. It was late, and there was very little movement about. Torches were lit along the seawalls but there were enough dark spaces for the pirates to move around in. Molly ordered Ikemba, Charles, and James to come with her. The rest would hide with the boat.

"Jesse, you and the others stay here and stay out of sight. I'm hoping this goes quickly and quietly. If it doesn't, be ready to leave in a hurry. If they capture us... leave this place and scurry back to the ship. Let Kate know she is captain. She won't want to leave. Make sure she does. If she won't, Séamus will know what to do."

"Aye, Captain," Jesse agreed somberly.

Molly and the others moved through the city as quickly as they could. They avoided any movement or lighted area, sticking firmly to the shadows. Finally, they reached the home they were looking for. It was a large home set alone on a small hill overlooking the city. The beautiful yellow plaster and white trim displayed the wealth of the occupants. It was a warm evening and the upper-level double doors were open. There were small balconies at some of the doors. On one wall there was two balconies with open doors close together. They decided that those would lead into the master's bedroom. They threw a rope with a hook up to the balcony. It took Ikemba two tries but on the second throw, the hook caught. Molly climbed up first, then Ikemba, followed by James. Charles stayed on the street as a lookout.

The three moved into the villa bedroom. It was large with heavy, dark wood furniture. The owners were soundly sleeping in an immense bed that seemed to be as tall as it was wide. There were steps on each side for the husband and wife to climb into their respective sides.

Molly motioned for Ikemba and James to take the man's side. Molly moved up the steps and waited for Ikemba to wake the man of the house. Ikemba clapped his hand over the man's mouth and he tried to sit up with a start. Ikemba's large hand muffled his yell. Séamus held a knife to the man's throat "Keep quiet, man, and you will live to see the sun rise in the morn." The man nodded, eyes wide. He understood. He would keep quiet.

Molly placed her hand over the woman's mouth. The woman's eyes flew open, and she tried to scream. Molly held her small push knife just under the woman's eye. "If you want to lose an eye, try and scream again."

The woman nodded and glanced fearfully toward her husband. Seeing that he would be no help, the woman whispered in hesitant English, "What do you want? Money? We have little in our *casa*. In *mi esposo's* desk. There are gold coins. Take those and go."

Her husband made a small objection and Ikemba punched him. The man fell back into his pillow. Quiet and no longer a problem.

"No. It isn't gold coins that we are after, it's a treasure. A treasure fit for a queen."

The woman instinctively put her hand between her breasts. "We do not have treasure here. You have come to the wrong *casa*."

Molly cocked her head and smiled. She leaned forward and kissed the woman on the cheek. "What is your name, *Señora*?"

"Cataline."

"Cataline, that's a beautiful name. It fits you." Molly leaned close and breathed the woman in. "You smell like a garden. What flower smells so wonderful on a lovely woman such as you?"

Molly's compliment shocked the woman. She was shocked but not un-happy. With a slight smile, she quietly answered, "I do not know the name in English."

"No matter." Molly trailed her blade down the woman's cheek to her neck. There she felt a chain hanging from Cataline's neck. Molly tapped it with her knife. "What is this?"

Cataline shook her head, looking down. She resisted the urge to grab the pendant again.

Molly smiled and raised Cataline's chin to meet her gaze. "Is this part of the dowry? Are you willing to keep the treasure safe at the risk of your own life?" Molly stroked Cataline's graying hair away from her face. "You are a beauty, Cataline. I do not want to mar this face but I will if you force me."

Cataline reached up and pulled the chain out from under her night-dress. The chain was thick and glittering gold but the pendant on the end made Molly catch her breath. It was a large uncut ruby nestled in golden vines wrapping around the stone. At the end of each vine were three leaves with small diamonds on the edge of each leaf.

"Is this the Queen's Heart?"

"*Sí, El Corazon de la Reina.*" Cataline slipped it off of her neck, kissed the ruby, and then handed it to Molly. Molly hung it around her own neck and tucked the ruby into her vest.

"Where is the rest of dowry?"

Cataline jutted her chin toward a wardrobe close by.

Molly hurried to the wardrobe and threw open the doors. There sat a chest all on its own. Molly opened the lid. It was full of velvet-wrapped items. Sitting directly on top was a ring with a large sapphire cut into the shape of an eye. The blue eye was looking directly at her. Molly paused for a moment. An evil eye to protect the contents? Molly shook herself. Now was not the time to be bothered by Spanish magic. She grabbed the ring and put it in her pocket. She then reached back into the chest and unwrapped one velvet package and gasped at the jewels inside. She motioned for Ikemba and James to come over and get the chest. While they lowered the chest to the ground, Molly returned to the bed and sat with Cataline to keep her quiet.

"All is clear! Let's go!"

Molly put both hands on either side of Cataline's face and kissed her mouth. "Thank you, Cataline. I will remember this short time we've had together and I will always wonder what it would have been to have more than a few moments with you."

Molly raced to the window and slid down the rope. The group hurried away from the villa when a man's shout went up. Cataline's husband had woken up and he was on the balcony calling for help.

"I hope you can run, old man," James called out to Charles as he and Ikemba began running with the chest.

They heard shouting and gunshots coming their way. Molly saw a group of soldiers running toward them.

"Oh shit! Come on Charles! Run!" Molly grabbed Charles's arm, and they ran after Ikemba and James.

As the four ran down the road toward their boat, shots hit the walls beside them, blowing pieces of plaster and brick toward them.

One hit the wall beside Molly as she ran. She instinctively ducked. "We have to get off this road! Charles, where do we go?"

"Up ahead. That alley to the port side!" Charles puffed as he struggled to run and breathe.

Ikemba looked back. Both Molly and Charles were pointing to the left. James and Ikemba ran to the alleyway. There was another small alley that was very dark where they might be able to rest for a moment. They rounded a corner, and the four ducked into the dark opening between two large buildings. They sat quietly, trying to slow their breaths. The sound of soldiers running down the road shouting passed them by. The soldiers hadn't seen where the four had disappeared to.

"How did those soldiers find us so quickly?" James whispered harshly.

"Maybe there was a lookout or guard that we didn't see?" Ikemba guessed.

Molly nodded. It had to be. How could they be so careless as to have missed the lookouts? Molly was angry with herself. She and the men should have scouted the area before climbing through the window of the villa. If they got through this alive, this would be a big lesson for all of them. If they got back to the ship and didn't die at the hands of the soldiers hunting them.

It had been quiet for a while. *Maybe we're going to be okay,* Molly thought. Just as a sliver of relief crossed her mind, someone above them was shouting. They looked up and there was a woman on a small balcony shouting and pointing down at them.

"Dammit!" James whispered.

Ikemba slipped on soft gravel, falling hard on one knee. He swore under his breath but quickly recovered. They were off running again, moving from alley to alley, trying to keep to the shadows and attempting to avoid people. Especially those with guns. Finally, they made it to their boat. The crew had the boat prepped and ready to shove off. Molly and Charles jumped in while Ikemba and James maneuvered the heavy chest to a spot mid-boat, then James boarded. Ikemba pushed the long boat off the shore and jumped in.

Everyone on the boat was silent, fearful that the guards would hear them. They were in open water, well on their way to the ship, when Molly felt Charles shaking. Molly grabbed his arm and shook him. "Are you okay, Charles?"

Charles sat up and laughed out loud. "I've not had that much fun since I was a young man. Thank you for taking me on this adventure with you, Captain. It was a good night."

Molly looked at James and Ikemba. They had huge smiles. Molly shook her head. She laughed. *Yes, it was a fun night.* As they rowed back to the ship, Charles relayed the tale of their night to the four crewmen that weren't with them. Molly suspected Charles would be telling this story until the day he died. On his deathbed, he would boast of being with Molly Malone on the night she stole a Spanish dowry. Molly imagined that each time Charles told the story, the treasure would be bigger, there would be more soldiers, and his role would be much greater.

Molly and her men made it back to the ship. Once the long boat and chest were safely stored aboard the *Revenge*, Séamus and Kate got the ship moving. They didn't need to be anywhere near Cartagena come morning. Molly stood on deck as the sails filled with wind and the ship shuddered and creaked as it slowly moved to open water. She could see the sun's rays just peeking out from the water's edge. Molly loved to watch the rising sun. It always made her feel hopeful. If the sun could find a way to rise each morning, Molly could find a way to push herself and her men to bigger and better things.

Once the ship was well underway, Séamus, James, Kate, Charles, Ikemba, and Molly convened in her cabin to assess the treasure. Ikemba was leaning back in Molly's chair with a pistol in his hand when they walked in.

"A pistol, Mr. Kamara?" His hyper-vigilance puzzled Molly. Usually, Ikemba was outwardly relaxed but ready to spring into action at any moment.

"I looked into the chest by light of day, Captain. We have a lot more here than we expected."

Molly and the rest gathered around her desk to peer into the chest. Most of the pieces were wrapped in velvet. Molly pulled pieces out, one by one, and unwrapped them. There was every kind of metal and gem one could imagine. Thick gold and silver chains with emeralds, diamonds, pearls, and rubies hanging from them. There were lady's hat pins with beautiful birds made of small gems. She unwrapped broaches so heavy with gems she wondered how anyone could wear one without it ripping the clothing it was pinned to. There was a tiara made of sapphires and diamonds, the gems held in place by delicate silver vines. Molly recognized the vines from the necklace she was wearing.

Once everything was laid out on Molly's desk, the group could only stare at it.

"We are in a lot of trouble," Kate whispered.

"Kate is right. We have to get this chest of jewels off this ship as soon as possible," Séamus stated, tension and worry evident in his voice.

"Agreed. But where do we take it? We cannot bring the Spanish vengeance down on Tortuga. The Spanish will raze that makeshift town to the ground to recover this chest. Anyone have any ideas?"

"I do," Charles interjected.

All eyes turned to him. "Well?" James demanded.

"Gemma Della Luna."

"Who?" Ikemba asked.

"Gemma Della Luna. She has a fortress on a small island. She deals in gems that most will not touch because they are too expensive or too dangerous," Charles stated. He was sure La Luna was their only answer. "She's tough and I would never cross her but if she chooses to take these gems, she will give us a good price."

"She?" Molly asked.

"She. She calls herself La Luna."

"The moon?" Molly asked. Charles nodded. "Where can we find her?"

"Her home is on Whale Island." Charles stabbed a finger at the chart lying open on Molly's desk. "It is here. The island isn't marked on any map but she is there. It's her own personal fortification. Most people who venture there don't leave the island alive. I believe that's because they are trying to rob her but if you are there for trade or sale of gems, then you stand a chance at life after Whale Island. Captain, you will need to go alone. You, and maybe one other. More than that and her men will kill you before you get anywhere close to her."

Séamus spoke up. "Ikemba and I will go. We won't risk the captain on a fool's errand." Everyone in the room echoed his concern for their captain. This didn't sound like a mission they wanted to send the captain on.

"Molly is a woman. If anyone on this ship has a chance of living through the meeting with La Luna, it would be her." An argument broke out amongst Ikemba, Séamus, James, and Charles. Charles was adamant in his conviction that it should be Molly who goes to Whale Island. The noise in the cabin became deafening.

"This doesn't sound safe for our captain." James protested, slamming his hand down on the chart.

"Enough!" Molly shouted. "I will go. Kate will go with me. I agree with Mr. Fisher. A female captain willing to trespass on her island should impress La Luna more than a captain who cowers aboard her ship."

Ikemba shook his head. "I don't like this, Captain. Is this really the only way to unload the dowry? There must be merchants in Tortuga who will buy these jewels from us. We don't need to risk your life with a woman none of us know except him." Ikemba jabbed his finger toward Charles.

"Listen, all of you. We robbed the Spanish of a rich dowry." Molly gestured toward the chest. "That chest is filled with jewels the likes none of us have ever beheld. The Spanish won't take kindly to our theft of them. They will be hunting us down to recover those gems. We won't bring that wrath down on Tortuga. I want the chest off this ship. To my mind, Gemma Della Luna is our only option. Mr. Fisher, please go to the helm and set a course for Whale Island. The rest of you, we will take shifts guarding the chest." Charles Fisher made his way toward the cabin door when Molly asked, "Mr. Fisher, how long until we reach the island?"

"At a steady pace, we should be there by nightfall tomorrow, Captain."

"Be sure we do, Mr. Fisher."

"Aye, Captain."

Molly looked at Kate. "What say you? Are you willing to go with me to this island?"

Kate smiled, "I would be angry if you left me on the ship for this little adventure, Captain. I'm eager to meet this La Luna."

Molly began putting the pieces back in the chest. "Séamus, go with Charles and set us on course to take us to this Gemma Della Luna. Kate, Ikemba, James—we'll take shifts watching the chest. I don't want the men to know what we have in here." Molly wasn't sure they could hold the men back if they had any idea just how much treasure was sitting so close to them.

Gemma Della Luna
Whale Island

Molly and her most trusted crew barely slept over the next twenty-four hours. True to Mr. Fisher's calculations, they arrived at the island the following nightfall. They anchored off the island well away from any cannon fire that might be aimed their way.

Séamus found Molly looking through a spyglass, appraising the island's fortifications. She handed him the glass. "It looks like she's been on the island for a good while. Look at the seawalls. Charles was correct. They do have cannons on those walls."

Séamus swept his gaze across the front of the island. It looked formidable. How could anyone reach this La Luna? Finally, he spied what looked like a place for boats to make landfall on the beach. There was a wooden slide leading from the water to the beach and at the top, two wooden beams for tying off boats. Séamus pointed it out to Molly, handing the spyglass back to her. Molly nodded in agreement.

"That's a good sign. She must be willing to welcome visitors if she made a place to come ashore." Molly felt a small measure of relief. With a short laugh meant to reassure herself and Séamus, she quipped, "Kate and I might live through tomorrow after all."

Séamus frowned at Molly. "I haven't changed my mind, Molly. I still think Ikemba and I should go."

"No. I don't want to talk about this again, Séamus. Kate and I will go at first light on the morrow."

"I know you gave Kate a choice but, do you think she realizes how dangerous this is? "

Molly cocked and raised an eyebrow. "You think there's any chance on hell or earth that Kate wouldn't accompany me on this?"

Séamus sighed. "Of course she's going to go. She's becoming a little too fond of danger for my taste. A lot like her friend, Molly Malone."

"You worry too much, Séamus. You are becoming an old woman."

Agitated, Séamus snapped the spyglass closed and handed it back to Molly. "An old woman? An old woman! No. I'm an old man. When I met you, I was already an old man and you are making me older by the day! One day I'm going to be walking across this deck and drop dead because of my worry about you. You! You are the reason I worry. You are the reason I look older than I am. Old woman. Ha!" Séamus stalked off mumbling something about an ungrateful, redheaded child.

Molly shook her head, laughing. She extended the spyglass and continued to study the island before her. She was feeling nervous about tomorrow. Molly was certain her men could batter those walls and break into the fortress. Her ship alone had enough cannon fire to demolish the walls. Not that it would do her or Kate any good. Once they were inside La Luna's stronghold, they could be overwhelmed and killed before her men realized they were in danger.

Kate found Molly scanning the walls. "What do you think? Will you and I survive tomorrow?" Molly asked Kate. She was teasing but she had a hint of true worry about their trip to see La Luna.

Molly handed Kate the looking glass. "There is a break in the wall for long boats to come ashore. That's a good sign. I'm worried but I'm more excited to meet this woman. She built a fortified home on a deserted island and has a thriving gem trade. She sounds like a woman you and I will very much enjoy meeting."

Kate nodded, handing the spyglass back to Molly. "I agree. It's not often a person can meet a woman who is queen of an empire of her own making. I'm curious as well... and don't worry about our visit to the island. It will go as planned. She will take our jewels and we will return with a chest of gold pieces."

Molly glanced at Kate, wondering about that future sight she seemed to possess. Molly hoped Kate was correct. For their sakes, let La Luna be a queen who was more interested in trade than taking lives of strangers.

Early the next morning, Molly and Kate prepared to board a long boat along with four men to row them to shore. Ikemba fixed a white flag on the front of the boat. Séamus and James brought the chest and loaded into the boat. Both men were quiet as they loaded it. The rest of the crew stood watching as the group readied the boat. The sounds of the ropes pulling, sails moving gently in the breeze, and the groan of the wooden ship were the only sounds on the ship.

Ikemba handed Kate a loaded pistol. "If you get into trouble, shoot this pistol. This is a loud gun. I think it will be loud enough for the sound to reach us. We will listen for the single shot. We hear that, and we will come ashore to find you."

"Do you think her men will allow me to keep it?"

"Keep it in your belt where they can see it plainly. Do not look like you are trying to hide it. Maybe they will let you keep it if they think it's for show only."

Kate placed the pistol in the belt that crossed from her shoulder down across her chest. Normally, she carried two weapons. Having only one felt odd.

"Kate, are you ready?" Molly asked.

"Aye, Captain! I'm ready."

As her men rowed toward the shore, Molly could see movement on the beach. A group was gathering to greet them. At least Molly was hoping they were going to greet them. As the boat slid up the wooden ramp, a few men ran forward and slid the boat to the top of the ramp. They tied Molly's boat between the two poles. Several other heavily armed men surrounded the boat. One woman strolled forward through the line of armed men. Her clothing was bright and beautiful. She had beautiful brown skin and dark hair. Molly and Kate exchanged glances. Was this La Luna?

As the woman moved closer, they could see that it wasn't a woman, but a man dressed in what looked like women's clothing. He was wearing a red velvet shirt with gold beaded trim around the short sleeves and neck. The dress was a beautiful red wrap with green beading throughout. It was draped beautifully around his body. He was adorned in gold jewelry and had a red dot just above his brows in the middle of his forehead. He was wearing red lip coloring and had rouged cheeks. Kate glanced at Molly. Molly didn't take her eyes off of the person walking toward them.

He stopped in front of Kate and Molly. He seemed to absorb their clothing and most importantly, their weapons. Molly smelled a wonderful aroma of flowers drifting off this beautiful young man.

"My appearance confuses you," he stated flatly. This was obviously not his first time addressing his appearance.

Kate and Molly didn't answer and waiting for him to lead their conversation.

"In my country, I am what they call a Hijar. I am both man and woman and neither man nor woman. I and others like me are our own sex. Does this frighten you?" He spoke in a smooth, lilting accent. His skin was a beautiful shade of golden brown. Both Kate and Molly were enthralled by him.

"Frighten? No. You are one of the most beautiful people I have ever laid eyes on. You are from India?" Molly couldn't take her eyes from the person standing in front of her.

The hijar smiled, beautiful white teeth showing through ruby lips. "Yes. Yes, I am. You have been there?"

"No, but I have met others from there."

"What about you?" The question was directed to Kate.

"I was raised in a Native tribe. We called our... Hjars? Two-Spirits."

"Two-Spirits. I love that. My parents named me, Lakshmireet, but I prefer to be called, Laxmi."

"Very good to meet you, Laxmi. We are here to see, Gemma Della Luna. We have a chest of jewels we need to be rid of." Molly gestured to the chest still in the boat.

"How did you hear of La Luna?" Laxmi asked.

"A member of my crew."

"Your crew? You are captain of a pirate vessel?" He smiled at Kate, motioning toward Molly. "Do you call her Two-Spirits as well?"

"No, but it does fit Molly Malone." Kate glanced at Molly, a mischievous spark in her eye.

Molly grew impatient. "May we meet with La Luna or no? If you won't allow it, we need to leave and find a merchant who will purchase the contents of this chest from us."

Laxmi waived a hand toward Molly. "You are in impatient one. Open the chest so I may be sure you are bringing gems and not weapons to harm our queen."

Molly instructed one of her men to open the chest. The man lifted a velvet wrapped necklace and showed it to Laxmi.

Laxmi motioned to the single pistol in Kate's belt. "Is that for signaling your crew if you are in trouble?"

Kate nodded, "It is."

Laxmi considered Kate for a moment. "I will allow you to keep it. Now, come with me."

The soldiers with Laxmi grabbed the chest and fell in line behind Kate and Molly as they followed Laxmi toward the fortress.

As they reached the gate, Laxmi paused with a serious expression. "Be warned, we will not allow anything to happen to our queen. One thousand elephants will trample you to dust before we would allow you to harm our goddess, La Luna. Do you understand?"

Molly and Kate both nodded.

Kate leaned close to Molly and whispered, "What's an elephant?"

Molly's eye widened as she shrugged and shook her head. She didn't know what an elephant was either. She was sure she didn't want to find out.

Laxmi called out and men rushed to the gate to open it. It was tall. Taller than Molly expected. It looked like it was made of bone. Extremely large bones. Probably whale.

They walked through the gates into a large opening bustling with people. Women, children, and men. Kate and Molly could see small houses built into the side of the rocks and in the trees.

"How many people live here?" Molly asked Laxmi.

"There are fifty men, forty women, and ten children that live here in the fortress. We have another village more inland, that is much larger. La Luna does not like to turn away anyone in need, but the fortress cannot handle many people. The village is quite beautiful. For many who were shipwrecked on the reef and have survived, this place has become heaven on earth for them. Many lived poor and were the lowest of class in their lives prior to landing here. We do not have classes here. A person has a job in our community. Either you do it and do it well or you are sent away. La Luna only allows people to stay who are happy to be here and contribute to the needs of all."

"Sounds much like a pirate ship," Kate interjected.

Laxmi stopped and turned to face them. "Yes, I can see how it would be very similar. Captain Molly, maybe you and La Luna will have many things in common."

Molly hoped so. She needed to be free of the chest of gems.

They moved toward a large opening on the side of the hill. The guards stationed at the opening eyed Molly and Kate suspiciously.

They walked deeper into the cave. As they walked, the cave appeared to be getting smaller. Kate and Molly exchanged glances. This wasn't looking good. Finally, they reached a manmade wall and doorway. As they walked through, Kate and Molly stopped astonished at what was before them. The cave opened up into an enormous cavern. To the right, there was a pool of water with a small waterfall feeding it. All around the pool's edge there were lit candles, illuminating the rock wall around the pool. The candles flickered and danced, making it seem like a portal to another world. The scene in front of them mesmerized Kate and Molly. They were taking it all in when the top of the water broke and a women's head came to the surface. She swam to the edge of the pool and stood.

This must be La Luna, their goddess, Molly thought.

The woman had long dark hair that brushed the small of her back. She stood naked, waiting for Laxmi. The woman was beautiful in the candlelight flickering on her skin. She was indeed a goddess. Laxmi wrapped a golden dress around her body that wrapped snugly around her breasts and fell to the floor. There was an opening high on her thighs. Laxmi arranged the skirt so the dress would fall behind La Luna as she walked. Her strong legs were visible through the opening. Laxmi whispered something to the woman, and it was only then that she looked toward Kate and Molly.

"Take them to my throne room. I will be there shortly," she ordered.

The guards pushed Kate and Molly further into the cavern. There at the end stood a large throne. Again, this piece seemed to be made of whale bones. It had gold and silver highlighting some of the carvings in the bone. Molly could see whales, flowers, and symbols gleaming in the candlelight. Again, this part of the cavern was lit by candles. The guards placed the chest just in front of the throne and they ordered Kate and Molly to stand back from the chest.

They waited for about a half of an hour when, finally, the woman returned with Laxmi in tow. La Luna was stunning. Her long hair was half up and half down. She wore a jeweled tiara placed in the up sweep up her hair. Her dress was plain but obviously made for her. The pale gold cloth hugged every curve and moved with her. The jewels hanging from her neck and wrist were stunning. She was dripping in gold and emeralds. The sleeveless gown showed the golden arm bands on her upper arms. The cut of her muscles was accentuated by the gold bands. She took her place on the throne. Laxmi came behind, fussing with her dress to make sure it splayed out properly. The woman patiently waited until the task was done.

Finally, La Luna spoke to Molly and Kate. "And who might you be?" She spoke with a slight accent.

Italian maybe? Molly guessed. "I'm Captain Molly Malone of the pirate ship *Fortune's Revenge*. This is one of my crew, Kate The White."

"I see. Captain of a pirate ship? I have heard of female pirates, of course. But, I have not heard any tales of your exploits. I am quite sure I would remember hearing of a one-eyed, redheaded pirate sailing around these waters."

"I'm rather new as a captain... and as a woman. I played the part of a male sailor for some time. When I was found out to be a woman, they expelled me from the ship. It has taken me some effort to find my footing once again. None the less, here I am. This chest should prove my worth as a pirate. Female or not."

"Let us see about that, shall we? Bring a table!"

La Luna's men brought a table closer to her throne and began spreading the contents on it. La Luna descended from her throne to examine the jewels.

"These pieces are spectacular. From whom did you acquire them?"

"They were bound for Spain as dowry for a noblewoman's marriage," Molly answered.

La Luna dropped the piece she was holding and turned to Molly and Kate. Her voice tightly controlled, she asked, "You brought a stolen Spanish dowry to my home?"

"We were told that you could handle such a problem. Otherwise, we wouldn't have," Kate answered.

"My crew member felt certain that where they came from would be not be of great concern to you. He told tales of your dealings with Spain in the past. That is why we are here. You, of all people, will most likely live if found with this chest. Me and my crew, we will not."

La Luna sighed and turned back to the table. She ran her fingers over the pieces. Every gem was represented. Pearls, rubies, emeralds, and diamonds. "Did you keep anything from this collection?"

"Yes. I did." Molly affirmed. Kate gave her a quick glance. She wasn't aware that Molly had kept anything from the chest.

"And... what did you keep?" La Luna inquired of Molly.

"I kept two pieces. That is all that you need to know. Can you help us with the rest or do I need to search for someone who can?"

"I can help. Your crew member is correct. I am the only person who can negotiate a reward for the return of the dowry. Slightly less than I would normally receive since you have kept pieces for yourself. Can I surmise they are equally as fine as these pieces?"

"Yes." Molly affirmed.

"Are you hungry? I have not broken my fast and I need food. Would you like to join me and we can discuss price?"

"We would be happy to join you," Molly answered.

La Luna
Whale Island

The three women settled at a table while Laxmi supervised food being brought in. Plates filled with fish cooked in coconut milk and stuffed with fruit. Mango and dried coconut sprinkled with a brown spice. La Luna invited them to eat. Molly took a bite of the mango and spice. It was very good. Not sweet or bitter. It was fragrant and delicious.

"What is this spice?" Molly asked.

"Nutmeg. We trade with a nearby island. We have coconut and mango a plenty but no nutmeg. They are happy to trade with us. Inside the fish is something they call an apple. It is not like any apple I am familiar with. But it is tasty."

Kate took a bite of the fish and apple. "This is wonderful! The cook on the ship is good but the food isn't as fresh as this. It reminds me of home."

"Where was home, Kate?" La Luna asked.

"I grew up in French trapper territory outside of the colonies. We lived near a large river. My father and I would often catch fish for our supper. At eleven years of age, my family was killed by Indians. Those Indians took me to live with them. I was with them for ten summers. Again, my father and brother would allow me to fish with them. It is my favorite meal. It brings wonderful memories of both my families."

"What brought you here?" Kate asked La Luna.

La Luna was quiet for a moment. "My husband dropped me here."

Kate felt terrible for asking. "I'm sorry I asked. It must be a hard memory."

La Luna smiled. "He did me a kindness. Look at the life I have here. I know my life would have been sad and lonely if he had taken me to Columbia."

"Columbia?" Molly coaxed. She wanted to hear this woman's story.

"I was born to Italian nobility, and I grew up in a wealthy home. I wanted for nothing. Nothing, save adventure. I took to sneaking out of my home, donning men's clothing, and riding in the countryside, shooting guns, fighting the stable boys. Anything that would be on the edge of dangerous. I needed that feeling." She paused for a moment, looking away with a far-off stare. "I needed it." She said with force. "My family did not understand. My father used to tell me that if I was born a boy, he would be proud of me. Since I was not, I was bringing shame to the family. His words made the need in the bottom of my stomach grow. Soon I was coming home with bruises and blackened eyes from my fights. I won a lot of money from betting that I could win in a fight against boys." La Luna laughed softly and shook her head. "Perhaps, if we had been poor, maybe that would have made a difference to my family." She paused once again. Molly and Kate could see that the memories were difficult for her.

"They tried to lock me away. Nothing could keep me caged. They tried to marry me off but no man would have me. Until another nobleman, who was not as rich as my family, had a bastard son he needed to be rid of. My father had a similar problem—a child he needed to be rid of. They married us and put us on a ship bound for Columbia. My new husband had Basque family in that region. Both of our family's problems gone on one boat. I did not make it to Columbia. To be free of me, he dropped me here. It was a full moon the night he rowed me from the ship to the beach. There was a dead whale on the beach. The smell was beyond horrible. I begged him not to leave me. He coldly said that I was not a woman. I was a man in a woman's skin and clothing." Her face hardened with the memory. "He said I should be grateful. He could have thrown me overboard. By leaving me on this island, I had a chance at life. It was up to me if I lived or to died." La Luna took a deep breath in and slowly let it out. "I lived. I made a life here. Not only for myself but for others as well. He was correct. He could have thrown me overboard and let me drown. Instead, I have this life as Gemma Della Luna."

"I understand La Luna now, but how did you become Gemma?" Molly asked.

"All around this island, there are reefs. Reefs that are deadly for large ships. There have been many shipwrecks off these shores. Ship debris would wash up on the beach. I collected the pieces until I finally had enough that I could make a raft. I was able to weave ropes together to make a harness of sorts that would keep me connected to my raft. Each morning I paddled out and swam down to the wrecks and collected items. There were many gold pieces and other treasures I salvaged. I stored them in this very cavern. In my prayers, I would ask for a ship to find me and I could pay for passage with my bounty. While I was scavenging the reefs, I found a strange sea creature in a shell that moved about almost like a crab. But not. I collected a few. The shells were beautiful, and I was hoping I could eat the creature inside. It took me several tries, but I finally removed one from its shell. When the meat came out, so did a pearl. It was the most amazing pink color I had ever laid eyes on." She removed a chain from her neck and handed it to Molly. "Here is one. Look at the color. When you turn it, the color changes."

Molly and Kate examined the large pink pearl. Molly handed it back. "That is a pearl?"

"Yes, I have come to understand the creatures are called conchs. On rare occasions, they can produce this stunning pink pearl. Slowly I built up my island. I rescued a few people from shipwrecks and brought them here. One day, a merchant ship anchored off my shores. I had a choice to make. Buy my passage off the island, or stay and make this place my home. I stayed. That merchant was the first ship I traded with. Word spread and more merchant ships arrived wanting my salvaged items. These pearls brought me the most goods and gold."

"The people here are all shipwreck survivors?" Kate asked La Luna.

"Some. Some heard of me and came to the island in search of a better life. If I can make a place for them, I welcome them."

"What about Laxmi?" Molly glanced in Laxmi's direction.

"Laxmi was a shipwreck survivor and I am blessed the gods brought me such a wonderful companion and helper. Laxmi made this dress for me. Is it not gorgeous? Laxmi is the one that started calling me goddess." La Luna smiled, "I cannot complain. I rather like it. For the first time in my life, I may be who I am. A woman who is strong and beautiful."

Molly nodded. She understood exactly what La Luna was saying. Molly and La Luna locked eyes. In that moment, they both understood the other perfectly.

"As for your gems. I will buy them from you. I am certain I can send word to the Spanish and collect a reward for returning them. Plus, it will earn some well-needed favor with them."

"Thank you, La Luna." It relieved Molly to be free of the dowry.

"Please, call me Valentina. La Luna is what I use for trade. You are now my friends."

"Valentina. What a lovely name." Kate interjected.

"Since we are friends, Valentina, is there anything I can do to coax you from telling the Spanish how you came across these treasures? There are few redheaded females captaining pirate ships around here." Molly was hoping to not be the focus of a Spanish hunt.

"I can do that for you, Molly. I would hate for the Spanish to hunt down and kill such interesting women. Especially women that I hope to forge a lasting friendship and working relationship with."

Kate spoke up, "Yes. Yes, to all of that. The women of this world need to band together not only for our survival but for our success."

Valentina and Molly nodded in agreement. Both were very aware of the trouble men could bring a powerful woman that did not bend to their ideas of how a woman should fit into their world.

The three sat around the table negotiating price and regaling each other with their stories of adventure. Valentina was fascinated with Kate's time living as an Indian and she couldn't get enough stories of Molly's time as a male pirate on the *Hades Curse*.

The day wore on and Laxmi appeared at Valentina's side, reminding that another group would arrive soon. Valentina sighed. "This is has been a special pleasure but Laxmi has reminded me I have another buyer arriving soon. He does not like to share my time and refuses to come here if he is not the only visitor on my island. Sadly, it is time for us to say our goodbyes. I will be back in a moment with your payment."

Molly and Kate stood. "Be ready. If this doesn't go according to plan, we may have to fight our way out of here," Molly whispered.

Kate nodded her agreement and stood next to Molly, ready to take on anything that may come their way in the next few moments.

Valentina and Laxmi returned with a different chest carried by two of the fortress guards. Valentina looked at Kate and Molly. Their stance screamed they were ready to fight if they had to. Valentina smiled to herself. She understood their hesitation to trust anyone besides themselves. She was of the same mindset. Having been betrayed by those closest to you will make a person suspicious of everyone.

The men set the chest on the table and Valentina flipped the lid open. "Come, look. Laxmi counted the gold, but if you do not trust that count, you have my permission to count it yourself."

Molly made her way to the chest while Kate stood back, watching. Molly dug through the gold. There wasn't anything in the chest to take up space so it looked like there was more gold than there actually was. Molly was certain that this was their agreed-upon amount. She looked at Kate and nodded.

"Laxmi, make sure the chest is placed upon their boat safely." Laxmi and the men hurried from the cavern toward Molly's longboat.

"Ladies, I have had a most pleasurable day. Thank you. Please come back to visit me, whether for business or for friendship. I would be quite happy to see you again." Valentina hugged Molly. Molly hugged Valentina in return. She sincerely liked this woman and she hoped she would be back this way again.

Molly stepped back so Kate could hug Valentina goodbye. Molly watched Valentina's face and hands. Her face seemed to be genuine in her regard for them. Her hands were open and relaxed. No weapons. No clenched fists. Molly relaxed only slightly. They still had to make it off the island with the gold and their lives.

Laxmi waited for them next to their longboat. To Molly, Laxmi was a bright, shining light in a dull world.

"Your men checked the gold, it made it all the way to your boat unmolested," Laxmi assured Molly.

"I'm certain it did but for my own peace of mind, Joseph, open the chest lid, if you please." One of the crew opened the lid so Molly could peer in. "Dig around and make sure there is nothing else in the gold." Joseph did so.

"It is all clear, Captain." Joseph assured Molly.

"Good! Laxmi, it was wonderful to meet you. I hope we will meet again." Laxmi's head bowed slightly in agreement.

Kate walked to Laxmi. "I feel very lucky to have met another Two-Spirits, especially one so beautiful. In my tribe, they are considered good luck. Touching a Two-Spirit is said to gift some of that good luck to you. With your say, I would very much like to hug you!"

With tears and a smile, Laxmi grabbed Kate and hugged her. "Until we meet again, Kate, may you have all the good luck you need."

The men rowed the longboat back to the *Fortune's Revenge*. It had been a successful day. The gold would split easily amongst the crew and they were rid of the dowry that would have meant their deaths had they kept it on board the ship.

Back on the ship, they stored the gold while Kate and Molly told of their day on Gemma Della Luna's island. Molly could hear Charles shouting orders for the men to get the ship ready to sail. Molly looked at Séamus and Ikemba with a raised brow.

"Did Mr. Fisher receive a bump in station while I was away?"

"Not officially, Captain. That would require your blessing." Ikemba hurried to assure Molly.

"Which we hope you will give, Molly. He is a good man and an expert sailor. He helped us earn a large bounty for this crew. We would like to reward him for that." His expression and tone of voice told her he didn't want no for an answer.

"Very well. When we are well away from here and on our course, we will promote him."

"Thank you, Captain." Both men answered at the same time.

"Now, both of you leave me. I haven't slept in days. I need some rest. Please send Maurice in with some tea."

"Aye, Captain," Ikemba answered.

A short while later, Maurice entered Molly's cabin with tea and biscuits. He found her asleep fully clothed on her bed. He set the tea tray down, retrieved a blanket, and covered Molly. Maurice quietly went to Molly's desk and pulled out the small box with his gun. He loaded the gun and sat in Molly's chair to watch over her until early the next morning.

Molly woke and found him sitting in her chair, nodding off while holding the small pistol. She took the gun and put it back in its box in her top drawer. Molly then lovingly picked Maurice up and cradled him in her arms for a long while before she placed him in her bed. As she looked down at him, she realized how much he had changed since she found him on the slave block. His hair was growing, and he had gained weight. He looked taller. Molly leaned down, kissed his forehead, and quietly left her cabin so her young protector could rest.

"Mr. Fisher, please take the helm. Make way for Tortuga."

"Tortuga, Captain?" Mr. Fisher wasn't sure he heard Molly correctly.

"Yes, Mr. Fisher. I have some business that I must attend to in Tortuga. Make way in all haste."

"Aye, Captain!"

Molly looked around the deck of the ship and found the person she was looking for. "Mr. Ikemba! Please see me in my cabin."

"I will be there in a short few, Captain."

Molly nodded and strode to her cabin. She needed Ikemba to ready the men's earnings for port and make plans for provisioning the ship.

Ikemba knocked on Molly's door. "Enter!" Molly called out to him.

"So, we are to go ashore, Captain?" Ikemba asked as he took a seat opposite Molly.

Molly pulled the ship's ledger from her desk and slid it over to Ikemba. "We need to give the men their portion of the gold we brought on board from La Luna. I don't like having that much on board this ship. If we distribute the men's portion and they spend it in Tortuga, there is less temptation."

"Agreed. The men will be happy to release some of their pent-up manhood," Ikemba said with a smile.

Molly ignored his comment. "I will be busy while we are in port. I need you to take care of provisioning the ship."

"I can do that. Is everything right with you, Molly? Do you need me to accompany you?"

"I'll be fine. I'll take Mr. Reese with me if he is so inclined."

Ikemba nodded. He was still puzzled over how quickly Molly had taken to their latest crew member. She was very vague about their meeting. She would only say that he helped her get out of a tough situation. If Molly thought the situation was tough, Ikemba mused, he could only guess what really happened and how bad it must have been.

"I need to find James so we can decide what the ship needs for provisions. I haven't seen him on deck this morning. Have you seen him?"

Molly shook her head no. "I'll find him. You start on the men's portion of the gold in yon chest." Molly motioned toward the chest locked in one of her cabinets.

Ikemba agreed and took the key Molly produced from her desk. Molly was glad to have at a good portion of that gold out of her cabin and into the hands of the men. Molly left her cabin and made her way to Kate's cabin. The crew should be happy once they arrived in Tortuga. Molly made a mental note to talk to Séamus and Ikemba about replenishing any crew they would lose on this trip. The men will be holding a lot of coin, a few wouldn't be coming back to the ship. Some would be killed for what they have and some will make passage back to their homes. It happened each time the men had a lot of coins in their pockets.

Molly stood in front of Kate's door. She could hear people quietly talking inside. Molly raised her hand to knock but hesitated. Finally, Molly knocked and called out Kate's name. Molly could hear movement inside and after a few moments, Kate cracked the door and blocked Molly's entrance with her body.

"Good morning, Captain. Did you need me for something?" Kate asked breathlessly. Her face was red and she couldn't look Molly in the eye.

"No, I'm looking for James Barlow. No-one has seen him. Since you two seem to be close, I wanted to see if you have seen him before I turn the ship upside down until he shakes out. Have you? Have you seen him, Kate?"

Kate finally looked at Molly squarely in the face and took a deep breath and letting it out before she answered. "If I had seen him this morning, is that the business of the captain? I can see any crew member that I please."

"Yes, yes you can, Kate. However, when your time with a member of my crew interferes with their duty on this ship, that's when it is my business. If a member of my crew is derelict in his duties, then it's up to me to take that person to task and make sure he answers for that misstep. James Barlow is teetering on that line. Another wrong step and he could be brought to the mast."

Kate's voice was no longer breathless, and she was no longer nervous. She stood tall and answered Molly, "I understand, Captain, that your crew is under your command to do with us as you will. It would be a mistake for you to bring Mr. Barlow to the mast. It would do more damage than you realize to the crew... and to me."

The door jerked open and James stood next to Kate in only his pants. "Please, Captain. I am most apologetic for losing time. I'll be on deck in a moment. It won't happen again."

Molly nodded and turned to leave. The image of Kate's defiance was burned in her memory. Molly needed to go ashore. She needed answers. She knew only one person who could give them to her. Corisande Lowe. She would ask Jesse Reese to go with her. He didn't frighten easily. Molly hoped that bravery would hold when he came face to face with a witch.

A few days later, the *Revenge* moored off the shores of Tortuga. The men were going ashore in the longboats. Molly and Jesse Reese were on the first boat to shore. They made their way to the edge of town where a large makeshift barn stood. It looked like it was a house at one time. The front door had been widened and a ramp replaced the stairs that once led into the home. Molly entered first and let her eyes adjust to the darkness inside the building. She loved coming here. The smell and sounds of horses always soothed Molly's soul. One horse reached out from a stall and nudged Molly with its nose. Molly moved closer to rub the horse's face and neck.

Both Molly and the horse jumped when a man yelled, "Who the hell are you and what are you doing touching my horse?"

"Lloyd! It's Molly Malone." Molly answered the man standing in the shadows. Molly couldn't see him clearly until he moved further toward the door and the sun illuminated his body.

"Molly?" The man laughed and hurried to her. "It's so good to see you, girl! How are you doing with that ship of yours?"

Molly hugged Lloyd. He was getting older. His hair was more gray than brown. He was a tall man, but his shoulders were slightly hunched, making him appear shorter than he was. Though, his hug was strong as ever when Lloyd returned Molly's affection.

"I'm doing quite well, thank you! I see you have more horses."

"Yes, I do. More horses mean more gold when you mangy pirates need a quick ride somewhere." He absently reached out to the horse and gently ran his hand down the face. To Molly, his blue eyes seemed faded since the last time she saw him. Maybe it was the light? She hoped his sight wasn't going.

Molly laughed. "This mangy pirate needs two horses for the day. Maybe two days. I won't know how long I will be gone until I get to where I'm going."

Lloyd laughed loudly. "Yep, you sound more like a pirate captain these days. Two horses? I only see you."

Molly called out to Jesse, "Mr. Reese! Can you join us, please?"

Jesse hesitantly entered the building. Lloyd glanced at Molly, unsure of the man that was with her.

"Mr. Reese, have you ever been on horseback?" Molly asked Jesse.

"No, Captain. I haven't had the occasion," Jesse responded warily, eyeing the horses.

Molly turned her attention back to Lloyd. "Do you have a horse that will suit Mr. Reese's inexperience… and fear?" Molly whispered the last two words. She didn't want Jesse to be embarrassed.

It didn't work. "I'm not afraid, Captain! Give me a beast and I will make due."

"I'm sorry, Mr. Reese. I did not mean to offend. We only need to find a proper mount for you, that's all. I have every confidence in your ability to adapt." Molly's raised brow and side look to Lloyd said differently.

"Not to worry, my good sir. I have just the horse for you. His name is Lucifer." Molly started to speak, but Lloyd hurried to explain. "That was his name when I bought him from a missionary set on bringing God to the godless here on the island. The horse and that missionary didn't see eye to eye on most things. The horse left that man dumped in the dirt on more than one occasion. He traded me for another horse. One that didn't have such a high opinion of itself. Ole Lucifer only needed someone to listen to him now and again. He has been as docile as a lamb ever since. Perfect for those that are new to horses."

"Mr. Reese, does that sound agreeable to you?" Molly asked Jesse.

"Aye, Captain. Though I wish I had known about the horses before I agreed to come with you." Jesse replied sullenly.

"Please ready the horses, Lloyd. I'm anxious to depart." Molly was feeling restless. She wanted to get this done and return to the ship.

Jesse and Molly rode away from Lloyd's barn. Jesse didn't ask where they were going. Molly hadn't offered an explanation of their destination and he wasn't the type to ask. In truth, he didn't want to know. It must be dangerous or she wouldn't have brought him along. He was happy she already trusted him with her safety.

They rode for two hours and were making their way deeper into the jungle. There were times it was too difficult for the horse and rider to pass together. Molly and Jesse would dismount and move tree branches or fallen trunks out of the path so the horses could get through. Once on the ground, Jesse could see that they were following some sort of trail. It didn't look like anything as large as a horse had been on the trail for some time.

Finally, Jesse could smell wood burning. They must be close to the location they were searching for. As if reading his mind, Molly said softly, "We're close."

They came to a clearing in the jungle. A small house sat at the back of the open space. The house was covered with moss and it leaned slightly to the left. It had two windows that appeared to have glass in them. A garden with a short fence around it occupied most of the right side of the clearing. It was overgrown with herbs of all kinds. Directly in front of the house was a large fire pit rimmed with rocks. There was a tall tripod spanning it. The three pole ends buried in the ground just outside of the rocks. In the middle of the tripod hung a large cauldron attached by a heavy chain. Jesse was taking in the scene before him with dread. Then he noticed an old woman standing on the narrow porch watching them.

Jesse's first instinct was to run. His captain clearly had come to see a witch. Jesse had heard many stories told by other sailors about witches. He didn't want to be turned into a lizard or have his flesh eaten so the witch could steal his soul. Just as he was going to run, the woman called out.

"Molly Malone! Is that you?" The old woman tapped her cane on the porch. "It has been too long. Come up here and give an old woman a hug!"

Molly wrapped her horse's reins around a low tree branch and hurried to the woman. They embraced for a long while. Molly stepped back and turned to Jesse.

"I've brought one of my men with me. Mr. Reese, I would like to present Mrs. Corisande Lowe."

"Oh, no need to be so formal out here in the jungle, Molly. He can call me Coris. That is, if he deems to come anywhere near me." Corisande was used to people being afraid of her. It didn't bother her. In fact, it was very helpful in keeping those that would harm her away from her home.

"Mr. Reese, would you like to come in and have some tea?" Corisande called out to Jesse. He didn't seem to be coming any closer to her than he had to, but she wanted to offer, anyway.

"No thank you, ma'am. I'll stay here and tend to the horses." Jesse turned his back and pretended to check on the horses.

The two women exchanged smiles. "Come in, dear. Let us get you some tea and talk about what brings you back to my doorstep."

Molly glanced back at Jesse before she entered the house. He didn't look like he was going to run. He wasn't interested in going into a witch's house but she didn't think he would leave her behind. She saw him take a long drink from a bottle. Molly didn't blame him for drinking rum to keep his courage about him. She knew how sailors talked. She had heard the stories told late at night to frighten fellow sailors. Poor Jesse. Molly contemplated his bravery. Despite probably being scared to death, he was staying to protect his captain. Molly wondered if Mambo Nicole's spirits sent Jesse to help protect her. She couldn't explain his sudden appearance and his willingness to put himself in harm's way for her safety.

Molly entered the small house and, at Corisande's invitation, sat at a small table and waited for the tea to be made. Molly's eye scanned the room. The entire house was just one room. A small bed piled with blankets sat in the back corner. Next to it on the back wall were shelves holding books and jars of all kinds. A pair of lizards ran across the shelf and disappeared through a crack in the wall. Opposite Molly and the small table was a wood stove that Corisande was standing in front as she heated water. Another set of shelves lined this portion of the house. There were plates and a tea set, along with various canisters of food, herbs, and teas. A comfortable chair and footstool sat to the right of the stove. A large rug covered the middle of the floor. Two cats lounged on the rug, taking in the heat from the stove. Molly remembered the black cat. She tried to recall his name. Shadow? Molly was sure that was it. She had no memory of the other cat, a large black and white cat with gold eyes.

"Did you have that black and white cat the last time I was here, Coris?"

"No. She found her way to me during a terrible storm. I thought as soon as the storm passed, she would move along. She didn't. She has been good company to me and Shadow."

It was Shadow, Molly mused. "Did you name her?"

"Yes, I named her Stormy because she found me during a storm."

Corisande brought two teacups to the table and sat opposite of Molly. Molly took a deep breath. The tea smelled heavenly. She didn't ask what was in the tea. She was certain she didn't want to know. They sipped their tea and Molly caught Corisande up on her life as a pirate captain. When Molly took the last sip of tea, she handed the cup and saucer to Corisande. Corisande swirled the small amount of the liquid in the cup and peered intently into the cup.

"I see why you are here. You think that someone close to you is going to betray you. No, not betray... leave you." Corisande looked up from the cup to Molly's face. She knew enough about Molly to know that someone leaving her would be painful. Molly didn't like her close relationships to be uncertain or unpredictable. Yes, it was clear why Molly made the trip to her.

Molly's shoulder's hunched with the weight of Corisande's affirmation of what Molly was feeling. "So, she will be leaving."

"Yes, who is she to you?" Corisande asked gently.

"A friend. Almost a sister. I found her in New Orleans and she has been with me ever since. We are close. As you know, I don't have many females in this life that I have chosen. She is strong and getting stronger each day. I feel she will want to go her own way soon."

"As always, your feelings have not misled you. You know she won't be truly happy until she is her own woman. Until she is in command of her own life. Molly, this isn't bad. You have given your friend the way to her happiness. Don't you want that for your sister?"

"I do. I do want that for Kate."

"Then let her go. You need to leave her behind so that she may take her own journey. The same as you have. What if Molly Malone had never left Ireland? What if you had never joined a pirate ship? What would your life have been reduced to? Not the captain that you are now. I am sure you would be dead. I don't need to read the tea leaves to know that much."

"When do I do this? When do I leave her behind?"

"You will know." Corisande set the cup down firmly. "You have another purpose for coming here."

Molly took the Queen's Heart necklace from around her neck and placed it on the table. Then she took the Queen's Eye ring and laid it next to the necklace. "I need blessings on these two pieces. The necklace for me and the ring for Kate."

Corisande picked up the ring and smiled sadly at Molly. She had already started preparing for Kate's leaving. The two talked about what Molly wanted for the ring. Then Corisande touched the necklace. "And for yourself? What do you wish?"

"I want to be strong of heart. Even when the decisions I make hurt me to my very depths. I want the ability to make those difficult choices. I don't want this weak heart of mine to make my will weak as well. I need this necklace to take some of the pain from me. Any of the pain. I need to feel loss less than I do, so that I may be a strong captain."

Corisande bowed her head over the pieces. "I will do as you ask, Molly. As you go forth, even with the necklace charmed, I want you to remember that feeling pain does not make you weak. Though you are a captain on a pirate ship, you are still a woman. Our depth of heart and soul is what makes us who we are."

Molly wasn't so sure.

STORY 7
IT IS TIME

Molly And Kate Clash
The Fortune's Revenge

For the next year, the crew sailed the Caribbean, taking ships as they presented themselves. When the men would get restless, they would make port to be spend their money and do what men did with a pocket full of coins. Molly loved her ship and crew. They were a fearsome lot when in battle and family when they were on board. There were only minor discipline problems that had to be dealt with. The men didn't dare push their captain. No one wanted to be on the receiving end of a flogging.

Kate's progress as a pirate impressed Molly. She was ferocious in battle and she could fight as well as the best of her men. Kate was learning how to be a warrior, a sailor, and a leader. Charles continued his lessons and she could navigate almost as well as he could. James was eager to teach Kate the basics of the ship. She could name the parts of the ship and had learned how to repair many items.

Molly kept a keen eye on Kate. Knowing that the time of Kate's independence was looming, Molly pushed Kate to become stronger and faster in battle, more adept at the helm, and knowledgeable about the sea. She made sure that Kate could lead the men under any circumstance. Kate was becoming a forceful leader. Molly's concern for her diminished with each passing day.

Despite Molly pushing so hard, she and Kate remained close. They could hide away in Molly's cabin and laugh the night away with childhood stories. Kate and Molly became more and more like sisters as the year passed.

One early morning, Molly awoke with the sun's rays shining through her window, warming her face. She smiled and stretched. She loved the Caribbean. Growing up in Ireland, she had her fill of rain, cold, and clouds. The warmth felt wonderful on her skin. She craved its touch, its heat. She lay in her bed, allowing the sun to caress her skin and spread its heat over her as if it were a secret lover. Finally, Molly got up and walked over to her double doors. She opened them and stepped out onto her small balcony. Molly inhaled the salty smell of the water deeply. She leaned over the railing to take in as much sun as she could. Yes, she loved the Caribbean.

There was a knock on her door. She recognized the soft but firm rap.

"Enter!"

Maurice came in with her breakfast and set it on her desk. Molly turned to study him as he set up her plates and tea. He was growing. He was taller and more confident. As always, it amazed Molly how different he was from the boy she had bought at the slave auction in New Orleans. His pants were getting too short on him. He wasn't wearing shoes. Maybe he outgrew them? It was time to purchase more clothing for him. This time, she would purchase additional sizes. Molly had never considered that he would grow so quickly. She frowned in thought. Why did he still refuse to speak most days? She knew he understood her and the crew. He spoke to her but rarely. He was very intelligent, and he learned tasks quickly. She could see the recognition of words being spoken to him.

Maurice cocked his head to the right, waiting for Molly to come eat her breakfast. She met his gaze with a smile. He smiled back at her and motioned to the food. Molly sat at her desk and looked at the food. Cured meat and hard bread again. The cook seemed to be hoarding the better food for dinner. At least she had that to look forward to. It was time to find land and get some supplies. Molly took and bite of bread. "Maurice, where are your shoes?" He shrugged. "Do they hurt your feet?" He nodded. Just as she suspected, he had outgrown them. "We will remedy that soon, okay?" He nodded again.

Maurice helped Molly dress. She noticed he had a large knife strapped to his side. How had she not seen it before? "Someone gave you a knife?" He nodded. "One of the men?" Again, he nodded. It would do no good to ask who. "Did they at least teach you how to use it? I'm not sure I like you having such a large weapon strapped to your side unless you know how to use it properly." He frowned at her. He looked angry that she was questioning him about his ability to use the blade. Molly reached her flat palm out. "Give it to me. You don't need a knife such as that one. We will get one more fitting of your size and skill." He stood taller, arms crossed his chest, a deep scowl on his face. He shook his head No. Molly raised one eyebrow. More confident is an understatement. Maurice was quickly becoming a pirate.

"I could have you flogged for disobeying my orders." Doubt crossed his face. He quickly shook it off. He stared straight at Molly, daring her to try and take his knife. This rare display of defiance irritated Molly. "Take me to the one who gave you this knife." He looked uncertain, then turned to leave her cabin. Maurice stopped at the open door, waiting for her to follow. Once he was sure she was behind him, he ran to find Ikemba.

Molly watched Maurice run to Ikemba and hug his legs. She should have known. Only Séamus or Ikemba would dare give Maurice a weapon without her permission. Ikemba looked up from the boy and met Molly's icy stare with a slight smile.

"Is there a problem, Captain?" Ikemba asked.

"Come to my cabin. Both of you!"

Molly heard Ikemba reassure Maurice that everything will be fine as they followed her to her cabin away from curious eyes and ears. Molly quietly shut the doors and rested her head against them, trying to curb her anger. She wanted neither of these two to pay a price for not obeying their captain. She didn't recall putting out a general order that Maurice must not be armed. It was more of a motherly instinct she guessed – this anger she had toward them both. Without training, a weapon like this one would do more harm than good.

Molly sat in her chair and faced the two of them. "You gave Maurice that knife?"

"I did, Captain."

"Why?"

"The boy needs to know how to defend himself. Molly, even on this ship, a boy this young isn't safe from harm. He came to me one night frightened from an encounter with one of the men. He managed to get away unharmed but just barely. You and I cannot always be with him. He needs to know how to protect himself. He trains with me every day. I didn't just strap a knife to him and hope he could figure it out. We train every day." Ikemba stressed the point. "He is getting quite good too!" He saw Molly's face soften. She had less of a scowl. "Molly, I'm very sorry. I should have asked your permission before giving it to him."

"Yes, you should have. However, I agree with you. Our little man needs to know how to protect himself."

"I will expect a demonstration of his progress soon." Maurice smiled so big Molly wasn't sure his face could contain it. Molly dismissed Maurice. He ran around her desk and hugged her. Molly could barely contain the lump in her throat. "Run along, you. Mr. Kamara and I have ship's business to discuss." He nodded enthusiastically and ran out of her cabin.

As soon as her door slammed shut, Molly turned to Ikemba with a disapproving glare. He smiled and walked around her desk. He leaned on the edge in front of her. "You cannot be angry that I'm teaching a member of your crew to fight. What is really upsetting you, Molly?"

Molly raised an eyebrow and leaned forward. She ran her hands up his thighs. "As captain of this vessel, I expect to be given the last word on decisions that are made in respects to my crew."

Kem leaned forward and kissed her, "Aye, Captain."

Molly leaned back in her chair and dragged her push knives from their holsters behind her hips and laid them on her desk. The two short knives were about four inches long. Their metal blades intricately carved with roses. The thick handles were made of Brazilian Rosewood. The wood was richly hued, with dark veins of color and polished to a high shine. Ikemba looked down at the two knives lying on Molly's desk. They were beautiful, but deadly, just like their owner.

Molly absently ran her finger over one of the blades. "Now, I need a name."

"A name?"

"The name of the person on my ship who would dare force himself on my ward. I need his name."

"Molly, I took care of it already."

"How? What did you do? Is he still sailing on this vessel?"

"No."

"Ikemba, my patience is wearing thin. Either explain the circumstances of this man's demise or give me his name."

"It doesn't happen often but there are times we lose a man overboard. We lost one of our crew on the night's watch just a week ago. Do you remember? We held a gathering for him the next morning when it was discovered that he was gone."

Molly nodded slowly. "That was him?"

"It was. His disappearance wasn't questioned. The crew knew him to steal rum from the rations. More than once, they had to subdue his drunken rages. They accepted that he probably became drunk and fell overboard."

"Very well..."

They heard a shout from the deck, "All eyes look sharp! Sails to the starboard side!" Molly and Ikemba jumped up and ran to the deck. They could see that it was a British ship. Séamus brought Molly a telescope. "It's a British Naval ship all right. It isn't a warship. A frigate, perhaps?" She handed the scope to Séamus.

"Yes, a frigate. It has guns, they could deliver heavy fire on us but I'm not certain that the captain is very experienced. His sails aren't full. An experienced sailor would adjust his course slightly and make full sail." He looked at Molly. "We could use the weapons and stores that are on that ship."

Molly shouted, "All hands on deck! Make ready the boarding party! Mr. Kamara, put us on a collision course with that ship!"

The ship came alive as men scurried to gather weapons, boarding ladders, and ropes with hooks. The boarding party was with Kate painting their faces with fearsome war paint. Molly went to her cabin to gather her weapons. She loved this time. The time just before they attacked another ship. This is when the ship is most alive. The sounds of ropes, sails, and men all getting ready for battle.

Molly hurried back to the helm. "Mr. Kamara! Run up astern so we may avoid those guns!"

"Aye, Captain. Running astern!"

"Boarding party! Make ready!"

Molly stood fast next to Ikemba, who was holding steady at the helm. "Their port side is lower in the water. Either they have more cannons on that side or they didn't bother to distribute the weight of their cargo." She handed Ikemba the telescope. He could easily see each side of the Naval ship. "I believe it to be the guns, Captain. They look to only be opening the hatches on the port side." Molly couldn't understand why a captain would only have guns on one side of this ship. Was it a trick?

"Head to their starboard side, Mr. Kamara."

Molly hurried down to the main deck to get everyone set to board the other ship.

Séamus took his place at the helm so Ikemba could join the boarding party. Ikemba stripped down to a loincloth. He stood next to Molly, mostly naked, holding two machetes. Ikemba's size and scars made him a frightening person to behold. She gave him a quick glance and smiled. "Is there a problem, Captain?"

"No. Every time I see you ready for battle, I cannot help but feel a bit sorry for the sailors about to lay eyes upon you for the first time."

Ikemba laughed, "Good."

Kate and the rest of the boarding crew flanked Molly. Their bodies and faces were painted with red and black paint. The rest of the crew got the ropes and ladders ready for Molly's command.

Séamus shouted, "Drop the mainsheet! Drop the anchor and back wind the mainsail!" The men worked quickly and the ship came shuddering to a slower pace. As they came alongside of the Naval ship, Molly ordered the men to throw the ropes. They quickly tied the hooks that grabbed a hold of the other ship off. By now, the ships were traveling side by side. The crew dropped the ladders between the ships. Molly motioned to Kate. She began her war cry and the rest of the crew joined in. With that, they made their way across the ladders to the other ship. The Naval crew stood still with fear, eyes wide, mouths agape. A few of the men met the pirates with guns and swords but they were no match for Molly's crew. Before long, they had the British crewmen in a group on the main deck.

Ikemba brought the captain face to face with Molly. The officer was crying and begging for mercy. Molly and Ikemba exchanged glances. No wonder the ship didn't put up much of a fight. Their captain was a coward. Molly dispatched some of her crew to search the ship for rations and items to sell.

Kate made her way to the bottom of the ship to inspect the holds there. She could see deep into the dark hollow what looked like a makeshift cell. She ignored the cell, and the man in the cell, to look through barrels and trunks. The barrels held rum, and the trunks held old rations. Most likely nothing they needed on their ship. She turned to leave when she heard a man softly say, "Wait." Kate paused for a moment but continued toward the stairs.

The man shouted, "Wait!" as he gripped the bars with both hands and shook them.

Kate turned and finally looked at the man who had shouted at her. In the dim light, she could make out a tall man. She walked closer to him so she could see him better. He was wearing an officer's uniform but it was in disrepair. It looked like he was beaten, thrown down here, and forgotten. His blond hair was dirty and had dried blood caked in several places. His blond beard was full after weeks of not shaving. He looked worn out, wounded, and desperate.

"Please. If you leave me here, I will die."

"If I take you with me, you will die." Kate countered.

"I would rather die in the sun like a man than in the dark like a rat."

Kate moved closer despite her better judgment. There was something about him that drew her to him. Kate was conflicted. She wanted to release this man but knew she should leave him. Kate stood facing him. His blue eyes drew her in. At that moment, she knew what it was. He looked very much like her father. Tall, broad, blond, and blue-eyed all the things she remembered about her father. She drew her knife, stepped closer to the cage, and looked him deeply in the eyes.

"Why are you down here?"

He met her pointed gaze without blinking. "The captain of this ship is not a sailor. He received his commission as a favor to his father. They put him on this boat without experience or training. Because of that, his decisions are not generally wise or safe. They gave him a strong first mate, me, but our dear captain is not a man that feels he needs advise."

"You were first mate?" Kate asked.

The man nodded and sighed. "There was no advising him. He is a cruel man with no feelings for his crew. On one such occasion, against all words of advice and discouragement, our captain ordered a harsh punishment on a young cabin boy who was approximately the age of seven. This boy dropped the captain's favorite tea set during a severe storm and it broke. A storm, mind you, we could have sailed around. The captain ordered a lash for each year he owned the set. It was a gift from his mother when he left for boarding school. He had that damnable tea set for thirty-five years!" The man shook his head, still seeing the event in his mind. "He was going to level thirty-five lashes on that small boy. I could not allow it. I stepped in. The captain did not take my interference as respectful guidance. He had me beaten and thrown down here. He still had the boy lashed... When I was first thrown down here, someone came to bring me food and water daily. One sailor told me that the boy died from his injuries. It has been several days since someone has been here to bring me food. I have a bucket of water, but soon that will be empty. So, it seems, that I will die too. In the dark, starving to death like the unkempt creature that I now am. My actions were for naught. Such a waste of life."

Kate heard one of her fellow pirates shout, "Kate! Kate! Did you find anything down there? Kate! Can you hear me?"

Kate yelled back, "No! Nothing of value! I'm coming up!"

"I 'm very sorry for your plight but I'm not the person to free you." Kate felt for this man, but she couldn't help him.

The man sighed. "I understand. You are part of a pirate crew? Saving the enemy is not part of your code. It is fine. I had already resigned myself to dying down here like an animal. My one regret in this degrading death is that I will not make it home to watch the eagles soar once again."

"Eagles?" Kate murmured.

"Yes, they are enormous birds. They are unimaginably beautiful. On the rare occasions when I am home, I ride out into the countryside to watch them fly. Sometimes I can find their spent feathers on the ground. They are unique. The tips are dark and transition to white." The man shook his head and laughed softly. "I have quite the collection at my home. No wife or children, just eagle feathers. A very sad ending for a man indeed. The only thing to show for his time on this earth is a life at sea and eagle feathers."

"I'm familiar with eagles. Their feathers are beautiful." Kate answered quietly, thinking of that same color eagle feather in her cabin back on the *Fortune's Revenge*.

"There are eagles where you are from?" The man asked Kate.

"Yes," Kate said simply.

Kate knew she had to save him. If her ancestors were not telling her she had to save this man... she couldn't think of another reason that she had found him and something connected him to eagles like she was. She turned to the man and blurted, "What is your name?"

He stood tall for the first time, "I am Benedict Edward Goodsir." He bowed to Kate. "A pleasure to meet you, madame, whether or not you release me."

In a split second, she made a fateful decision. Kate grabbed the key, and without another thought, unlocked the cage. She ran in and put her arm around his waist and his arm over her shoulder. She moved to the stairs and doorway as quickly as she could with the British officer in tow. He was very weak but Kate used her height and strength to keep him upright.

Kate's mind was racing as they struggled up the steep, narrow stairs toward the open hatch. She had to take him with her. If she left him, they would execute him as a traitor. Kate heard the stories other sailors told of the harsh punishments ordered by the British Navy. Finally, they made it to the main deck and out into the daylight. The strength of the sun hit Ben hard. He dropped his head and covered his eyes with his free hand.

Kate's eyes frantically darted around the ship. She took in the scene. Molly and some of the crew were guarding the British sailors while the rest of the pirates ransacked the ship. There was very little bloodshed that had taken place. To Kate, this gave confirmation of Ben's assessment of his captain. Kate made her way to the ladders spanning the two ships. Ben was getting weaker and she was almost dragging him to keep him moving. Kate stopped just shy of one ladder. Ben was so weak, how could he get himself across.

"Kate, may I ask what you are planning on doing with that man?"

Kate steadied Ben against the side of the ship. She gave him a slight, reassuring smile. Slowly, Kate turned toward Molly. Molly had fresh blood dripping from her sword. Kate looked past her. The captain that was standing a moment ago was now crumpled on the deck, blood draining from his body.

Molly cocked her head to the left. "Explain yourself!"

"I'm taking him to our ship. He is a good man in need of help. I believe he will be an excellent addition to our crew."

"You mean my crew?"

Kate nodded, "Yes, Captain. Your crew."

"You must have hit your head during this fight and suffered an injury that's muddling your judgment if you think I will allow you to bring a British officer on to my ship."

Kate stood tall, "I am bringing this man with me across those planks, Molly. Please, I feel strongly about rescuing this man. My ancestors sent me a sign. I'm meant to save him."

Molly sheathed her sword with force. She crossed her arms and quietly stated, "Leave this man and make your way back to the ship before I decide to leave you here as well. I promise, our crew won't kill him. He may or may not have to answer for his misdeeds. I killed his captain. He will probably go unscathed if left on this ship."

Kate drew her sword and faced Molly. "Captain, I am not in alignment with your decision. I feel that I am to relieve this man of the confinements of this ship. I am bringing him with me… At all costs to my personal well being."

Molly's face gave no indication as to her feelings. Kate couldn't tell how she would react. She held fast, waiting for her swift death. Molly didn't break eye contact with Kate.

"All hands back to the ship!"

Benedict Edward Goodsir
The Fortune's Revenge

As ordered, the men raced to the planks. They carried the last of the bounty with them. Two of the pirates unhooked the ropes and swung them to the crew on their ship. As all of this activity went on around them, Kate and Molly never broke eye contact. Molly's body was relaxed but Kate knew that at any moment she could spring into action and cut her and Ben down.

As the men left the naval ship, it became quieter and quieter. All Kate could hear were the dying British sailors softly moaning. The last two pirates flanked Molly, awaiting her orders.

"Take him to our ship." They both glanced in her direction, surprised by her order. "Take him down to the brig and I will decide what to do about him later. Please confine Katherine to her quarters. Post a guard outside to make sure she doesn't leave and no one enters without permission."

Kate desperately tried to talk to Molly but the men forced her and Ben toward the ladders. Ben shouted at Molly, "Please! Please do not punish her. I will stay! I will stay!" The pirates pushed Kate and Ben over the ladders to the deck of The Curse.

As Molly's boots hit the deck, she shouted, "Mr. Kamara! Get us out of here!"

"Aye, Captain! Is there a heading?"

"At your pleasure, Mr. Kamara!"

"Thank you, Captain!"

Ikemba shouted orders to the crew as Molly went to Kate's cabin. She dismissed the guard at the door. Molly put her hand on the latch and paused. She still wasn't sure what to do. She leaned her head on the door. Why would Kate do this? She challenged Molly's authority in front of the crew. Pulling her sword on her captain is a transgression that cannot go unpunished.

After a few moments, Molly left Kate's door and made her way to Ikemba. She quietly gave him a new heading. He tried to talk to her, but Molly turned and called for Séamus to join her.

The crew went about their business but were quieter than usual. They only spoke when absolutely necessary. They watched their captain. Some closer than others. The fate of Kate was in Molly's hands. Kate had supporters. If Molly decided Kate needed to die, would there be a fight amongst the crew? The men were on edge, waiting.

Molly and Séamus headed to the small, two cell brig in the belly of the ship. Molly had yet to send anyone to this hole. She hated the idea of locking people up. She preferred to give them punishment and move on. Captivity seemed cruel to her. Even now, she didn't like keeping this Englishman in a cage. It was necessary, though. She needed to keep the crew safe from him and him safe from the crew. She had to decide Kate's fate and quick. The crew was already feeling the strain of the conflict.

Molly sent the brig's guard to get some food and rum for the prisoner. Molly took her sword out of the sheath. Ben looked up at the sound. *Well,* he thought, *at least I will be killed by a beautiful sword.*

Molly sat on a barrel, took a rag from her pocket and began rubbing the blood from the blade. Molly glanced up and noticed Ben studying her sword.

"Do you like my sword?" Molly asked.

"It is beautiful. I have only seen Arab sailors with swords like that. Where did you get it?"

"I saved my captain's life. He was grateful for my sacrifice in doing so." Molly motioned to her missing eye. "This was his way of saying thank you." Molly ran her fingers over the golden lion's head with ruby eyes that crowed the hilt of the sword. She ran a finger down the chain from the lion's mouth to the hilt guard. The gold inlay continued down the length of the sword. As she studied her sword, Molly mused, *It truly is a magnificent sword... was it worth giving my eye in trade?* She wasn't sure.

"Your captain must have been a great man for you to make that kind of sacrifice for him," Ben whispered.

Molly thought about it. "I'm not sure that he was worth losing my eye for. At least I didn't lose my life." Molly softly laughed. "What does not kill you scars you for life. Would you not agree?"

"I would agree with the sentiment," Ben said.

"At least I have this sword. What do you have for your troubles?"

Ben didn't answer. He wasn't sure what his future held at this point. He was clearly at their mercy. Judging by the way the man standing behind the captain was glaring at him, his future was not looking good. Ben waited. At this point, he was so tired and weak, he could barely stand on his own. If they meant to kill him, it wouldn't be a hard feat.

Finally, the guard returned with the food and rum. He unlocked the cell and handed the food and drink to the prisoner.

At first Ben didn't eat. He kept his eyes on Molly and Séamus. Molly stopped cleaning her sword and laid it in her lap. "We will wait for you to finish your meal. So, by all means, feel free to begin eating."

Ben hesitated, then tore into the food and gulped down the rum. When he was finished, he sighed and leaned his head against the bulkhead. It was the first time in weeks that he wasn't hungry.

"We have good food on this ship."

Ben raised his head and smiled. "Yes, you do."

"How did you like the rum?" Molly asked.

"Not the best I've had, but most certainly not the worst either."

Molly nodded. "I purchase it from a friend of mine. She's new to the craft, but I believe she's showing promise."

Ben waited. Any moment, this friendly conversation would end and he would learn his fate.

Yet, Molly continued to casually sit on the barrel, sword across her lap, watching Ben. Studying him. The man behind her never seemed to blink. Clearly, she was the captain of this vessel, but who was he?

Ben had to ask. "You are the captain?"

"Yes, I'm Molly Malone, captain of the *Fortune's Revenge*. The ship on which you are now a prisoner."

"You do not see many female captains on these seas," Ben commented.

Molly raised her eyebrow. Ben rushed to continue.

"I personally do not have a problem with a woman as captain. I want my captain to be fair, experienced, and make smart decisions. What sex that person is, does not bloody matter to me."

"Is that what you told Kate? Did you promise to back her as captain if she freed you?"

"No!"

"Then why? Why would she free you? Why would she raise her sword to me if I didn't allow you on to our ship?"

"I do not know why she set me free. Maybe it was my story? I told her my sad tale in order to plead my case with her. I was in that hold because I was trying to save a young lad from a horrible beating that our captain had ordered."

"You broke with your captain's orders?"

"Yes, I did. I did not believe that a young boy could handle, or deserved, thirty-five lashes over a broken teapot."

For the first time, Molly dropped her eyes. She felt unsure of what to do next.

"You did not tell Kate that you would back her for captain?"

Ben struggled to stand. He slowly walked to the bars. He stood straight in a military parade rest and met Molly's harsh glare. "No, Captain. On my honor as a gentleman and an officer in his Majesty's Royal Navy, I did not exchange a promise of mutiny for my freedom."

Molly stood and without another word went back on deck, Séamus following close behind her.

Ben collapsed in the corner. He knew no more about his fate than when she first came to see him.

The End
The Caribbean

Séamus and Molly adjourned to her cabin. Molly sat at her desk. Séamus poured them both a dram of rum. Séamus drained his glass with one gulp. Molly didn't touch her glass. She stared down into the liquid.

"What are you going to do about Kate?"

"I should kill them both..."

"But, you are not going to do that."

"No."

"You have chosen the punishment?"

"I have one or two options open to me."

"Your mind is set, then?"

"Yes."

"We may have members of the crew that won't like Kate's consequences. We may have to deal with them when the time comes."

Molly nodded, well aware that she will lose additional members of her crew.

Séamus stood. "Do you need anything else from me, Captain?"

"No. You may go."

At the door, Séamus paused. "Molly... You have the final say in this matter. You decide the outcome. There is no pirate law that says the consequences need be dire in these matters." Molly didn't look up from her contemplation of the rum in her glass. Séamus left Molly to her thoughts. He made his way on deck to feel out the mood of the crew.

Molly sat at her desk, feeling very alone in the world. She couldn't allow Kate, Ben, and any crew members who backed Kate to stay on the ship. Molly sipped her rum and pondered her options. Maurice uncurled himself out of the corner and came to Molly. He had tear streaks down his face. He hugged Molly and let out a desperate cry of sadness. Molly took both his shoulders in her hands and pushed him back. She took a cloth out of her pocket and wiped his face.

"Now, now, little man. Is this how pirates behave?" He shook his head no and stood tall. "Very good. We both love Kate and we will miss her terribly but we have to allow her to find her own way in this life." In that moment, Molly remembered the words of Corisande Lowe and suddenly knew Kate's future course. She would go with the decision to let Kate and her compatriots live. She would drop them off on an island. From there, it was up to them if they lived or died. "Do we not want what is best for her?" Maurice nodded in agreement. "All right then. Enough of this."

Molly stood up and walked over to a long box sitting on her shelf. She walked back to Maurice, laid it on her desk, and flipped open the lid. Inside was a matching pair of swords. One wood and one steel. "I had this set made for you. What do you think?" Maurice looked up at Molly with a rare huge grin on his face. Molly laughed, "I will assume by that smile that you are pleased." Maurice nodded his head up and down enthusiastically. "I think it's time to start your swordsmanship training, don't you?" Maurice nodded. "Run along and find Séamus. He will know what to do." Maurice grabbed the box and turned to run out of her cabin.

He paused on his way out of her door, "Thank you, Captain!" and with that, he was off to find Séamus. Molly watched him run with the large box. How did he capture her heart so securely? Three words from him, and she was an emotional mess. Molly laughed to herself. Some fearsome pirate she was when a small waif's words could bring her to tears. Molly sat back at her desk to plan the next day's unfortunate events.

The next morning, a shout awoke Molly. "Land ho!" There was a knock at Molly's door. "Captain! We have reached your heading."

"Thank you! Fetch Maurice for me."

Maurice returned to the cabin and helped Molly dress. Both were silent as Molly prepared to let the crew know her decision about Kate's fate. As Molly prepared to leave her cabin and face Kate and crew, she paused.

"Maurice, go to Kate's cabin and pack her belongings. Make sure you get everything ready for her to travel. When you finish, bring them to me on deck. Understood?"

Maurice nodded. "Aye, Captain. Understood."

Ikemba gathered the crew on the main deck. They brought out Kate and Ben.

Molly faced the crew, Kate, and Benedict. She called out, "Katherine

Ersland, we have summoned you here for your crime of disobeying an order, raising your weapon to your captain, and taking up arms against the crew in defense of an enemy. These crimes are punishable by death."

The crew shifted uncomfortably. Molly looked at the crew, "Do you disagree with your captain?"

James Barlow stepped forward. "Aye, Captain! I disagree!"

"James! No!" Kate called out.

"Mr. Kamara, please make sure the prisoner does not speak." Ikemba put the tip of his knife to Kate's throat. "You will not speak," he whispered. "The next word you utter will be your last."

"What is the nature of your disagreement? Did she not disobey my orders? Did she not pull her sword on her captain in defense of our enemy?"

"Aye, she did." James mumbled.

"Then speak up, man! What exactly is your disagreement?"

"I don't want Kate to die, Captain. I'm willing to give my life to save that of Kate's."

Five other men rushed to James and stood by him, their arms at the ready.

"I see. Anyone else feel that Kate's life is worth more than their own?"

Charles Fisher stepped forward. "I'm sorry, Captain, but I stand with Kate The White. She has become like a daughter to me. I would gladly lay down my life for her life."

Molly's heart sank. She liked Mr. Fisher. He was a valued member of her crew. Molly didn't try to dissuade him. She only motioned for him to take his place with James and the others.

When no others stepped up. Molly called for the crew to surround the defectors.

"Drop your weapons and surrender. Otherwise, the crew will see to your surrender with force." Molly's voice sounded hard. She didn't want them to think that she wouldn't follow through with her intentions. None of these people were getting out of this unscathed. The crew surrounded the seven men and waited. James motioned for Kate's supporters to drop their weapons. James went to his knees in surrender and the rest followed his lead. There was no winning against the rest of the crew. It was best not to test Molly Malone's resolve in the matter.

Molly raised her voice and called out so the entire crew could hear her. "Though I am well within my right as captain to order death for this group, I have decided that the punishment will not be death... but marooning. The island you see just off of the bow is to be your new home until you either perish or find your way off." Molly leveled her gaze at Kate. "Your fate is in your hands."

Molly ordered two longboats dropped into the water. She had the crew pack bags of weapons, gold, food, and their belongings into one boat and ordered the prisoners split between both boats. Molly and Kate sat face to face during the long row to the island. Neither showed any emotion to each other or to their crew members. All the men, both Kate and Molly's, kept a close watch on Molly. They were sure that Molly would change her mind. None of them could believe that the captain would maroon her closest friend on a deserted island. This had to be a bluff to teach Kate not to cross her and to not question her authority on the ship.

In silence, the men rowed the two boats toward the island. It surprised everyone on board when the boats slammed on the shore. No one moved until Molly stood up and barked, "Get moving! Get these boats unloaded!" The men scrambled into action. They jumped into the water, dragging the boats onto the beach. Kate, Ben, James, and the rest of the men were ordered out of the boats. They dropped the bags of provisions onto the sand. While Ikemba and the rest of her men stood guard, Molly grabbed Kate by the arm and walked her away from the group.

Molly took a ring out of her pocket and handed it to Kate. She marveled at the beautiful sapphire in the shape of an eye. The color was a rich, deep blue. The eye rimmed with small diamonds and set into a thick, tall silver setting. Kate slipped it on her middle finger. Kate wasn't a petite woman, and yet the ring still dominated her fingers. With tears in her eyes, she looked up from the ring to Molly.

"Why? Why are you doing any of this?" Kate asked.

Molly wiped a tear from her eye. "I got this ring in the same raid as the Queen's Heart. I have named it the Queen's Eye and I had it blessed by the witch on Tortuga. It will enhance your vision and sight to see the way forward in all situations. It will also protect you from your enemies by giving you sight into their motives." Molly grabbed Kate and hugged her tight and choked out a sob. Tears ran down her face. "Do not take it off. I want you to survive this. I believe you can survive this. Katherine Ersland, you have changed since I found you in New Orleans. You have found the strength within yourself and you showed that to me, and the crew, when you challenged me. I cannot have you on my ship any longer because now I and my crew will always question your loyalty. It is time anyway. It is time for you to make your life your own."

Kate held Molly sobbing. "I'm so sorry. I'm so sorry. I should never have challenged you." Kate and Molly hugged for a few seconds, both of their bodies convulsing with tears and pain. Then, Kate dropped her arms, took a step back and whispered, "I understand why you have to do this." She looked down at her hand. "Thank you for the ring. Truly, thank you. I hope to see you again someday, Molly Malone."

Molly nodded and smiled slightly. She turned and ordered her men back on the boats. Molly stood at the bow, keeping her eye on Kate. When they reached the *Revenge*, Molly ordered the men to make sail. Molly stood at the railing, still keeping her eye on the tall figure with blond hair. Séamus stood beside her and leaned on the rail, glancing toward land, then watching Molly, concern showing on his weathered face.

"Are you sure about this, Captain?"

"Séamus, do you think we get what we deserve? Do we earn the difficulties that we experience or do some of us come to this life burdened with pain and loss, our fates already set? Nothing good in my life seems to last. Am I getting what I deserve or was I born under a cursed flag destined for sorrow and misery?"

"You don't have to do this, Molly. You can stop this now and go back to retrieve them. Your point has been made."

Molly reluctantly took her sight from shore and faced Séamus. "I could have killed her. Would that have been better? There's no room for two captains on any vessel. If Kate survives this, she will have found the deep well of strength I know she has in the very pit of her soul." Molly turned back to watch the island fading from view. "She will either find her way off that island and begin anew or she will find a ship and become its captain. Either way, she will be alive."

"And if neither of those things happen and she dies?"

Molly considered for a long moment. "If she dies, may I not hear of it for many, many years." She turned, strode toward her cabin, and shouted, "Mr. Flanagan, find me a ship to attack! The crew and I need a good fight!"

"Aye, Captain! Mr. Ikemba, make ready the ship!"

Ikemba began shouting orders to the crew, and they jumped into action. "Mr. Davis and Mr. Jareth, scurry to your crow's nests. The first one of you to spot a ship will receive an extra cup of rum with their meal on that eve."

The two young crew members, excited at the prospect of an extra rum ration, scurried up the ropes to get to the crow's nest. One of the crew members shouted out, "I wager two pieces of eight that Mr. Davis will be the first to spy a ship!"

Another answered, "I will take that bet! Mr. Jareth will put some coin in my pocket when he makes the discovery!"

Ikemba laughed. "Captain, it seems that the crew would like to make a wager on the luck and vision of our young mates. Are you so inclined to allow this wager?"

Molly stopped and turned to the crew. "Mr. Ikemba! Put me down for three pieces of eight on Mr. Davis!"

The crew cheered. Molly stood on the quarterdeck listening to her ship come alive as the crew sang and worked their magic on the *Fortune's Revenge*. Captain Molly Malone was happiest on her ship, surrounded by her men. A bird flew by, screaming at the ship, upset that they had encroached on its territory. Molly looked up at the clear blue sky. The sun shone down. Yes, she truly loved the Caribbean and this pirate life that had chosen her. On her ship, she was finally home.

WHAT'S NEXT

K&M.

hat's next for Kate and Molly? Vicki has at least four more books planned in The Saga of Kate & Molly series. The next book, *Meet Molly Malone* (working title), will introduce the readers to Molly, tell the tale of her unhappy beginnings, and disclose how she became a pirate. Kate's fate will also be revealed, and an old enemy will emerge. *Meet Molly Malone* is scheduled to be released late 2022.

ABOUT THE AUTHOR

Vicki Pearson is an adventurer and world traveler who has collected experiences and inspiration from places near and far. Whether at the helm of a sailboat, SCUBA diving in tropical waters, cruising the Amazon River in Peru, exploring fortifications in Cartagena and castles in Finland, watching the sunset at Mallory Square, island-hopping across the Caribbean and West Indies, investigating the history of New Orleans's French Quarter, taking in the grandeur of the Egyptian pyramids, or climbing hundreds of steps to reach Buddhist temples in Hong Kong and China – she lives her life in pursuit of new experiences. Vicki feels fortunate to have a husband and two adult children who share her sense of delight in discovery. They often travel together and enjoy a deep family bond.

Vicki has always been a storyteller. As a child, she would make up ghostly fables around the campfire, and in adulthood, she relishes telling tales of travel to anyone who will listen. Stories are her passion. Vicki also enjoys photography. Visually illustrating adventure, pursuing moments in time, and aspiring to capture an entire narrative through a single image. Just as in her life of adventure, Vicki craved more and decided that writing a novel was her next endeavor. The Saga of Kate and Molly is an exciting project of the heart. Her love of the Golden Age of Piracy, her fondness of rum, and her time spent in tropical locales help bring her tales alive. Now that she has released *The Rise of Kate,* Vicki has several more books planned. Stay tuned, this is going to be fun.

Visit Vicki's Website

www.ingramcontent.com/pod-product-compliance
Lightning Source LLC
Chambersburg PA
CBHW071214260626
47162CB00004B/1291